the unfinished kiss

Tim Weller

The Unfinished Kiss

First Print Edition: July 2018

Cover and Formatting: Streetlight Graphics

This novel is dedicated to every fine American who ever served, or is serving in the military, especially the United States Marine Corps. Thank you for your courage, patriotism and sacrifices.

Chapter One

MICHAEL LA RUE DIDN'T REALIZE it when he woke up that day, but at 5:08 in the afternoon his life would change forever.

Sure, every day affects our lives, even if in the smallest way. On that otherwise typical Friday, July 29th, his future would swerve in a totally new direction. And he wouldn't even be aware of it when it happened.

Michael was a waiter at The Mansion, an expensive Newark, New Jersey restaurant where the waiters - no waitresses - wore tuxedos. And the cost of dinner for two couples could easily zoom into monthly payment territory for a new Mercedes. If you felt daring when you ordered wine, you could double or triple that without breaking a sweat.

Michael liked to arrive early and enjoy a leisurely espresso in the huge kitchen that nightly produced about two hundred beautiful to behold, and delicious to eat, continental meals. Michael wasn't sure what 'continental dining' meant, other than it cost more. While showing an apple tart from the dessert tray to a table of very satisfied customers recently, someone asked, "What is the difference between a slice of apple pie and an apple tart?"

Michael replied, "About five dollars."

On that life altering day, Michael reached for the small white ceramic cup filled by the large, polished, no fingerprints allowed, silver espresso machine capable of making four beverages at once. He sprinkled in a little sugar, stirred it with a small espresso spoon and sipped the hot, strong, slightly sweet beverage. Michael gently said, "Excellent." That word described how Michael felt about his life as well. He was twenty-nine years old, in great shape, and enjoyed his work. Michael structured his life to include no debt, no attachments, and a couple morsels of money in the bank. What else could a young guy ask for?

Michael's thoughts were interrupted by movement to his right. He turned and saw Oskar Schultes, the German executive chef, and Juergen Werner, the German director of operations, on either side of a young female stranger. The trio moved to the middle of the kitchen and stopped. Oskar and Juergen were pointing at things and speaking their native language as the stranger nodded and replied in soft-spoken words.

She was one of the most attractive women Michael had ever seen. The mystery woman's bare legs pulled his eyes to them like a powerful magnet. She wore a short, not too short, light grey skirt that emphasized long, delightful legs, with magnificent calves and ankles. Michael had a great appreciation and fondness for women's legs.

His expert scan quickly moved up past her slender waist to her white blouse that enjoyed the pleasure of stretching across breasts that fit in the slightly-larger-than-medium category without being excessive. Michael also possessed an appreciation and fondness for breasts. Somewhat wavy blond hair gently fondled her shoulders. *I've got to meet her. I don't care how rude this is.* He put his espresso cup down and walked over to the three Germans. As he got closer, the two men stopped talking, and fired a 'Why-are-you-interrupting-us?' look. Michael didn't care.

He ignored them, and looked into the blue eyes of the

stranger. "Hi. Sorry to hold-up your tour. I'm Michael, one of the waiters." He held out his hand.

She hesitated for a heartbeat. "I'm Evelyn." Her whiff of an accent was as alluring as the rest of her. She grasped his hand. Her skin was smooth, her grip was strong. Michael was impressed. He didn't hold on long, but it required effort to let go. Evelyn smiled as if she knew this.

Michael wasn't sure, he believed it was Evelyn's smile that did it. He might have resisted her individual physical qualities, though cumulatively they added up to awesome. When she smiled, Michael knew he was defeated. Never had he been graced with an irresistible smile like that. This was not a fake, practiced until I've got it right, 'look at me, aren't I adorable' smile. Evelyn possessed a slightly uneven, perfect in its imperfection, smile.

Evelyn and Michael stared at each.

Oskar said, "You'll have time to chat with Evelyn next week. She's starting here on Monday, working in the kitchen."

Michael accepted his polite dismissal. Oskar was a good guy and handled this tactfully. The chef smiled, amused by what he had witnessed between Evelyn and Michael. Maybe he wished he were young, single, and Cupid's target again.

Michael said, "I need to get back to work. Evelyn, it was a pleasure to meet you." He wanted to snap his heels together with a loud click, then bow, and bring her hand to his mouth for a quick kiss, as he'd seen in movies about German officers during World War II. Michael knew it probably wasn't a clever idea.

He did put his hand out. Michael needed to feel her touch again. He hoped Evelyn might give him some indication that she was glad she met him. She didn't.

Michael had Mondays and Tuesdays off, the two

slowest and least profitable days in the restaurant business. He wouldn't see Evelyn until Wednesday. He wondered if one of the other waiters would have glommed onto her by then. Five days was a long time to leave the hen house unguarded, especially with a new prize visitor. He knew that Evelyn would be the hottest item on every waiter's dream list. Well, not every waiter. A few were gay.

Then reality tossed icy cold water in Michael's face. *What if I'm being a world-class idiot? It won't be the first time.* He'd been too distracted by her spectacular body, face, and presence to look for a ring. And even if he had, the absence of one wouldn't prove anything. Maybe she was married, and didn't wear one. Maybe she was married, and had children at home. Or a serious boyfriend. Maybe a lot of things.

Michael decided not to think of the what-ifs. *I'm not going to waste time thinking about things I have no control over. Let's keep my fingers crossed and see what Wednesday brings. Or doesn't.* There was no point in kidding himself. Michael knew that he would not stop thinking about Evelyn.

That weekend at The Mansion, as he feared, Evelyn was the talk of the kitchen. The wolves were hungry. And circling. What would happen in his absence on Monday and Tuesday?

Chapter Two

On Wednesday, Michael held himself back from running into the kitchen at The Mansion. He'd never been this early for the dinner shift before. A scattering of guests lingered from lunch. He entered the kitchen and searched for Evelyn. Michael saw her in the pantry section where cold items such as salads and certain appetizers were prepared. She was leaning over and putting something together on the long counter. He ignored greetings from the waiters who'd worked the lunch shift. All his attention was zeroed in on Evelyn.

Michael walked over and said, "Hi."

She stopped, straightened up and beamed that magnificent smile again. Was it possible she'd missed him?

Evelyn's voice gave nothing away when she said, "Hello."

Maybe she's controlling herself. Or maybe she's politely uninterested.

"How's work at The Mansion so far?" He regretted the lame words as soon as they spilled out.

"I like it."

"How about going out for a drink after work tonight?" Michael believed a straight line was the shortest distance between where he was and where he wanted to be.

"I'm sorry. I have plans to go to a jazz club with the other Germans."

Michael didn't hesitate. "I love jazz. What time shall I pick you up?"

Evelyn stared at him. She said nothing and revealed nothing. He was certain that an American girl's face would have shown something, anything.

Is this a German trait? A European one? An Evelyn mannerism?

Finally, she spoke. "Ten-thirty would be acceptable." She added that she and four other Germans lived in the two-story brick building that was on the restaurant property. The owner lived there before he'd moved into a small palace in a nearby luxurious and private gated community when The Mansion zoomed from profitable to super successful.

Michael said, "I'll try to be on time. I'll ask the maître d' not to give me any late tables. The other waiters won't mind, that means extra cash for them."

Michael felt like he was having an out-of-body experience during his dinner shift. He genuinely enjoyed being a waiter. However, that night his normal focus on everything around him was not as sharp as usual. Michael was so skilled at both the big things and the details of his job that no one detected this. But he could not pull his mind away from his date with Evelyn. And the evening seemed to torture him by slowing down. He finally handed his last customer their credit card voucher to sign.

Michael barely had time after that last table to rush to his apartment and change out of his tuxedo. Even the quickest of showers was out of the question. Michael didn't want to smell like the restaurant kitchen, so he searched for a gift bottle of after-shave that he hadn't used, and accidentally splashed on too much.

Damn, I don't have time to rinse this off. She'll think she's out with a Frenchman, not an American.

He knocked on the door to Evelyn's temporary home five minutes early. Michael knew the house had transitioned to a fancy barracks for the Germans, but he'd never been inside. Marc, one of the German cooks, opened the door, and was rather cool with his greeting. Michael was friendly with Marc, so he was surprised at the lack of usual pleasantness. He quickly dismissed it and stepped into the large entrance way.

Marc said, "Have you ever dated a German?"

"No."

"Then I will say nothing. Good luck." Marc emphasized the last two words.

Michael stayed silent. Marc led him through a hallway into the living room. Marc used his chin to point at Evelyn, and said, "Here's the Empress of Germany."

With a lighter tone those words might have been a friendly joke. Marc coated them with obvious dislike.

Michael wondered, *What's that all about?* He tossed away the question as he noticed the room. Dark wood trim around dreary wallpaper, and windows covered by heavy drapes that looked like they were from an old movie, made the room gloomy and somewhat creepy. *This is like living in a cave. Who would have decorated like this on purpose? I guess having money doesn't guarantee taste.*

There were no chairs. Evelyn sat on the floor to Michael's left with her back against the wall, watching a small TV on the floor near the opposite wall. The antenna sticking up from the back of the television looked like an empty flagpole. A tall, inexpensive-looking lamp with a single bulb and no lampshade stood in the corner. The owners must have taken the rest of the furniture with them when they moved up and out.

Evelyn didn't stand as she turned her attention away from the TV. She looked terrific. "Hello. Please don't think me rude, in Germany we don't get these channels. I don't care for television. I prefer living life, not watching it. But this show is interesting."

Michael smiled. "I know what you mean about life not being a spectator sport. I don't even own a TV."

Evelyn's knees were drawn up toward her chest, her feet were flat on the carpeted floor. And she wore a short skirt. A loud warning blasted in Michael's head. His 'I-Am-A-Pig Meter' was screaming at full volume.

If I walk in front of Evelyn, I'll have a direct view up her skirt. All the way to the Promised Land.

For a second, he considered doing exactly that. But Michael knew there was no way in the world that Evelyn would not instantly catch on. He was certain that no amount of looking around casually would disguise his intent, or fool her. With effort, Michael stayed far to Evelyn's right, he didn't trust himself to be anywhere near the front of her. The tantalizing appeal of even a brief glimpse up her skirt was too strong to risk it. He felt some moisture forming on his forehead.

Michael smiled. *I can't believe I'm nervous. Am I back in high school?*

Evelyn stood up and stared at him. "Michael, are you feeling alright? You seem to be, what is the word, inspiring?"

"I think it's *per*spiring. I'm fine. I rushed to get here on time."

Marc looked at his watch and said, "We should go now. We are missing what I have been told is a decent band. Evelyn, our small car will be crowded. Can you ride with Michael?"

Michael wondered whose benefit Marc was doing that for?

Evelyn looked back and forth between Marc and Michael. Maybe she was asking the same question. She finally said, "That will be acceptable."

Outside, Michael opened the passenger door to his five-year-old Toyota. Although he was being polite, his main purpose was to see how Evelyn handled scooting into the low seat with her long legs and short skirt. He hoped that this might make up for his missed opportunity inside the house. Evelyn kept her knees totally together as she effortlessly glided in. He scanned her legs during that brief movement, sending urgent messages to the skirt to slide higher, or for Evelyn to be even slightly careless. It didn't work.

Wallace's was about ten minutes away. Michael drove slowly. He wanted to get to know Evelyn at least a little before they entered the noisy jazz bar. All he knew of this young woman was that he found something about her to be irresistible. It wasn't her impressive looks, or her captivating accent. It was something beyond them. Although Evelyn's attractiveness was a fine beginning, that was not enough for Michael. The world was filled with attractive women. He wanted substance to go with the beauty. He looked toward Evelyn and said, "Have you ever been to the U.S. before?"

"No. I've always wanted to come here."

"Why?"

"I enjoy travel to new places. And we are near to New York City, yes?"

"Yup. It's about twenty minutes away."

"Yup? What does that mean?"

Michael glanced at Evelyn. "It means yes. So does uh-huh, sure, okay, right, yeah, and certainly. I could probably think of more with enough time."

She smiled. "The way you Americans speak is interesting. In Germany, I liked to watch American movies to listen to the actors talk. It is entertaining."

"Well, on behalf of our language, welcome to America."

"You are the official American representative? I am honored." Her smile lit up the interior of the car. Michael sensed he was swimming into water that was way over his head. *I hope there are no sharks prowling out here.*

Chapter Three

MICHAEL PARKED ACROSS THE STREET from Wallace's and rushed around his car to open Evelyn's door. Too late. She had already swung her legs out. If she knew what he was trying to do, her face kept it a secret.

When he opened the big wooden door to Wallace's, they were blasted by a small cloud of cigarette smoke, a large burst of music, and the smell of beer. The dominant flavor of the music was a bluesy guitar racing to keep up with a smooth saxophone. Michael looked around, the four German cooks were at a table that barely held them, with no further room.

Several empty stools beckoned at the bar. Michael touched Evelyn's arm and pointed at them. She nodded, and they went over and sat down. The bartender leaned toward them, his expression asked, "What do you want?"

Michael pivoted to his left, to face Evelyn. "What would you like?"

"I have heard of a drink, a Long Island Iced Tea. I like the name, no one in Germany knows how to make it. I will have that, please."

Michael nodded to the bartender. "What do you have on tap?"

A verbal short list got tossed back and he picked one. This was not a single's bar. It was a no-frills jazz joint. And it planned to stay that way. Too many beer choices, or anything other than basic décor might attract the wrong crowd.

Their drinks arrived. Michael picked up his beer and said, “What shall we toast to?”

Evelyn looked at him, “In Germany we say ‘Prost.’ We are not in Germany, so you decide.”

Possibilities flitted around like fireflies on a dark summer night. Michael didn’t want to seem aggressive, “To new friends.”

“What makes you think we are going to be friends?”

Michael felt like he’d been slapped. He was stunned. And disappointed. He tried not to show it. Evelyn must have seen this. She attempted to smile and said, “I was making a joke. It seems that it was not a good one. Please forgive me. I am a little nervous, and was trying too hard.”

She briefly placed one of her hands over his and smiled. “Michael, you are my first American friend.”

The warmth of Evelyn’s hand felt sensual. Michael returned her smile. He gently clicked his glass against hers. They raised them to their mouths.

“Now that you’ve tasted a Long Island Iced Tea, was it worth traveling three thousand miles for?”

“Frankfurt is four thousand miles. And, yes, I like it.”

The band stopped. The guitarist thanked the audience for the loud, long applause. He gave a brief preamble to their next song. The four members, guitar, sax, upright bass, and drummer looked to each other for timing. Each musician began tapping a foot, and then they started playing. The music roared down the runway and took flight. The sax provided propulsion and lift. Michael became aware of his left foot keeping time in appreciation.

He turned to Evelyn, “Do you like the sax?”

She stared at him. "Are you always this direct with women?"

"What do you mean?"

"Asking me if I like sex? Are *you* now making a bad joke?"

Michael smiled. "I realize that it's noisy in here with the talking and the music, I asked if you liked the sax. You know, the saxophone." He made a gesture of playing one.

Evelyn blushed lightly. "That is a question I will answer. Yes, the sax is alright." She shrugged. "I am not a fan of jazz."

"You're not? Then why did you come here?"

"I did not have a choice. The other Germans were coming here. They like to drink beer, smoke cigarettes, and chat each other up in dark, noisy bars. I wanted to get out of that house and do something. Since I do not have a car," she shrugged her shoulders. "Here I am."

Evelyn continued, "You did me a favor by wanting to join me, or I would have to sit at their table and pretend to listen to stories about sports games they have won, and women they have conquered."

She sipped some of her drink. "I think many of the victories, on or off a playing field, took place in their minds."

Michael smiled at her openness. Evelyn seemed honest and direct without needing to wear it as a badge of honor.

He said, "I know them from their work in the kitchen, I'll have to trust your opinion on that."

"I do not like to put people in a group," she said, "they are common of some men in Germany - more interested in being with their sports buddies than with their girlfriends or wives. My girlfriends and I laugh when we mention this. It's wonderful that they haven't forgotten their male friends and have interests outside of the relationship, they don't seem to want to balance this with their home life.

"Some of my girlfriends complain that their men play football, I think you call it soccer, two or three nights a week. Then, out for beers with their comrades. When they finally go home, they want only to shower and sleep. There is no talk, no spending time together.

"On Fridays, they go to bars with their teammates. By Saturday, my friends want to go out, their men are tired and want to sit on the sofa, watch television, and drink beer. I hear this sad song often." Evelyn paused, and then said, "I'm sorry, I did not mean to talk on and on." She smiled. "It must be the Long Island Iced Tea."

Michael looked at her drink. A couple drops were left. Half of his beer remained. He didn't want Evelyn to feel self-conscious, so Michael held up two fingers when he gestured to the bartender.

Evelyn said, "Let's change the subject. Tell me about yourself."

"Okay, you asked for it. Here's the Reader's Digest version of my life."

"Reader's Digest version?"

"Sorry. Reader's Digest is a magazine that has the short version of books. For people in a hurry, I guess. Anyway, that means I'll make this brief and light on the details. I served in the Marine Corps for four years right after high school. Then I traveled around the U.S. for nearly two years, doing any work to pay the rent and buy some beer. It was great, and I saw a lot of the U.S.

"After two years, I knew I should think about growing up and getting a real job. A guy I knew from the gym was an x-ray tech. He drove a cool car, had a nice apartment, and a powerful stereo. These were very important to me when I was twenty-four. I started to think, hmm, hospital work – heated in the winter, air-conditioned in the summer, nurses in short skirts – hey, I could do that."

Evelyn laughed. It was just right. Not too much, or too little.

Michael thought, *Is there anything about her that isn't going to knock me out?*

She asked, "And did you?"

He nodded. "I went to x-ray school at a hospital on the G.I. Bill."

Michael noticed that a question mark worked its way onto Evelyn's attractive face. "The G.I. Bill helps veterans to go to school with government help. Well, it's really taxpayer money. It's the country's way of saying, 'Thanks.'"

Evelyn nodded her understanding. "And now you are a waiter."

"I enjoyed taking x-rays, and may go back to doing it." Michael shrugged. "I wanted a break." He drank some of his beer. "I think life is to be savored, like a tasty meal. And just as there are various courses to a meal, there are different phases in our lives. Each part of the meal, and your life, should stand on its own, yet build on what was before it. And prepare you for what is to follow. After the final course of a meal, or stage of your life, you should look back, satisfied with your pleasurable experience."

"And then?"

"Whether it is your meal or your life, then you pay the bill."

They both smiled. Michael said, "Okay, your turn. I want to hear the Evelyn story. And not the Reader's Digest version."

She smiled again. "I feel like I am being interviewed. Is that what you are doing?"

"Yeah, you figured it out. A photographer is waiting outside. I'll sell the photos and the story to checkout line magazines and get lots of money for them. And more money if you're drunk. So, keep drinking."

Evelyn laughed. "If you need information to be able to sell your story, here it is. Do you want to get a pen and some paper first?"

"No, I've got a bottomless memory, that won't be necessary. Let's start with how old you are. Wait, don't tell me. I'm excellent at people's ages. I'll bet that I can guess your age to within ten minutes of when you were born."

"You cannot! No one could do that."

Michael smiled. "You're right, I can't. I was joking."

"American humor. I may never understand it."

"OK, no jokes. Since we've decided that I can't guess your age that closely, how old are you?"

"Twenty-six. How old are you?"

"Fifteen."

This earned a 'No, you aren't.' look from Evelyn.

Michael said, "No, really. I'm fifteen. I've had a rough life."

She laughed.

Michael said, "All right, I'm twenty-nine. I'm sorry, please continue."

"When I graduated from school, I wanted to become an interpreter. I went to a French language program for two years."

"French is such a beautiful language."

"Not when spoken by a German it isn't."

Michael laughed. Evelyn didn't even smile. He wasn't sure if she was being modest, or displaying a very dry sense of humor.

"Then what?"

"After the language school, I realized that working in an office was not my cup of coffee."

"I think that's 'not my cup of tea.'"

"Oh. Thank you for correcting me. It's annoying when

people think that your language mistakes are cute, and they do not say anything. How can I learn if they do not tell me? Where did I stop?"

Evelyn closed her eyes briefly, and then she opened them. "I have it. First, do you think you could order another of these iced teas?"

Michael did, and Evelyn continued. "I did not enjoy working in an office, sitting in the same chair, at the same desk, doing the same task each day. I enrolled in a hotel apprenticeship program."

"I know what apprenticeship means, how does that work in Germany?"

"You need to complete a three-year apprenticeship to get most jobs, unless you went to a university. I did mine at the InterContinental Hotel in Frankfurt. I grew up fifteen kilometers away."

Michael did a rough conversion. It was about ten miles.

"When I was nearly finished, one of my co-workers told me about a restaurant in the U.S. that arranged with Inter to bring over five or six Germans to work in the kitchen for a year. I would get paid and provided a place to live."

Evelyn sipped her drink. "I could visit, and hopefully travel in the U.S., and put the work on my resume. International work experience from the U.S. is a positive thing to have in Germany. We look up to nearly everything about America.

"I applied, submitted letters of recommendation, and here I am with a one-year visa in my passport. The Mansion sent a driver to the airport to pick me up. I was in the U.S. about one hour when we met. And now I am sitting here with you, drinking more than I should. I will stop now." She paused, and then said, "I don't want to talk about myself. What about you? Your family?"

Evelyn, if only I could tell you.

Chapter Four

MICHAEL NEEDED TO CHANGE THE subject. And quickly. The band provided a diversion as they prepared to launch into some sweetness. Michael said, "Look, they're getting ready to play again. Hold that question. I'll get to it later." *Much later. Preferably never.*

They turned in their seats to watch the four musicians play. After about a minute, Michael realized that his left foot was again tapping to the music on its own. He smiled, glad that his foot was enjoying itself. And so was he, sitting with Evelyn.

She turned toward the bar and pushed her glass away. Then Evelyn changed her mind, picked it up again, and put the straw in her mouth. She kept her eyes down as she swallowed before once again moving the glass across the bar. She smiled at Michael. That smile. It was official: Michael was her prisoner.

Evelyn said, "This time I mean it. No more alcohol."

The band kicked into overdrive with a number that got the small crowd cheering. Michael briefly joined in the clapping of approval, and then asked Evelyn a question. The music and the cheering were too loud. She mouthed, "I can't hear you."

He repeated himself. She shook her head. Michael moved his head within inches of hers. Evelyn kept her face toward him. He slid closer, nearer than needed. She hesitated, and then also moved in a bit.

Their noses nearly touched. Evelyn stared into Michael's brown eyes and tilted her head, gifting him with a clear approach to her lips. Then she shut her eyes. Their mouths were separated by a distance nearly too small to measure. He could already taste their first kiss.

Until he felt a hand on his shoulder. Marc loudly said, "This band is strong, yes?"

Michael realized instantly that Marc had consumed at least one beer beyond the sobriety level. His words were a bit slurred and more accented than normal.

Michael straightened up on his barstool. The magic of that near kiss was officially over. "Yes, they are." Michael was frustrated and annoyed. He tried not to let his voice convey it.

Marc said, "How could you tell? It seems that you have not been listening."

Michael was caught off guard by the boldness of Marc's rude statement. He rolled responses around, trying to pick one that would deliver the right message.

"Evelyn was telling me that German men are the finest in the world. Especially the ones who work at The Mansion. I said she was mistaken, that it was American men. She replied that if she was lying, her nose would grow. I wanted to get a closer look at it, to be sure."

Marc looked as if he swallowed some lemon juice, so Michael decided to pour him a little extra. "Does that sound about right to you, Evelyn?"

"Yes."

The German glared at Evelyn so forcefully that Michael believed Marc swayed right on the edge of pushing this further. Michael tensed his body, ready to jump off the stool and restrain the cook if necessary.

Marc continued his ugly look, and muttered something in German that Michael was sure Evelyn heard. Then he turned and walked back to his table. Michael followed him with his eyes, not trusting Marc.

The other three Germans watched silently and cheered after Marc sat down and spoke to them. One of them slapped Marc on the back like a congratulatory gesture, and handed him his beer. They put their bottles together with a loud German toast. Michael relaxed and turned back to Evelyn, certain that in Marc's version of their encounter he'd slain Michael with his superiority.

"You handled him quite well," said Evelyn.

"Thanks. I get the feeling that there's something going on between you two."

"There is. Or to be precise, there is not. But Marc hoped there was. This past weekend, I was unpacking and making my room in the house to my taste when Marc came in without knocking. He said that the others talked, and decided that he was the one to be with me." Evelyn paused before adding, "He was serious."

Evelyn continued. "I said, 'That's very thoughtful,' as sarcastically as I could. Marc repeated that we would make good German lovers. When he said that, he shut the door to my room...with him in it."

Michael shook his head in amazement and disgust.

Evelyn said, "I walked past him, opened the door, and stood in front of it, keeping it open. Marc looked surprised when I told him, 'Let me be certain that I understand this. The four of you talked about me like I was an object, a prize, not a human being. And then you decided who should be awarded that prize. That's quite flattering. Or it would be if we were in a land of arranged marriages in the Middle Ages, and not in America today.'"

Michael realized that Evelyn's voice contained enough steel to build a large, German luxury car. She reached for the glass she banished and put the straw in her mouth.

Michael asked, "What did he say to that?"

After two swallows, Evelyn looked back at Michael. "He tried once again to convince me how lucky I was. His tone suggested that I should shut the door, take off my clothes, lie on the bed, and be grateful."

Michael swiveled and stared at Marc's table, nearly hoping that he would notice this and rise to the challenge. Michael turned back to Evelyn. "I'm sorry. That must have been unpleasant enough to make you regret that you came here."

Evelyn turned and held both of Michael's hands. "You don't need to be sorry. He is an idiot."

She didn't let go of Michael's hands. This was his first extended touching with her and he liked it a lot. "Marc finally realized that I was not, how do you say it - playing hard to get? Then he said that I was a typical cold German bitch."

Michael shook his head. "Very classy."

Evelyn nodded. "I said that if German women were such bitches, why did he bother with me? Could it be that the American women were too smart to want to be with him, and that he no choice except to turn to icy bitches?

"He had no answer for that. He stomped out of my room the way a five-year-old does when he does not get the toy he wants. I wasn't surprised when Marc slammed the door to my room, and then his. He has been rude to me since." Evelyn smiled. "I try not to lose sleep over it. So far, I have been successful." She released Michael's hands, and he wished she hadn't.

"Wow. That's quite a story. I'm going to have to include it in the article I write about you."

Evelyn rewarded Michael with another laugh. "I needed something funny after that, thank you." She glanced quickly at Marc's table where he and the others were loudly talking. "Being here is not so enjoyable any longer. Would you mind if we left?"

"No, not at all." He pulled his wallet and left enough to make the bartender's night. Like many people in the food and beverage industry, Michael generously over-tipped.

Evelyn slid her fingers between Michael's as he led her toward the door. He travelled the long way, far from Marc's table. Michael didn't run from trouble, but he didn't like to look for it.

Considering it was the first week of August, this was a glorious night, not too humid. They walked across the street to Michael's car, he unlocked Evelyn's door. She turned to him. "I am curious. Marc looked angry enough to hit you when he talked to you at the bar. If he had, what would you have done?"

"*Me*? I was concerned he might hit *you*. To answer your question, I don't think he would have succeeded if he tried anything."

"Why? Are you a fighter?"

"No, I'm a pussycat. I don't like to fight. I feel that one way to end a fight is not to let it happen in the first place."

Evelyn nodded. "Fighting is primitive. How would you have prevented it?"

"I would have used some special words."

Evelyn tilted her head. "Really? And those special words work?" She was teasing and they both knew it.

"Every time."

"Would you please share them with me?"

"Sorry, it's a professional secret. But there are words I *can* share with you."

"And what might they be?"

Michael moved toward her. There was very little space between them. "That you are an appealing and attractive young woman."

Evelyn did not look away from his eyes. “Am I?”

“Yes. You are.”

Michael moved closer. He was nearly up against Evelyn.

Her voice was nearly a whisper. “Michael, what are you doing?”

“I believe it’s called unfinished business.”

“Is that what this is? Unfinished business?”

“Yes. Our first kiss never happened.”

“Then it is an unfinished kiss.”

He smiled.

She said, “And now it can be finished?”

“Yes.”

Evelyn closed her eyes. Michael was less than an inch from her lips.

“There’s the German bitch.” Marc was drunk, or close to it. The four cooks crossed the street toward Evelyn and Michael.

Chapter Five

MICHAEL PULLED HIMSELF AWAY FROM the startled Evelyn, and moved in front of her. Marc and the other three kitchen workers crossed the street, and arranged themselves in a semi-circle around Michael, about four feet away.

Michael swiveled his head staring each man in the eyes. He said, "You owe the lady an apology."

The four Germans laughed, and spoke to each other rapidly in their native language. Michael figured they were verbally drawing straws to see who would make the initial approach. The biggest one, Michael didn't remember his name, stepped about a foot closer.

Michael stood six feet one inch, and weighed one hundred and ninety pounds, none of it was fat. The cook was an inch or two taller than Michael. His tight black t-shirt revealed lots of hours lifting weights. And he was about six or seven years younger.

The cook taunted Michael with a medium accent, "If we do not apologize, what do you think you can do to four men? Beg? Cry for your mama?"

The cooks laughed again.

Michael knew his own fighting skills, he had no idea of what this cook was capable of. Maybe he'd earned a high degree belt in some martial art. It didn't matter to Michael. He owned the confidence that came from being a former Marine with two combat tours.

Michael said, "Let's do this the easy way. Why don't

you tell Evelyn you're sorry, and then get in your car and leave? We'll pretend this never happened."

The big German smiled. It wasn't a friendly one. "No. It has happened." His smile turned into a smirk. "And I don't like the easy way. I'm too tough for that. I prefer the hard way."

He looked at his friends, who smiled. And then back at Michael. "Hard for you. Not for me."

Michael thought, *I'm going to try once more.* "You're probably a smart person. And a smart person doesn't want to be in a world of pain."

The large German moved closer, now about two feet away. He was clenching and unclenching both fists. Michael noticed his big knuckles. And large silver rings. *I've got to avoid those.*

"You are the one who will feel any pain," the cook said. "And I will enjoy giving it to you." The others moved a little closer.

Michael felt like a sheep tied by a rope to a tree with the wolves creeping in. He could sense electricity snapping and crackling in the air. Michael knew that the twitching German was about to make his move.

The cook said. "Enough talk. It's party time."

The big man lunged. Maybe he believed he caught Michael by surprise.

He didn't.

Michael calmly stepped to his left as deftly as a matador avoiding a snorting, charging bull. Michael hated the sadism and cruelty of bull-fighting, yet acknowledged the comparison as *el toro* missed his target.

The cook's momentum carried him past Michael. The German stopped and turned. His smile was gone, replaced by anger and embarrassment. This time he walked toward Michael, maybe expecting him to back away. Michael didn't.

When the bigger man got within punching distance, he pulled back his right fist. The dangerous looking rings, one had short metal spikes sticking up from it, seemed even bigger now.

Michael ignored it. Before the cook could pull the trigger on his punch, Michael fired a burst of alternating lefts and rights to the cook's abdomen. The first punches stunned the cook with surprise and pain. Then he recovered enough to lower his arms to protect his body. He did exactly what Michael was hoping he would do.

Michael blasted the cook with a powerful, solid left to the unprotected right side of his face. The German dropped to one knee. Michael stepped back. He wasn't a sadist. He gave the bigger man the chance to end the fight by staying down or walking away.

The cook rose to his feet and swung his right hand, the one with the ring that would rip flesh open, at Michael's face. Michael's left arm rose and blocked the invading forearm, pushing the cook's arm outward. Then he resumed launching explosive lefts and rights at the cook's exposed abdomen. The cook's pain instantly became agony. Michael's brain flashed advice from the past. *Take out the body and the head will follow.*

The bigger man was muscular and tough. But he was still made of flesh. Flesh that covered millions of pain sensors. Five seconds isn't long when you're doing something you enjoy. Five seconds passes very slowly when someone is chopping away at you with strength, speed, and precision.

Michael's fists were a destructive blur as he landed hard punches.

The cook howled as if every one of those millions of pain receptors was splashed with gasoline and set on fire. Then he stepped back and fell to the ground where he curled up and moaned continuously. He muttered something in German that Michael did not understand, or care about.

Michael turned to face the other three cooks, checking his perimeter. *No further threats.* Instead, the trio slowly helped their groaning friend up. They supported him as they walked to their car and drove away.

Evelyn looked at Michael. “That was amazing. You handled him like he was a child on a playground. You said that you couldn’t fight.”

“I said that I didn’t like to fight. Not that I couldn’t.”

“Where did you learn to do that?”

“My father raised me to avoid fights. He said, ‘If it must happen, every fight has a winner and a loser. And it is better to be the winner.’ Dad taught me the skills to be the winner. I boxed in the Marine Corps and still do at the gym to stay fit.”

Michael smiled. “The world can sometimes be a concrete jungle. With no shortage of bullies and fools. You never know when one of them will try to make you their latest victim.”

Evelyn considered that. “Michael, this has been an interesting evening. I have enjoyed being with you, but Marc and the others have stolen the fun from it. Please take me back to my flat.”

When Michael pulled up in front of Evelyn’s quarters, she turned and looked at Michael for a moment. He searched her face and posture for clues, signals, permission. He detected none.

Evelyn got out of the car as Michael did. She walked right up to him. Evelyn stared at Michael, and then touched her lips lightly on his right cheek. Before the sensation on his skin faded, she was in her house.

Michael drove back to his apartment wondering, *Am I ever going to get to kiss her?*

Chapter Six

MICHAEL WALKED INTO THE KITCHEN at The Mansion a little early. He wanted to see Evelyn. And he wanted to keep their young relationship, if that's what it was, private. Michael was pretty sure that Evelyn felt that way, too. No one at work needed to know about them. *Let's be careful.* Michael knew that the waiters at The Mansion possessed an alert, animal-like sense of their environment. They would instantly detect any changes, however small.

The other reason Michael went in early was that he wasn't sure what to expect from Marc and the other three German kitchen workers. He hoped that they were adult enough to accept what happened, even if they blamed it on Michael, as he felt certain they would.

The sounds of the large and busy restaurant kitchen getting ready for that night's performance raced around, chased by the scents and aromas of wonderful sauces and other ingredients for fine-dining being prepared.

Michael saw Oskar Schultes slicing something and looking up every couple of seconds. *He's waiting for me.* Michael didn't believe in pretending things were fine, when they weren't, so he strode right over to Oskar. Oskar put his chef's knife down and come out from behind the counter.

He reached up, and placed one of his short, muscular arms on Michael's shoulder. "Let's go somewhere private and talk." Oskar had been living in the U.S. for about twenty-five years, his accent made it sound like twenty-five days.

"Okay."

Michael followed Oskar's short legs through a double door into a long hallway. Halfway down on the right they entered Oskar's small office. Michael knew where it was, and had walked by it during his two years at The Mansion. He had never been in there. Michael looked around. Oskar was probably used to this from first time visitors; he sat on his desk, watching Michael.

Oskar's legs didn't reach the floor, they swayed back and forth as he quietly whistled a tune that Michael didn't recognize. Two of the walls held wooden shelves, with cookbooks neatly arranged on them. Michael didn't think another book, no matter how thin, could have slid in there. He noticed that the titles were in German.

Oskar coughed politely. Michael realized, *Time to get to it.*

"Michael, when my kitchen crew came in today, I saw that one of them either fell down a flight of stairs, or been in a fight. When I asked what happened, they said that last night they came out of a bar, and saw you kissing Evelyn. You insulted them with curse words, and warned them to stay away from Evelyn, that she was yours. When they tried to talk to you, you attacked the biggest one. This is the story they told me."

Michael wanted to speak, Oskar held up a hand. "I asked what weapon you used to beat the big man. He looks like a car ran over him after he fell down the stairs. They turned to each other for a believable lie. The truth doesn't require thinking. Finally, Marc said, 'A baseball bat,'

"I asked him why were you were kissing Evelyn with a baseball bat in your hand? Perhaps describing the finer points of that game between kisses?"

Oskar sighed. "I know these men. They are solid

workers. They show up on time, and sober. They do their work, and they do it well. I would not want them for my sons. They should have less hormones, and more brains. I know you. You have not caused any problems. And you get along with everyone." Oskar smiled, "Now, it is nearly everyone."

The chef checked his watch. "My lobster ravioli sauce should be ready. Two items and we both get back to work, yes? First, I don't need to see all the pieces of a puzzle to know what the picture is. Thank you for protecting Evelyn. Second, if you find it necessary to fight with my kitchen staff, kick them in the balls. Facial injuries call for explanations, and that wastes my time."

Oskar jumped down from his desk, and slapped Michael on the back. "There is one final item. Evelyn is exceptional. Please don't hurt her."

"I promise to do my best."

"I'm sure you will."

Oskar opened the office door, and they headed back toward the kitchen, the chef in the lead. After they'd walked a few steps, Oskar stopped, and turned around. "Here's something that may make you smile. I told the four clowns that I know all that goes on in this restaurant. If Evelyn or you have any problems with them, I let them know that they will be on the first flight back to Germany.

"Then I reminded them that Juergen and I stay in touch with important people in the restaurant and hotel business in Germany. Germany is not so big as the U.S. If we spread the word, not one decent job will open for them. They will work long hours, for no money, in shitty little dumps. I will not let hooligans bother a fine young German woman."

"Thanks, Oskar."

They continued into kitchen. The chef went back to his ravioli sauce. He leaned over the big saucepan, and sniffed the vapors coming from it. A smile appeared on his round face, and he stirred the sauce with a large wooden spoon.

Michael saw Evelyn working behind the counter in her area of the kitchen. Her hands were doing something that he couldn't see from that angle. Maybe Evelyn sensed him. She looked up, and airmailed Michael a smile that was gone before it left her face. It was the specialness, not the duration of her smile that excited him each time she graced him with it. Then she continued her work.

Nice work, Evelyn. Let's keep this our secret.

When she finished her work that night, Evelyn waited for Michael in the employee parking lot. They were going to a nearby diner for a late coffee, and continuing to get to know each other.

Michael usually liked to get late tables to make added money. Not that night. Hurriedly, he counted his cash, and figured out how much to tip the busboy, bartender, and the maître d'.

Michael smiled to himself at how this must be what teenagers feel like in high school romances. Those usually end with the last day of school. He knew it was foolish to think ahead, he hadn't even kissed Evelyn. *I wonder what the last day of her one-year visa will bring?*

Chapter Seven

MICHAEL CONSIDERED ONE OF THE benefits of growing up in Newark, N.J. - maybe the only benefit - was that New York City was eleven miles away. It was his playground.

Evelyn and he sat in comfortable wooden chairs with thin cushions at a small corner table in one of Michael's favorite restaurants in Little Italy in New York City. They were sharing a flawless tiramisu, a rendering about as common as a UFO encounter. Two frothy cappuccinos competed for their attention. Some tourists knew of this place, but not too many. That night, this small, family run business on a side street off a side street, was largely filled with laughing, gesturing, well-fed people from the neighborhood.

The meal preceding their dessert had been as delicious as the menu promised, and that Michael remembered from previous visits, usually alone with a mystery novel. The teenaged grandson of the owner and cook cleared away their dinner plates, and served them what they were currently lingering over.

The conversation between Evelyn and Michael was as varied as the ingredients in their meals. And as tasty. Evelyn picked up the white ceramic cup, and sipped her hot beverage. "Michael, you haven't told me anything about your family."

He wanted to tell her. Michael wanted to know everything about Evelyn. And he wanted her to know

Michael. Even the secret Michael. And his problem. Michael kept the problem inside. No one in the world knew. If his relationship with Evelyn was going to continue, to deepen, and Michael hoped it would, it was fair that she should know.

I can't tell her. Part of that was because some of his feelings were a mystery, even to himself. How can you explain something you don't fully understand? You can't. And if the parts you do understand are bad, you keep them hidden. Locked away as deeply as necessary to bury the bitterness.

Michael was reasonably satisfied with the person he'd become, except for his problem. He didn't think it was his Achilles' heel. *This is Achilles' entire leg. I wish I could get over this.*

Memories, no, these weren't mere memories, they were highly detailed, brightly colored, 'Please don't make me watch this again' movies, that played without warning in Michael's mind. He never willingly watched these movies, they were forced on him. Michael didn't know what part of himself tortured him this way, or why.

The opening scene was almost always the same. Michael had been twelve-years-old, and sitting on a sofa at home with his parents, Christina and Marvin La Rue, watching TV. Their next-door neighbor and close friend, Jim Santucci, knocked on the door and asked Marvin if he would please drive his seventeen-year-old daughter to her high school junior prom. His car wouldn't start, and they were running late.

Christina answered, "We'll be glad to. I'll come along to check if Elizabeth needs any final touches before her big night."

His mother turned, and looked at Michael. "We'll be right back. And no popcorn for you while we're gone, young man." Her stern voice and finger wagging didn't fool him. Her wink told him the truth.

The La Rues were an exceptionally close and loving family, and did a lot of unembarrassed kissing. His mother kissed him when he got home from school, and Christina and Marvin always went with him to his bedroom and kissed him goodnight after they monitored him brushing his teeth.

Then, as Michael got under the covers, it was always Marvin who said, "Whose turn is it?"

That was the signal for The Magic Words. Marvin started them when Michael was very young, and afraid to sleep alone in his bedroom.

Michael pleaded with his father each night to check behind the window curtains for monsters. Marvin performed a patient and thorough examination of the curtains, Michael's closet, and even under the bed. He said, "Michael, there is nothing here when the lights are out that wasn't here when they were on."

Michael nodded that he understood. Twenty-four hours later he begged his father to again check for anything evil. That was when Marvin offered to share the protective power of The Magic Words.

Michael's eyes grew big. "What are the magic words?"

Marvin carefully looked around the dark bedroom, which was faintly illuminated by the overhead hall light, as if checking for listeners. He moved toward Michael and lowered his voice. "These magic words are so powerful that they must be kept secret."

Michael's open mouth was the letter 'O'.

Marvin said, "Abracadabra, Kalamazoo," then he made a 'Stop' motion with both hands before using them to point first to himself and then to Michael as he said the words that accompanied those gestures, "No bad dreams for me, or you."

Twelve-year-old Michael's fear of monsters was gone,

the family tradition remained. Each night, as either Michael or Marvin said those words, Christina comically refused to follow them. Instead of pointing with the words, she always waved her arms around, and garbled the words purposely. Marvin pretended to be annoyed at her lack of deference. Christina and Marvin sometimes privately wondered if Michael would continue this playfulness in the future with his children.

A different family ritual took place when Marvin got home each late afternoon. He always tapped the same sequence of short touches on his car horn that announced his arrival. Christina and Michael went to the door, waiting for him to open it and say to them, "Who gets the first kiss?"

Then Michael and his mother gently pushed and shoved each other to get at the smiling and delighted Marvin. Michael was nearly a teenager and approaching the phase in his life where he would probably be embarrassed being seen with his parents in public. But he loved them deeply. They were Mom and Dad in public, Mommy and Daddy at home.

That night, as his parents were getting ready to drive the neighbor's daughter to her prom, Michael turned his face up for them to kiss. Christina said, "We'll be home in about a half hour."

On Christina and Marvin's way home from dropping the neighbor's daughter off, a drunk driver stretched that half hour into forever. The drunk was treated for minor cuts, Michael became a twelve-year-old orphan. Because of his age, he had to be placed in a home with adults. The authorities asked a grieving Michael about aunts and uncles. When contacted, they told the officials that they were busy raising their own children and couldn't take in Michael. He didn't mind. He didn't like them much, or his cousins.

Christina and Marvin had a will, it didn't name a

guardian for Michael. They hadn't expected to die before Michael reached eighteen. Neatly paper-clipped behind the will in a drawer were adoption papers. A pleasant and sympathetic middle-aged woman from Family Services drew the assignment of telling Michael the truth.

That's how Michael found out that his parents weren't his parents. By love, yes. Not by blood. It didn't matter. Michael would always consider Christina and Marvin to be his family, and never stopped referring to them as his parents. The social services counselor was talking to him as Michael fought a tornado of competing emotions: grief, loss, confusion, shock, and others that he couldn't isolate well enough to stick a name on. He knew he was required to respond to the case worker's blur of words. What would Michael say? And where could he begin?

After a long, confusing, nearly dizzying silence, Michael said, "My birth mother gave me away just like that? Abandoned me without first seeing if I worked out?" Being slammed with this news immediately after losing the family he loved was nearly unbearable.

The social worker replied in a sympathetic voice, "I'm sure it wasn't like that. She must have had her reasons."

Michael struggled to stay calm, like the La Rues had taught him to behave in bad situations. "What reason could there be to toss away your own child like a bag of garbage?"

The counselor tried to soothe him. "Michael, I know you must be upset. We don't know what her situation was."

"No, we don't. But we know what her response was." He paused for a moment. "Do you have kids?"

She didn't want to answer. She knew where this was going. The force of Michael's stare gave her no choice. She spoke softly. "Yes."

"Could you ever have given any of them away?"

Once again, she knew that he deserved the truth.

His youth might not be over, but his years of protected innocence certainly were. Her voice was even weaker as she looked away, and confessed, "No. Never."

Michael nodded in agreement at the one answer she could truthfully give. "My father, Marvin La Rue, taught me to judge people by their actions, not their intentions."

She realized how mature and intelligent Michael was, and wondered what portion of that was learned, and what was inherited?

Michael continued. "I know you're trying to be kind to me, and I appreciate it. Nothing you can say is going to change my mind. Let's talk about the future, not the past. What happens now?"

Chapter Eight

THE AUTHORITIES DIDN'T RELY SOLELY on young Michael for the names of relatives. They searched thoroughly for anyone related to the La Rues. None were willing to take in the twelve-year-old. Michael spent the next six years of his life in various foster homes and orphanages.

Michael understood the need to carefully screen and select a young person before taking them into your home. But he felt that it could have been done in a way that didn't make him feel like he was a piece of equipment being examined for defects before being purchased.

He did a first-class job of fitting in at the houses of the foster families. Michael's problems were at school. At the first school he transferred to, a group of four boys decided to pick on and torment the new kid. Michael put up with it for a while. Christina and Marvin encouraged him to be bigger than other people, and to walk away from trouble.

Then the wolf pack started strolling by Michael in the hallways, and sneakily pushing him against the wall or lockers when no one was looking. His refusal to retaliate was seen as weakness, not strength, so they escalated their bullying. Michael's full lunch tray was 'accidentally' knocked out of his hands in the school cafeteria at least once a week. And he was often tripped by a quick foot while he looked around for an empty seat at a table.

Michael didn't mind the laughter of the other students when he picked himself up. However, the big, messy, wet blotches of food stains he wore on his clothes for the rest of the school day were uncomfortable.

After each incident, his foster parents asked about the stains. It didn't take long before Michael could no longer cover it up as clumsiness or unintentional bumping. The foster family phoned his teacher, who properly informed the principal, Mr. Stacy Moulton. Michael was spared identifying the trouble-makers. Their reputations and other recent problems accomplished that.

Mr. Moulton summoned the small gang to his office and finished his hard-boiled lecture with a warning before dismissing them. The four jerks displayed an obvious lack of concern, and waited until they snuck outside for a smoke before laughing about the principal, and cursing Michael, while promising to get even.

The following day, on his way home from seventh grade, Michael saw the goon squad blocking the sidewalk ahead of him. He knew this was fight or flight time. Marvin La Rue had served in the Marine Corps, and taught Michael that when walking away from a bad situation was not an option, don't fight defensively. Attack aggressively. Identify and exploit their weakness with your strength. And kick some ass. Mr. La Rue had skilled Michael in that philosophy on the heavy bag in the basement of their home until Michael possessed sore knuckles and lots of skill.

Marvin La Rue had been a quiet, peaceful man who believed that there was no drought of bad or evil people in the world. And that they would never obey the rules of a civilized society. Michael's father taught him that trying to have them respect others wouldn't work. Bad intentioned people lacked the honor or decency for that to succeed. The only way to keep them in line was to have them fear you. The single thing they understood was raw, abrupt, violent force. And the willingness to use it. That was exactly what Michael felt boiling inside of him as he faced the punks, and planned the strategy he hoped he wouldn't need.

"Here's the wimpy squealer himself," said one of the jerks. Michael didn't know their names and tagged him as the leader, he seemed to be the spokesman.

"Let him know who's the boss, Bobby," said one of the others.

Michael's father told him that in a situation like this, take out the top dog first. This should kill any fight the others have. Which probably wasn't much to start with, or they wouldn't be in a pack.

The jerks moved in closer. Bobby spoke again. "The principal isn't around now to protect you, asshole."

"I don't want to fight."

"No, shit."

Michael moved closer to him. They stood about two feet apart. Bobby looked startled. He backed up a step.

Michael said, "If I do fight, you won't like what happens."

Bobby looked at his friends, borrowing courage from their "Kick his ass," chorus. He knew his mask of swagger slipped. It was vital to put it back, and quickly. Bobby regained lost psychological territory by taking a step forward. Michael held his ground.

The two boys were nearly toe-to-toe. Michael calmly breathed through his nose, Bobby's lips were parted, and he was nearly hyperventilating. His friends shouted taunts.

"Hit him, Bobby."

"Show him he can't mess with us."

"Deck that clown."

Michael noticed Bobby nearly vibrating with eagerness. Michael's father extensively coached him in what signs to look for as indicators of aggression. This one was an alarm loudly blasting. Michael remained composed, even serene. "I'm going to give you one more chance. This is your last warning. Go home. Right now."

Bobby bent forward a little. His body language shouted his intentions.

Marvin La Rue always stressed, "Do all you can to avoid a fight. If you know it's inevitable, make sure to get in the first punch. And the second. And the third."

Bobby pulled his right arm back with his fist ready. Michael fired four powerful punches. Bobby fell to the ground like he'd been shot. Big drops of blood burst from Bobby's nose. And he held his belly where Michael doubled him up.

Bobby's friends looked on, not believing what they saw. Bobby shook his head. A spray of red flew into the breeze. He discovered where his feet were and slowly began to get up. Michael put him back down.

Bobby's three buddies were stunned. One of them stepped away, unwilling to get any closer to Michael. The other two looked at each other, nodded, and moved in, feeling invincible with four fists against two.

The two punks fought with anger, but not skill. Michael fought with the released white-hot fury of losing his loving adoptive parents, and being abandoned by his real mother. And he did it with the fighting ability his father drilled into him. The punks had no chance.

If a boxing referee had stood there, he would have raised Michael's hands in victory within a minute. Instead, Michael lowered his fists to his sides and stepped away backwards, he didn't trust the punks. This wasn't necessary. Bobby and the other two stayed on the ground, where Michael dropped them. One was crying, the other two were making wounded sounds, and couldn't decide where the pain was worst. The fourth one, who initially backed up, ran down the street, and was already two blocks away.

Michael calmly walked home. He said nothing. He knew tomorrow would bring another fight. Not involving kids and fists, but adults and angry words.

Early the next morning, outside the locked front door of the school, the outraged parents of the injured bullies sucked on cigarette stubs while repeatedly scowling at their watches.

Soon, Stacy Moulton, the principal, arrived, well before school hours. Mr. Moulton already knew the circumstances. The parental grapevine had worked efficiently. Mr. Moulton anticipated this confrontation.

The six parents, two of the couples were divorced, didn't bother with fake courtesy or introductions as they loudly and angrily demanded that Michael be thrown out of school for the rest of the year – permanently banned would be better - for savagely beating their innocent and pure sons without any provocation.

Then, without pausing to let Mr. Moulton respond, they threatened criminal charges with a lawsuit against the school, the principal, the school board, and the entire school district. Mr. Moulton wasn't mocking the seriousness of the incident, when he secretly smiled, and wondered why they left out the head of the state and federal Department of Education?

Mr. Moulton asked them to follow him as he unlocked the school front door, and led them down an unlit corridor of classrooms to his modest office. The parents stood, there were only two chairs. The group angrily repeated their demands, in loud voices that contained not a trace of restraint, politeness, or tact.

Mr. Moulton had earned his position with proficiency seasoned by years of experience. He was ready for this. He listened without comment. Then he opened his scuffed brown leather briefcase and removed some papers. As he always instructed the students, Mr. Moulton had done his homework.

He handed three sheets stapled together to each of the six curious and confused parents. Each document chronicled, in order by dates, and with devastating detail, the various and frequent infractions of school rules and policies that their offspring accumulated while attending his school. Two sheets were required to list all of them. The third page contained the legal definition of 'stalking' and added that the verbal threats Michael endured fulfilled the lawful threshold for 'assault.'

Mr. Moulton allowed them sufficient time to read the papers, and think about them. Then, he said, "You're right about the possibility of a lawsuit. And I think Michael has a powerful shot at winning it. Don't you agree?"

Later that day, Michael was suspended from school for one week. This was a token punishment. Bobby and the others were tossed out for three weeks. At first, Michael felt embarrassed about being home while school was in session. Then he saw it better: this was a vacation from school work that he already knew ,and was bored by. And as a bonus, it was a break from students he was either indifferent to, or didn't like.

Michael's foster parents didn't share his view of this. They were pressured by neighbors and friends to send Michael back to the orphanage with the excuse that it wasn't working out. Whether his foster parents believed that he instigated a fight against three cruel bullies, or they meekly surrendered to being squeezed, Michael would never know. Before his suspension ended, Michael was once again a guest of the state.

There were various versions of this until Michael graduated from high school. The other incidents weren't always violent, but they were always predictable. The new kid in school got taunted and shunned while rumors about his past were whispered to enough eager ears until they were accepted as 'truth.' Michael heard some of the rumors, and shook his head in amazement. He was given away by his birth family because he was a trouble-maker. He was an orphan because he rigged the family car to crash and kill his parents.

Michael coped with each incident by keeping increasingly to himself. He retreated within his private protective borders and stayed alone whenever possible, not sharing his feelings, or his life. And he liked it that way. Michael grew to prefer his own solitary company to that of others. He didn't feel lonely. Library books and his thoughts were sufficient companions. Michael bounced between foster homes and the orphanage until he graduated from high school. One week later he joined the United States Marine Corps for four years. If Marvin La Rue had been a Marine, so would he.

Something began growing inside of Michael. Something bad. Simply stated, Michael felt betrayed. Betrayed by his unknown biological father for never being around, and betrayed by his unknown biological mother for abandoning him.

It got worse. Michael felt betrayed by the La Rues for leaving him. He knew that made no sense at all, and he fought it while seething with shame. Yes, Michael realized they hadn't chosen to be killed by a drunk driver. But Michael was human. And humans are complex creatures, not driven exclusively by logic or intellect. Adding to the list, he'd been betrayed by each foster family that he'd lived with when they rejected and returned him like he was a broken or defective object.

Michael didn't like this complicated jumble that was metastasizing within him. And he hated that he couldn't make the feeling go away. Especially the bad ones about his parents, the La Rues.

Michael was proud of the self-discipline that his father, Marvin, lovingly taught him, and that the Marine Corps built upon. But, no amount of that discipline defused, destroyed, or reduced the nightmare of past betrayals. And maybe worse, the dread of future ones. Potential future betrayals joined with past ones to form a monster - a hideous, sneering, lurking demon that tortured Michael with its presence while waiting for the chance to wound him further. Michael's sensitivity to betrayal lay buried just under the surface, like a landmine, waiting to explode and destroy everything around it. Everything Michael loved.

That wasn't all. Neediness lived inside of him. A hunger for emotional intimacy. This was as unwanted as his feelings about betrayal. And it was confusing. Michael didn't understand how he could enjoy being alone, yet want Evelyn to desire him. *How in the world can I ever reveal this to her?*

Michael pulled himself back to the present and looked at his watch. He said to Evelyn, "My family? It's a long and not very interesting story. I'll tell you when we have time."

Chapter Nine

ON THE FOLLOWING MONDAY, EVELYN and Michael sat in a booth at a local diner, enjoying afternoon coffee, and the pleasure of their conversation. Michael still had not kissed Evelyn. That was by choice. He hungrily wanted to kiss her. *I think I'm more attracted to Evelyn than I ever was with any other woman. But I don't want kissing her to be something that I check-off on a list. I'll know when the time - and the mood - are exactly right. And I can wait until then.* He smiled inside. *I hope that moment doesn't get lost trying to find us.* Michael sensed that kissing Evelyn for the first time would be something he would remember for a long time. Maybe the rest of his life.

He pushed those thoughts aside and asked, "Do you stay in touch with any of your friends in Germany?"

Evelyn put down her coffee cup. "As you described yourself, I'm a private person. I have a few close friends, not a big collection. One of them is a girlfriend I stay in contact with, we grew up together. I received a letter from her last week telling me what is new in her life."

Evelyn sipped her coffee and continued. "She broke-up with her husband. He was very demanding. She felt like a maid and servant, not his wife. She said she tried for a long time to get him to improve, then finally realized that he wanted things that way. He didn't want to change. She hated to do it," Evelyn shrugged, "she gave up."

Michael said, "Relationships shouldn't have to be work. Yes, I know that effort and compromise are required sometimes. Being with the other person should flow naturally, like with close friends." Michael had a happy, yet sad, flash of the genuine friendship between Christina and Marvin La Rue.

He continued. "In a romantic relationship, they should be close friends. If they aren't, then what's the point? If statistics are to be believed, the average American watches television a bunch of hours each night. These couples sit there, staring at a big screen. They appear to be together, they're not. They're alone with their private passions, and secret desires. Silently bleeding their lives away. They're not killing time, they're torturing it to death."

Michael shook his head. "I feel sorry for them."

He pushed his nearly empty coffee cup away. Michael placed his forearms on the table. "This reminds me of the runner who doesn't win any races. One day a coach walks up to him at a track meet and says, 'Would you like to know the secret to win races?'"

"The runner says, 'Sure, I would.'"

"The coach replies, 'Run faster.'"

Evelyn laughed.

Michael continued, "I know this may sound like that, so obvious that it's not necessary to say, to me the answer is obvious. Become involved with the right person."

"You make it sound like it's easy to do."

"It is."

Evelyn drank from her cup as she patiently waited for the explanation she hoped would follow.

"I'm not a complicated person. I like to keep things basic," Michael said. "People are usually attracted to others based on looks. They probably knew very little about the other person to start. Here's where the simplicity comes in. After you get to know them, you either both sincerely enjoy being together, and fit well, or not. If not, move on. You owe it to them, and to yourself."

Michael smiled. "See, wasn't that easy?"

Evelyn nodded. "Yes."

He said, "And as you discover new things about them, there either are warning signs, or there aren't."

"Let me guess. If there are warning signs, you move on."

He smiled again. "Give our German visitor a gold star. I'm not saying that two people should be exactly alike, have all of the same tastes, or even agree on everything. That would be boring. But the more they have in common, particularly the important things, the better. The passion and excitement of a new relationship doesn't last forever, and that's probably a positive thing. So, once they come back down to earth from the heavenly cloud they've been on, if there isn't a genuine friendship, they've got problems."

Evelyn smiled again. "Are you speaking for yourself or as the spokesman for all men?"

Michael paused. *I'm sure she's at least somewhat teasing me.*

He said, "I am Everyman. I have two pairs of shoes. One is black, and the other is sneakers. My selection of trousers is quite varied, I have jeans in both blue and black. My idea of a satisfying meal is one that has no more than four ingredients. And one of them should be hot sauce. I eat it out of the frying pan unless I have company. With guests, I serve it on mismatched plates, chipped of course. I don't want anyone to think I'm a snob."

Evelyn watched silently as Michael continued. "The correct side dish is always an important decision. Personally, I think it's hard to go wrong with Cheetos.

This fine dinner must be accompanied by a suitable wine. After I twist off the cap, I sip from the bottle to make sure it's been aged long enough before I serve it. Two hours from vine to bottle should do, don't you think?"

Evelyn nodded her agreement, enjoying Michael's humor.

"Now for dessert. It's critical to end this fine experience with a flourish. And nothing does that as well as a package of Twinkies. It sends precisely the right message: I am a suave, sophisticated man of the world, and not ashamed to show it."

Michael nodded. "That's about it. The ideal feast from a man in touch with his sensitive side. Reservations not required. And neither are shoes, socks, or clean clothes. Just an appetite."

Evelyn's smile grew. "Michael, I don't know what to make of you. You don't fit into any categories."

"Is that good or bad?"

"It's refreshingly good." *And refreshingly appealing. I could fall for you, Michael. Maybe in a big way. I can't let myself.*

Chapter Ten

MICHAEL WAS THE LONE WAITER in the kitchen of The Mansion. It was that no man's land between lunch and dinner. Michael watched as the last drops of hot, dark liquid surrendered to gravity, and fell into his small cup at the espresso machine. Just like the day when Evelyn literally walked into his life.

The kitchen crew was already busy getting ready for the hectic dinner rush that would start sooner than they wanted. The sounds of knives chopping, pots and pans clanging, and ingredients arranged to be within easy reach reminded him of a symphony warming up. Michael felt like each evening was a performance. The customers were the audience, and they came here not merely to eat – any decent restaurant could satisfy that need. They wanted to be entertained, pampered, and pleased by the three-act event.

Act One opened with being greeted and charmed by Ron Grace, the tuxedoed head maître d' who asked if they had reservations. The answer was usually, "Of course."

Ron asked this not to challenge, but to give them the chance to boast a bit. To announce that, yes, they did have reserved seating at a probably booked-out, highly regarded restaurant. As if this were something they'd earned, not requested. The patrons felt flattered, and proud to say it. Ron was savvy enough to massage their egos by asking.

Ron then escorted them to a table that reflected their status. Only an insider knew that subtle advantages of table placement existed. But, there were no bad tables, such as placed near the highly trafficked kitchen doors. Ron always made each person feel like they were a V.I.P., whether they were a celebrity - and there were enough of them - a once a week regular, or a first timer. He was a true professional, and genuinely wanted them to enjoy their dining experience. The money that savvy customers discretely palmed to him while shaking hands didn't hurt Ron's feelings. Or their chances for a table upgrade.

Act Two began with the waiter introducing himself and presenting the menu. And, of course, the wine list. The waiter wouldn't return to the table until summoned by a small nod or a gesture. The former by polished patrons, the latter by rookies.

Act Two continued with the food, usually several courses. Soup was an excellent first option. The rich lobster bisque received raves all year, and was highly popular during the cold months. Or perhaps a tangy gazpacho. Next, an appetizer. The lobster raviolis, made by executive chef Oskar Schultes, were in demand, and more flavorful than any others that Michael ever tasted. The gravlax, not always available, also made by Oskar, presented another wonderful choice. Then, maybe a Caesar salad. This was prepared tableside for at least two people, in a large wooden bowl, with the right amount of flair – entertaining, not ostentatious. For main courses, the seasonally changing choices were extensive enough to please, though not so plentiful as to invite skepticism that the kitchen could successfully produce all of them.

The dessert cart was Act Three. The cart was a rolling beauty, with white marble handles, and two polished dark wood shelves. But, the beauty of the cart and its features were banished to the background, overwhelmed by the luscious creations from the experienced German pastry chef. He didn't invent anything new, he didn't need to. His versions of desserts such as Grand Marnier cheesecake, served with fresh raspberries and Grand Marnier sauce, tasted as delightful to your mouth as they did to your eyes.

And, as a bonus, the service throughout the meal was professional and unobtrusive, allowing patrons to focus on their meal, dining partner, or both.

Michael felt that each evening was as exciting as the opening of a new play. With an eager audience that wanted, hoped, and expected to be delighted. That adrenaline rush was a big part of why he worked as a waiter. Michael did not view himself as a member of the cast. He was too modest for that. He considered himself to be part of the backstage crew who anonymously made things happen.

However, Evelyn is leading lady material.

Finished with his hot beverage, Michael deposited the white ceramic espresso cup where it belonged, and went into the dining room to inspect his station of tables. He was checking for perfection. Michael slowly walked past each table, and scanned the fine linen table cloth, and the expertly folded and positioned napkins of the same material. His gaze approved of the highly polished and spotless silverware that rested exactly where it should be.

Michael held each wine and water glass toward the large, elegant chandelier that hung about five feet over his head and slowly rotated them, using the light to check for anything that didn't belong there. The hardworking and smart Brazilian bus boy, Michael's favorite, had done his usual fine work. *Super job, Galeno.*

One final glance into the mirror behind the beautiful wooden bar made sure that his tuxedo bow tie was correctly centered. Michael was ready for that evening's performance.

~ * * * ~

The dining room was finally empty of customers. The night had unrolled as expected, with just enough occasional tension to make the calmness comforting. Evelyn said she needed to write letters home, and to take care of some personal items, so Michael was on his own.

His last table thanked him for a pleasurable evening, and tipped accordingly. Michael went home to his apartment, and let a relaxing hot shower rinse away any residue of the kitchen and his work. He uncorked a bottle of red wine, read for a while, and went to bed.

Evelyn arranged to also have Mondays and Tuesdays off. Monday afternoon, after eating at a terrific local diner, they parked in front of the main branch of the library. Michael preferred its downtown location. He liked the area and the volume of books at that large facility. He needed to return two novels and check out three that he'd reserved.

First he went into the building right across the street. A clever and creative woman converted a small neighborhood church into a café which was made complete with a talented cook, and an even more talented pastry chef.

Michael exited the cafe with a white plastic container in one hand. He reached into the open car window and handed it to Evelyn. Then he ran into the library, and came out within minutes holding three books. Shortly after that they were in his apartment for her first visit. He positioned the new books on the top shelf of a dark wooden cabinet that was neatly organized, and nearly full with other books. Some were from the library, some were not. Michael noticed Evelyn watching. He shrugged. "I like to read."

"Me, too." She continued taking in the room with its empty walls and plain furniture. Her face disclosed nothing.

Michael walked over to Evelyn, and looked at the container that she held. "Did you take a bite of that lemon Bundt cake while I was in the library? Wait, that would be too obvious. Did you lick the lemon icing? Yeah, I bet that's what you did."

"I did not." Evelyn enjoyed his spontaneous humor.

"Uh-huh. That's exactly what anyone would say. Open the box, let's see."

She lifted the top of the container, and moved it to about three inches in front of his face. "Look for yourself."

Michael went through a pretense of inspecting the small cake carefully. He placed his hands on hers, and turned the box to look at its contents from different angles.

"I think I see the trail of a tongue in the icing. Yes, I'm sure I do. And since you were the only other person in the car, my list of suspects is a short one." He looked at Evelyn. "Open your mouth, I need to inspect for evidence."

She laughed. "I will not. Even if I did sneak a quick taste of the icing, and I didn't, it's dissolved and gone by now."

"I see you've already prepared an alibi, a sure sign of guilt. Yes, you're right, the icing may be gone, the distinctive lemon aroma will have lingered. Let me get a whiff of your breath."

Evelyn moved in a little. She was aware that things had shifted from joking around to borderline romantic. It wasn't solely Michael's words, it was their softer tone, and the increased closeness of their bodies.

Evelyn knew that if she continued, she'd be entering

a place she considered off-limits. A place where complications lived. A place that could jeopardize her plans to put the U.S. on her resume, and return to Germany without any entanglements.

This was decision time. Evelyn wasn't the kind of person to have a casual relationship. If she didn't stop now - right now - all her careful planning would be replaced by the uncertainty that accompanies any new relationship. She hesitated, as consequences zipped across her mind like a meteor shower on a clear night.

Then Evelyn moved closer to Michael.

Her mouth was an inch or two from his as she exhaled a small puff.

He inhaled audibly. "Hmm, that certainly seems lemony to me. I'm willing to give you the benefit of the doubt. I need to taste your lips to be sure."

"If you don't detect any lemon, do I get an apology?"

"No talking, please. I need to concentrate on gathering evidence."

Evelyn smiled with anticipation as she closed her eyes. Evelyn felt Michael's lips barely touch hers. An involuntary sound of pleasure escaped from her mouth. Michael lightly caressed her lips with his. Evelyn's eyes remained shut as Michael placed his hands on the back of Evelyn's head. The arousal continued to build. An authentic, not-to-be-interrupted, eager lips-seeking-lips, kiss began.

Evelyn and Michael's first kiss.

Chapter Eleven

THE KISS STARTED SLOWLY. THEN quickly gained passion. The intensity accelerated the way a rocket does to break free of the earth's gravity. Michael felt like he was riding a rocket, exploding into a new universe. A universe that revolved around the somewhat mysterious, and extremely desirable Evelyn.

Evelyn's hands moved to the sides of Michael's face as their kiss continued, and deepened. Then she ended it, and slowly pulled her head back.

"Michael, that was special. We need to stop."

"Why?"

"I can't continue. I mean I shouldn't continue."

He smiled. "Am I that bad a kisser? Maybe we should practice. Work on my technique."

Evelyn couldn't help laughing. "I'm trying to be serious. And you're not helping."

"OK, I'll stop. Why are you resisting me?"

"I'm not. I'm resisting myself."

Michael placed his hands on Evelyn's waist. "Now I'm totally confused."

She sighed. "This isn't easy. And a lot of it is putting words to unformed feelings, so please be patient. And don't judge me until I'm done. Or interrupt. I may not get my thinking back if you do."

"I promise."

Evelyn paused, and then said, "How should I put this?" She seemed to say it more to herself than to

Michael. "When I left Germany, my intention was to return when my J-1 visa expired in one year." Her voice revealed new seriousness, "That is still my plan."

Michael looked at Evelyn, waiting for her to continue. He realized that she wasn't going to. "That's it?"

"Yes."

"There isn't anything else?"

"No."

"Let me see if I have this right. We can't get romantic because in a year you're going back to Germany?"

"No, we can't get romantic, as you put it, because if we do, it might complicate my going back to Germany."

Evelyn sharpened her look. "That isn't going to happen. I won't let it happen."

She gave him time to consider this. "Now do you understand?" She added in a gentle voice, "I'm sorry. That came out, oh, what is the English word? Harsh? Harsher? Is that correct? More harsh than I intended. Please forgive me."

Michael struggled to get her words to align with his feelings and emotions. He felt like he was trying to make the pieces from two different jigsaw puzzles fit together. No matter how he turned the pieces, they didn't match.

Evelyn gazed at him. Her heart began to ache as she watched the dilemma spread to his face. "Michael..."

He raised his right hand. "Hold on, I've nearly got it." Michael closed his eyes. He opened them. "OK, now I have it."

"What? What is it you have?"

"The answer."

"You do?"

Michael smiled. "Of course. I once read a book - *The Ideal Solution to Everything* - and I memorized it. I needed some time to flip through it in my mind until I found what I needed."

She knew he was teasing. “That sounds interesting. Would you care to share it with me?”

His smile grew. “Sure. It’s obvious that I have feelings for you.”

“Your talent for observation is amazing. Yes, I suspected that.”

“And it’s equally clear that you like me.”

“Impressive. You should have been a detective.”

“Okay, we’re in agreement so far.”

Evelyn nodded as Michael continued. “The answer is in two parts. First, we should resume exactly where we left off.”

“Yes, I understand the first part,” she said. “The second part is the critical one. What is it?”

“It’s right in front of you. You were too smitten by me to realize it.”

“Smitten? What is smitten? It sounds like bitten. Are they the same?”

“Hmm, yes.”

“So, I’m bitten. Now what?”

“OK, this part is complicated. Please pay attention.”

“Yes, I’m listening.”

“I mean really, really listening.”

“Stop. I mean continue. Yes, I’m listening.”

“In a year, you either go home, or you stay here.”

Evelyn said nothing. And neither did her face. Finally, she said, “You’re serious?”

“As serious as lightning to a golfer.”

She laughed. “I can’t decide if that is brilliant in its simplicity, or merely simple-minded. Yes, you’re right. It is the answer. I think maybe I have been taking this, and myself, too seriously. What is it that you Americans say, ‘Loosen up?’ That is what I need to do.”

“Well, before you *loosen* up, how ‘bout if you *pucker* up?”

“Pucker up?”

"Never mind."

Evelyn started to speak, her words were lost in their kiss.

They embraced tenderly at first.

Then eagerly.

Then ferociously.

Michael held Evelyn's face in his hands as they kissed. She put her arms behind his back and pulled him tighter. Closer was not possible.

Evelyn hooked her right foot behind Michael's left calf. This pushed him to a higher level of arousal. He ran his hands over her back. The feel of her thin and skimpy bra through her clothes thrust his excitement even further.

Michael was a starved man groping for food. His hands travelled down Evelyn's sides to her short skirt. His fingers raised the material an inch as the warm, smooth, bare skin under it presented itself for caressing. The tempting, smooth skin of her legs was heaven. Michael slowly moved his hands higher along the back of her legs. Michael's fingertips found the edge of her panties.

Evelyn pulled away several inches.

Michael thought, *Damn. I blew it. Too much, too fast.*

She looked at him with half-closed eyes. "Why don't you carry me into your bedroom."

Chapter Twelve

NEITHER OF THEM EVER FORGOT that night. Evelyn woke slowly, and opened her eyes. She didn't want to move. She wanted to lie there, lingering, savoring where she was, who she was with, and how she felt. They lay on their left sides. Both were naked. Evelyn was pressed against Michael's back, her right arm around his chest. She sensed that he was waking, and whispered, "Good morning."

Evelyn added, "Are you sorry I'm still here?"

Michael rolled over and kissed her. "Good morning to you. And what kind of question is that?"

"Doesn't a man prefer that his one-nighters leave before the sun comes up?"

"Is that what this is? A one-nighter?"

"I'm not the man in this bed. Why don't you tell me?"

Michael yawned and smiled. "I try not to do any thinking on an empty stomach. Let's go out for breakfast, and we'll talk."

"Are you sure you don't want to drop me off at my flat? I'll understand."

He could tell by Evelyn's voice and face that she meant it.

Michael stared at her with the realization that Evelyn wasn't an American woman. She didn't have the cultural, social, or language background that he would normally take for granted. He couldn't speak in dating shorthand and expect Evelyn to understand. *This is going to be a challenge.* Michael sensed this might be not one challenge, but a series of huge ones. He smiled. *The bigger the test, the bigger the reward.*

Michael believed that relationships between men and women were interesting enough with the gender and possible priority differences. Now, toss in some international, cultural, and social disparities, sprinkle on some language difficulties, and this could be the Love Boat colliding with the Titanic. Michael smiled again. *Evelyn is probably worth it. Time will tell. I've been fooled before.*

"Evelyn, I'd like to get to know you better. All I know about you right now is that I like you, you're beautiful, and an exciting lover. Oh, and you don't snore."

She smiled. "Don't men think that women who give in quickly are easy?"

"If you assume that I think less of you because we went to bed, you're wrong." He paused, knowing this was an important moment in their young relationship. Michael tried to make his face and voice serious. "You didn't rape me last night, did you?"

Evelyn smiled, and shook her head.

"That means I had something to do with what happened. And I did it willingly."

She nodded. Then she yawned, covering her mouth with a hand. "Breakfast sounds fantastic. And some coffee."

Evelyn sat up, letting the sheet falling away. Michael tried not to stare. He enjoyed tasting her fabulous body with his eyes. She got out of his bed, obviously comfortable with her nudity.

"Which way is the bathroom?"

"Make a right, then the first door on the left."

As she gathered her clothes, Michael added, "I don't have an extra toothbrush. You can use mine."

Evelyn stopped, and faced him, holding her clothes,

not attempting to cover herself. "I'm glad you don't have that item here. I don't want to think that I am merely the latest overnight guest in Michael's sex hotel." Evelyn paused. "Or am I?"

Michael hesitated, trying different answers on for size. He wasn't going to lie. Michael considered himself to be thoroughly honest. Maybe too honest. He knew, however, that words could be dangerous weapons as well as powerful tools. He wanted to choose his words deliberately. This early in a relationship the trust factor had not been established. Michael believed that the wrong wording, even for the right answer, might cause Evelyn to call for a taxi and not come back.

Evelyn said, "Your silence has answered my question."

Damn.

"Michael, I didn't think that you were a virgin waiting to meet me so you could experience sex for the first time."

Evelyn surprised and impressed him with her disarming of the potential land-mine. She said, "Understand this, as long as we are together, the Michael Hotel is closed to others. I am a generous person, yet there are certain things I do not share."

Is there anything about this woman that isn't going to impress me? He said, "I can deal with that."

Evelyn nodded acceptance as she covered her mouth and yawned again. She started toward the door, and turned. "I need a few minutes. And then the American breakfast you promised."

~ * * * ~

Evelyn and Michael made love every night. And they continued getting to know each other and exchanging information about themselves. Evelyn was like a highlights film - no details. From even their first meeting, Michael was intrigued by Evelyn, and wanted to know more about her. He needed to probe for anything beneath the surface. "I'm not trying to be nosy. I'm fascinated by you."

Evelyn replied, "I don't like to talk about myself."

Michael smiled. "That's a welcome break from people who aren't happy unless the conversation is about them, and nothing except them. Don't worry, if there are any skeletons in your closet, they're safe with me."

"Skeletons in my closet?"

"Sorry. It means that you have dark secrets you don't want anyone to know about."

Evelyn's voice and posture shifted to a stiffened, slightly defensive tone. "I have no dark secrets. If I did, they would be my business."

Michael made a mock face of exasperation. "Let me make sure I understand. You're not keeping anything hidden. But if you were, you'd want to keep that fact hidden. Is that about right?"

Evelyn's strict look melted into an embarrassed smile. "Am I being as foolish as that sounds?"

"Do you want the polite answer, or the honest one?"

"I always want the truth."

"Then, yes, you are." Michael paused and said, "On the mistake scale, this barely shows up. You're going to have to do a lot better if you want to come anywhere near my record breaking blunders."

Evelyn put her hands on his. "You have a way of making my mistake seem harmless. This is an unusual quality, and I value it. Thank you."

~ * * * ~

One day soon after that, Evelyn asked, "Michael, do you know where the Excelsior Room is in New York City?"

"I believe it's one of the top floors of some tall building in Rockefeller Center. Why?"

"I've heard of it from Germany and it sounded romantic. Do you think we could go there for a drink sometime?"

"Of course." Michael suspected that Evelyn really wanted to go there for dinner. He already knew her well enough to know that she would never suggest that, the cost was extravagant. And she would vigorously refuse to go for dinner if he made the offer.

Michael didn't know all he wanted to about Evelyn, though he'd observed enough to know that she was quite aware of the value of money. They ate in restaurants on their nights together and Evelyn insisted, over his protests - both as a gentleman, and in recognition of their income disparities - to alternate paying the bill. She always considered menus carefully. Michael could tell by what she ordered, that Evelyn's purse, not her taste buds, influenced the decisions, especially when he paid. He knew that she would object to him spending more than a minimal amount on her. However, Evelyn's twenty-seventh birthday was coming up.

Michael said, "Let's go to the Excelsior Room for your birthday. We can have a drink, and then go to Chinatown for an inexpensive dinner. I'm thinking that some steamed dumplings and pork chow fun might hit the spot. Then we can walk across Canal Street to Little Italy for cappuccinos and cannoli. How does that sound?"

"That will be excellent. Thank you, Michael." She rewarded him with a tight hug and a kiss.

They chatted as Michael drove the thirty minutes into Manhattan on the night of Evelyn's birthday. Traffic was surprisingly moderate approaching the Lincoln Tunnel, and he was lucky enough to find a parking space on the street near Rockefeller Center. Michael didn't mind spending whatever money it cost to eat or be entertained in New York, he hated to have to pay a private parking lot a big surcharge on top of that.

As always, Evelyn looked spectacular. She was attired exactly right, the result of neither too much attention, nor too little. She bestowed beauty to an uncomplicated black dress. Michael knew that some people needed an item, perhaps an accessory, to complete how they looked. Evelyn's only extra was the occasional amazing smile that she flashed for him. She required nothing else.

They exited the elevator on the sixty-fifth floor of the correct building and walked to where a handsome, middle-aged man in a black tuxedo guarded his podium in the large and open lobby of the Excelsior Room.

The host smiled. "May I help you?"

"Yes, we have reservations for drinks. The last name is La Rue."

The man glanced down at his scheduling book. "Of course, Mr. La Rue. Please come with me."

Michael waved his arm for Evelyn to proceed, and then followed. They walked past tall glass panels that provided a glittering display of nighttime Manhattan. This led to the tastefully decorated lounge area. Their guide pulled Evelyn's chair out from their small table while Michael took care of his.

When they were alone, Evelyn said, "Did you enjoy the view?"

"Yes. New York at night is always spectacular."

"I'm not referring to New York."

"What makes you think I was watching you?"

"Michael, please don't tell me that I bought this dress for nothing."

He smiled. "Guilty, as charged, your honor. And, no, you didn't waste a single penny of whatever you paid for it."

Michael spoke quietly in the big, hushed,

cosmopolitan room. "For the record, every woman in here hates you. Each man stopped chatting with their wives, and girlfriends, and swiveled their heads to follow you. They were tempted to jump up and applaud." He added, "I could be wrong, I think I saw three of them half-way out of their seats to do that."

Even by the candlelight of their table, in the subdued lighting, he noticed Evelyn blush. She said nothing.

A waiter came by holding a silver tray with two full champagne glasses. He carefully placed one in front of Evelyn's right hand, and did the same for Michael before leaving. Evelyn's eyes discreetly traveled from the champagne to Michael's face. He said, "You do like champagne, I hope. I ordered ahead. It's Moet, the one they serve by the glass."

Evelyn nodded. "Thank you. Moet is an excellent choice."

Michael raised his glass. Evelyn did the same. He said, "To your first birthday in the U.S." *I wonder if it will be your last?*

Evelyn enjoyed the panorama of Manhattan while Michael enjoyed savoring her. Although he tried to be subtle, he felt sure that her radar picked up on it. She gave no indication, one more example of her sophistication.

They chatted about different things. Michael asked some questions about Evelyn's childhood, and teenage years. He wanted to know everything about her. She handed out information as readily as a miser gives away hundred-dollar bills. Evelyn wasn't being secretive, she freely admitted that she didn't enjoy talking about herself. Michael teased her a little about making him work so hard to get past her short answers. "Evelyn, if I wanted to pull teeth, I would have become a dentist."

She asked Michael to explain what that meant. Evelyn smiled, promised to try harder, and responded to his next question with another three or four-word answer.

Michael lifted his champagne glass before he noticed it was empty. It wasn't a surprise when the waiter returned. He leaned in a little and spoke quietly. "Mr. La Rue, your table is ready."

Evelyn looked at Michael. "Your table is ready?"

Michael stood, and held out his hand to her. He smiled. "Did I forget to mention that we're having dinner here?"

Chapter Thirteen

LINGERING OVER COFFEE AT ONE of their favorite diners soon after that night, Evelyn and Michael shared travel destinations. She mentioned that before she moved to the U.S., she went to Italy with her boyfriend. She said this in a matter-of-fact way, neither avoiding nor boasting of going as part of a couple.

When she finished describing Italy, Michael said, "Please don't mention past boyfriends again. And just so it never comes up, I don't want to know how many lovers you've had."

"You're the third," Evelyn said before he could stop her.

He hesitated. *A beautiful woman like her, twenty-seven years old, and two other lovers?* Michael said, "You don't have to say that."

Evelyn put her coffee cup down, and looked at Michael the way a hungry eagle looks at a scared and scurrying rodent before it plunges its razor tipped talons into it. "I don't lie. I told you the truth. You're my third lover. You can believe it or not. It's up to you."

He steered away from that topic. The tension disappeared, and was overlooked, as the conversation sailed into safer waters. In a while, Evelyn said, "I don't know anything about your friends. We spend all our time away from The Mansion together. Michael, I don't want you to feel that you must be with me. Please don't take this the wrong way; I look forward to being with you. I have seen relationships develop resentment over that issue. I don't want that to happen with us."

Michael shook his head. "I like being alone. Maybe I got spoiled by the tightness I felt with some of my Marine buddies, and how I could always count on them. I don't have any close civilian friends."

He changed the subject. "You're attractive enough to have been a model. Have you ever considered that?"

"In high school I was offered some modeling jobs for teen magazines. There was nothing about that life-style that appealed to me. So, I declined."

"Are you sorry?"

"No. And I never have been. Having people see my picture, and any fame that goes with it, is not important to me." Evelyn smiled. "I wouldn't mind the money, or the travel." Evelyn shook her head. "Not if I had to surrender my privacy. I am exactly as you previously described yourself – an uncomplicated person with simple tastes."

Michael thought, *Perhaps. Except you left out that you are simply beautiful. And more importantly, you have a simple goodness about you.*

"Tell me about young Evelyn when she was growing up."

She ate a forkful of the cloud-like topping on their lemon meringue pie, and followed it with some coffee. Then, she began. Evelyn's father sold linens and cloth items to restaurants and hotels, one hundred percent on commission. If he didn't sell, he went home with empty pockets. And some years contained more lean months than fat ones. Her father insisted that his wife stay home to raise Evelyn, so there was no back-up salary as a safety net.

When Evelyn was twelve, her father borrowed money from a local bank to build a house on a somewhat narrow, deep lot that he'd already bought and paid for. There wasn't enough money to hire a builder to put up the house, so her father became the general contractor, hiring local craftsman and helping them whenever he could. It was lot of night work, with long hours on weekends.

The large, two-level brick home was eventually finished, and included a full basement apartment for Evelyn's widowed maternal grandmother, Oma, to live with them.

Behind the home was about a half-acre of land which became the family's primary source of vegetables and fruit. The family budget permitted a once-a-week, tired, old chicken from the local market on Saturday, which was strictly rationed out as the star of the meal on Sunday. Then, some remaining chicken, with garden grown vegetables on Monday, more vegetables with even less chicken on Tuesday, and vegetable soup boiled with a chicken carcass and bones for flavor until Sunday.

Evelyn didn't complain about this. She didn't even perceive it as being deprived. Instead, she saw it as a solid foundation to appreciate whatever rewards life tossed her way. And she knew that most people in Asia and Africa were far worse off than her family. Rather than being resentful for what she hadn't possessed, Evelyn was grateful for anything they did have. Being in America did not diminish that exceptional quality, and Michael admired her for it.

Evelyn's upbringing didn't allow for vacations. Instead, maybe more for her parent's benefit, Evelyn spent weeks each summer as a child visiting her other grandmother several hours away.

Her first real vacation came when she was fifteen. Her parents allowed Evelyn to use money she'd earned to pay for a one-week package to the Costa Del Sol in Spain. She went with two other girlfriends, and the twelve-year-old sister of one friend who couldn't make it.

Michael laughed when Evelyn told him of the younger

sister's inclusion. Evelyn said that one of her friends had gotten sick right before they left. The parents were not about to let their non-refundable price go to waste. So, they sent their twelve-year-old daughter off with the three fifteen-year-olds to Spain.

Michael was amazed that the parents of the four girls were okay with their underage daughters going totally unsupervised. Not merely out of the country to Spain, but to the party capital of Spain. And with the addition of the twelve-year old.

He said, "I can hear everyone's parents when they spoke about it. 'Let's see, our young daughters will be completely un-chaperoned. Surrounded by discos, liquor, horny boys, and in an area famous throughout the world for its wild nightlife. Yeah, that's a brilliant idea. Oh, and send the twelve-year-old.'"

~ * * * ~

Franco was an assistant maître d at The Mansion. No one liked him. Not even the two Italian waiters from the same region. Franco enjoyed doing whatever he could to annoy the waiters, he was a classic bully. One of his typical moves was to respond to a waiter's request not to have late tables by making sure that any late customers went directly to that waiter's section. And, the later, the better.

One night at The Mansion, Michael saw Evelyn through the floor-to-ceiling windows on the wall of the dining room that looked out on an elegant garden area. Evelyn patrolled in and out of the light from the lamps showcasing the impressive display of multi-colored flowers.

She had asked Michael to meet her there. It was too enjoyable a summer's night to wait inside. Michael glanced at his watch. He hoped no other customers straggled in. He knew better than to approach Franco to leave early. Motion to his left caused Michael to turn. Franco was approaching. And he didn't look happy.

What garbage does he have for me?

Franco got closer, and looked out at Evelyn. "You don't keep a woman like that waiting. Finish up and get out of here."

Soon, Evelyn and Michael were sipping coffee and sharing a piece of chocolate cake at a nearby diner. They each had cake in their mouths. Evelyn put her fork down, swallowed, and quietly announced, "Michael, I like you."

Michael was surprised. He recovered, and teased, "That's the best you can do?"

Evelyn stiffened somewhat. "What do you want me to say?"

Michael suddenly wasn't teasing. Yet, he wanted to keep this light. "Nothing that you don't honestly feel."

"Alright. I honestly like you."

I won't let my frustration show. "Evelyn, you're an intelligent woman with an extensive vocabulary. In three languages. I'll bet you a donut that you can do better than that."

Evelyn knew that Michael was right. She could - and should - express herself more. After all, she liked the feeling it gave her when Michael told her how he felt about her. *Doesn't he deserve the same warmth?* For some unknown inhibition, she couldn't say it out loud.

She didn't understand why she was like this. It was as if instead of a speech impediment, she was stricken with a communication impediment. Evelyn knew that she experienced strong, intimate feelings for Michael. But those feelings remained trapped in her heart, never escaping through her lips. Evelyn kept her eyes down. She was embarrassed to look up. She knew Michael was staring at her for an answer. She didn't have one.

Chapter Fourteen

EVELYN AND MICHAEL SAT IN a back booth along a large picture window at a popular diner on Route 3 in Little Falls. The diner's Monday night specials were tasty and inexpensive. Two coffee cups and one empty dessert plate with two forks crossed on it decorated their table. The waitress didn't need the table, and left them alone after her second offer of re-fills of coffee was politely refused.

Evelyn asked Michael again about his early family life. His mind circled Evelyn's question like a large bird nearing its target. He would always consider Christina and Marvin La Rue as his family. The adage about blood being thicker than water may be true, but Michael believed that love was thicker than blood.

Whoever his biological parents were, he didn't care enough to want to find out. The rare times that Michael considered them, they were The Sperm Donor and The Incubator.

The La Rues took Michael in when they didn't have to, and loved him openly, unselfishly, and totally.

Michael looked at Evelyn and said, "My mother and father, Christina and Marvin La Rue, always provided positive examples of how to be an adult, a spouse and a parent. I didn't fully realize that when they were killed by a drunk driver. I was twelve. I'd really like to tell you the rest of that story some time."

Evelyn nodded her agreement. "And I'd like to hear

it. I'm sorry about your parents." They held each other's eyes, knowing that a door had opened, and a previously closed area stepped into.

Michael said, "I didn't know how lucky I'd been to be raised by Marvin and his wife. There's an old song, I forget the title, and it doesn't matter; one of the lines is, 'You don't know what you've got 'til it's gone.'"

Michael had a faraway look on his face as he added, maybe to himself, "And ain't that the truth."

Evelyn kept looking at him, and nodded again.

"I've always tried to live my life as if Mom and Dad were around, watching." Michael shrugged. "Who knows? Maybe they are."

Evelyn stayed silent. Then she said, "Do you believe that?"

"I'm not sure. I think I do. I know I'd like to believe that. The people we love live in our hearts forever. Wouldn't it be great if they were somehow, in some way, still with us?"

"Yes, it would. How would we know?"

"That's the question du jour, isn't it? Okay, here's a story for you. You don't have to accept it. Please don't make any decisions until I'm finished. And try to keep an open mind."

Evelyn sipped some room temperature coffee. "Alright."

"I came home from work recently and walked into my bedroom. Something about the bed caught my eye. There, right in the middle, perfectly centered, was a shiny penny."

Michael stopped for a moment. "I know what you're thinking. Maybe I somehow caused it to be there without realizing it."

Evelyn said nothing.

"That was my first take on it. Okay, maybe the penny fell out of my pocket. My first stop when I get home is always to empty my pockets, and then change into shorts, and a t-shirt. I do that in the spare room that I use as an office. And before I take off my trousers, all coins go into an empty coffee can. Let's say the penny did manage to somehow escape from my trouser pocket. Not likely, though it could happen. How did it travel into the other room, and to the absolute center of my bed? Not the edge, not near the center, but the exact center."

Evelyn was astonished. She couldn't say anything. Finally, one word came out. "Wow."

"That's how I felt. Yes, I know, sometimes we see what we want to see. I don't think that's the case here." Michael paused to let Evelyn absorb everything. "Do you have any comments?"

"I'm certain I will. I need to think about this first. That's quite a story. I'm sure you've got a theory. I'd like to hear it."

Michael said, "I always try to look at all of the explanations. Sometimes, no matter how unlikely, or improbable an event is, it does occur. Okay, now that I got that disclaimer out of the way, here's my opinion. Let's say that I'm mistaken, that I did go into the bedroom first. Did the penny jump out of my pocket, defy gravity, and leap sideways so it could land in the center of my bed, instead of onto the floor? I seriously doubt it."

He sipped some water. "The explanation that makes sense to me is that it was placed there, in open view, as a message. A signal."

"Don't keep me wondering. What was the message? And who sent it?"

Michael paused, somewhat reluctant. He'd already shared more of himself than he felt comfortable with. The last safe exit on this conversational highway was just ahead. He ignored it.

"I can't be sure, and I never will be; I think someone, or something, was letting me know that they're around.

Perhaps looking out for me. Such as my parents, or my guardian angel. Maybe they're the same. Whoever, or whatever, can't talk to me, or perform anything overtly physical like writing a note, so they communicated their presence this way."

"If they can't even write, how did they move the penny there?"

Michael grinned. "I don't know. You may have to wait until I contact you from the other side for a better answer."

Evelyn slapped his forearm. "I know you've given this some examination."

He said, "I always look for the straightforward solution first. I'm guessing that whoever placed the penny there has the ability, maybe through some power we don't understand, to move light objects."

Evelyn was silent. She closed her eyes. Her concentration reminded Michael of a blindfolded person struggling to identify some food placed in their mouth. She was tasting what Michael told her, trying to figure out what the ingredients added up to. He patiently waited, then said, "Are you ready for one extra bit of evidence?"

Evelyn opened her eyes. "Yes, please," she said quickly.

"I know you mentioned that when you were a teenager you had a cat, Mickey. Did he ever sleep on your bed?"

"Each night. Against my chest."

"Lucky cat. Okay, now think of how it felt when Mickey jumped up on your bed at night, and moved around, picking out exactly where he wanted to be." Michael paused for a second or two. "Got it?"

"Yes. I know exactly how that feels."

"I grew up with a cat, too. I know that feeling well. This doesn't happen to me often, maybe every couple months or so. In the middle of the night, when I'm asleep, there is precisely that same sensation. It feels like a small cat jumped onto my bed, and is walking around to find the right place to curl up and sleep. I wake up, groggy, and momentarily confused, not sure if I have a cat or not. That's how realistic it feels."

Evelyn's mouth opened, in amazement. Then she said, "Are you sure you weren't dreaming? You said this happens when you're sleeping."

Michael smiled again. "Brilliant minds think alike. Yes, I thought that it was a dream. And that even the waking up was part of it. Then I woke up completely, and laid there in the dark, totally still, with my senses alert. Like I was back in the Marine Corps on a combat deployment. There was light pressure moving around within a small area of the bed near my feet. Exactly the way it feels when a cat is turning around before lying down."

Evelyn's face had the eager look of being about to read the last page of a mystery to discover the identity of the killer. "And then what?"

"I said out loud, 'I get it. I know you're there. I'm not sure who you are, but thanks for looking out for me.' I added that last part because I've always believed I was the luckiest person I've ever known. Maybe it wasn't good luck following me around. Right after I spoke, the pressure on the bed stopped."

When Michael did not continue, Evelyn said, "Then what happened?"

"I turned over and went back to sleep."

"Weren't you afraid?"

"Of what?"

"You believed there was a spirit in your bedroom. Maybe on your bed. Didn't that concern you?"

Michael shook his head. "No. I didn't see this as anything other than an innocent and harmless way of letting me know that she, he, they, it, whatever, was there."

Evelyn stared at him, sorting out her feelings about this, and Michael's belief in it.

Chapter Fifteen

It was Michael's thirtieth birthday. He was sitting in his car in front of the house that Evelyn shared. She knew his birthday was approaching, and had asked him what he wanted as a gift.

He replied that he didn't want anything. Michael said that birthdays weren't a big deal to him, just a date on a calendar. That answer omitted that while his birthday wasn't important, Evelyn was, and Michael hoped she felt the same way about him. He wasn't sure, however, since she never said anything about her feelings, or their relationship. Michael wanted Evelyn to do something for his birthday from her heart, not as compliance to a request. He didn't ask for anything.

Michael considered birthdays ending with zeroes to be significant. You probably got less than ten of them in your lifetime. Maybe much less. Although he hadn't revealed that feeling to Evelyn, he knew she would make it suitably memorable. As she maintained her apparent vow of secrecy, Michael was impressed with her self-control, and even more convinced Evelyn was planning something notable. Something he wouldn't forget.

When the day before his birthday arrived, Evelyn reinforced the mystery and suspense by acting as if she wasn't even aware of it. Evelyn said she needed to write overdue letters, and asked to skip an evening together the next day.

Michael played along and said, "No problem."

Well, tomorrow was here. But Evelyn wasn't. *I guess I was wrong. She wasn't faking having nothing planned for me.*

Michael looked at his watch. *She isn't expecting me. If we're as close as I think we are, she'll know that I'm here. I'll wait five more minutes.*

After twenty minutes, not the five he decided on, Michael started his car and drove home. When he got there, his phone didn't ring. But an alarm inside of Michael did. *Well, I was right. Evelyn did make this a birthday that I won't forget. It won't be easy, I'm going to ignore this incident, and my internal warning. I won't pretend it didn't happen, I'll overlook it.*

Even as that notion formed, Michael knew that something had shifted inside of him. Something he wasn't certain would swing back. He hoped he was wrong about that. Michael avoided any mention of his birthday to Evelyn, unsure of where it would lead.

~ * * * ~

Over diner coffee on a rainy day that hadn't seen a single minute of sunshine, Michael put his cup down. He nervously adjusted the unused silverware in front of him, and looked at Evelyn. He got ready to say what he had spent quite a bit of time thinking about, and preparing for.

"Evelyn, as difficult as it is sometimes for me to be serious, this is important. I know you're on a one-year visa. I have strong feelings for you," Michael shook his head, "I'm not ready to get married. That's not a comment on you, it's about my feelings regarding relationships. I have a trust problem with people in general. And, other than my parents, I've never seen a long-term relationship that was successful. They may exist - I'd like to be in one someday – but I believe in what I see, not what I hope to see.

"I'm not ready for a big-time relationship. And I suspect that you aren't either, for your own reasons, which we can discuss whenever you want. Whether my theories about relationships are correct or not, I'm willing to marry you to give you the choices that come with a green card."

Michael searched Evelyn's face for a reaction. Surely, this important, life-changing statement would provoke one.

Nope. Nothing. I would hate to play poker, or negotiate against her.

He continued. "If we do this, this green card marriage, you keep your apartment, your bank accounts, and I'll keep mine. We'll open joint checking and savings accounts for appearances, and keep a small amount in them. If we stay together, fantastic. If not, that's okay, too. But you won't be forced to leave the U.S. *You* will make the choices about your life, not an overworked, underpaid, stressed-out government clerk somewhere. How does that sound?"

"I'll think about it."

"What is it you need to think about?"

"I just want to think about it."

"Okay. Let's talk about it."

"No, that won't be necessary."

Michael didn't push, he let it drop. *This is typical Evelyn. Not letting me into her private world.* Michael wasn't holding a grudge, he wasn't that kind of person. However, a question mark lingered, hiding somewhere in his mind - or maybe in his heart - about Evelyn. This wasn't a decision he made, merely a reflexive response. Michael wasn't sure what it meant. But he didn't have a good feeling about it.

That night, Evelyn turned over in her bed, alone. She didn't want to look at the glow of the alarm clock. Knowing what time it was would frustrate her further. She tried all the relaxation techniques and tricks in her arsenal to get the rush hour traffic jam of distractions out of her mind. Evelyn knew they probably weren't going to work.

Michael wants out. I can tell. He's a gentleman, and won't just stop calling. That may change if things don't get better. What a couple we are. He won't talk about his past, and I won't talk about our present. If we keep this up, there won't be a future.

Evelyn shook her head in the darkness. *I wish I could change this as easily as I discipline myself to work out, and eat sensibly. This involves changes on the subconscious level, and that isn't easy.*

As she squirmed around, and turned her pillow over again, Evelyn's mind wandered back. She was fifteen years old, sitting at the dinner table with her mother and father. There were less than a dozen words of conversation during the meal. Neither of her parents asked about her day in school, or each other's day. Her parents ate without talking, their heads down. The silence was interrupted solely by silverware clinking against the plates.

Evelyn loved her mother and father. And she felt sorry for them. She was certain that they married for convenience, not love. Their relationship was as practical as two accounting firms merging - and as romantic.

Evelyn wasn't being judgmental. She was merely making an honest assessment based upon her observations. Very revealing was the absence of emotion. She never saw, or heard them use encouraging or affectionate gestures and words, or ever embrace.

She shook her head. *They don't know any better. This is probably how they were raised. But why am I doing it? I'm not as extreme as they are, but I'm far from open and loving. Michael deserves better. I deserve better. So why am I not doing what I know I should?*

The sun came up and Evelyn didn't have an answer.

Chapter Sixteen

TWO MONTHS CREPT ALONG, ABOUT as fast as a condemned man walking to the gallows.

They were at a diner on Route 46. Evelyn said, "Michael, I am getting closer to when my J-1 visa expires. I don't want to wait until the last minute, so I would like to accept your arrangement to get my green card."

"Arrangement? How romantic. And are you proposing to me?"

She smiled slightly. It was a nervous one. "No, *you* proposed to *me*. Don't you remember?"

"I seem to be having memory problems. How long ago did this alleged conversation take place?"

Evelyn blushed. "I needed a little time to decide."

"A *little* time? I suppose the Grand Canyon is a *little* hole in the ground?"

"This isn't easy for me. Please don't make it more difficult."

Michael's tone, while not angry, carried an unintended edge. "You mean unlike how you've made my life? By not knowing how you feel about me, and our relationship? Or, if you were planning to return to Germany and be completely out of my life? Do you have any idea how that tortured me?"

She crossed her arms on her chest. "Is this going to be our first argument?"

"It will be if we're not careful."

Evelyn was silent. Michael searched her face for clues. There weren't any. But she uncrossed her arms, and lowered them to her sides. When she spoke, the steel was gone from her voice. "That delay in answering your gracious offer, and not talking to you about it, was unkind of me. And probably selfish for me not to overcome my reluctance to speak my thoughts and feelings."

Evelyn breathed deeply and let it out. "I didn't mean to hurt you. And I don't want us to fight. Please forgive me."

Michael stared at her. Different answers, and various ways to say them, zipped through his mind. He rejected the first few, they were sharp or cranky. He grabbed the one that was the authentic Michael. "Of course, I forgive you. I'm not sure I can stay mad at you even if I wanted to. And I do want to, a little." He sort of smiled.

Evelyn exhaled, relieved. "I won't be angry if you don't marry me so that I can get my green card. I probably don't deserve that huge favor from you."

"Well, then we have a problem."

"We do?"

"Yes, because when I was honorably discharged from the Marine Corps, they made me sign a document that I would never make a promise that I didn't deliver on. It's part of the code of Semper Fi. I believe it was form DD-3241. I have my copy of it somewhere." Michael shrugged. "I have to do this."

She looked astonished. "The Marine Corps does that? There really is a form, uh, whatever you called it?"

"No. It sounded believable, didn't it?"

Evelyn answered by slapping his hand. "I need us to be serious now. I meant what I said. If you don't want to do this, I understand. I really do. And I won't think less of you. If my visa runs out, and I go back to Germany, I must start making plans."

"OK, there is no form DD-3241. Those were the numbers of two of my favorite athletes. I am a man of my word. Besides, I can think of worse things than being married to you." Michael looked up, as if searching for something. "Maybe not many. At least a couple."

Evelyn gave him 'the look.'

He continued. "I checked into this months ago, just in case. The mayor's office performs marriages for fifty dollars. I don't know the details, so tomorrow I'm going to call, and ask them how to go about this."

Early the following morning, Michael called City Hall, and got through to the right department. Later, he told Evelyn, "OK, here's how it works. We need to get a blood test, then bring the results, and apply for a marriage license. They mentioned something interesting."

"What was it?"

"I asked about the fees. They said the marriage license costs ten dollars. I know that a dog license costs twenty dollars. I'm sure there's a message there somewhere."

Evelyn needed a second or two to before she realized that he wasn't serious. She mumbled, "American humor." Evelyn stepped toward her purse. "I'll pay for the blood tests and marriage license."

Michael held up a hand. "Oh, no. You're marrying me for a green card. I'm marrying you for your body and your money. Hold on to your cash, I'll let you spend it on me later. We can find uses for your body right now"

She smiled. "Michael, you're impossible."

"Ah, recognition is a beautiful thing" He clapped his hands together twice. "C'mon, grab your ID, and move your sexy butt. We've got to get to the lab before they get busy."

~ * * * ~

Within a week the blood tests were completed, and the marriage license was submitted. While enjoying their afternoon coffee, Evelyn said, "Michael, you make everything sound so easy, possibly because you think that life is a happy adventure. And maybe it is. I know that you are doing something important for me."

Evelyn paused, and then said, "I know I should say this more. I care about you, and I hope that we can continue like this. As you said, the future is not for us to know. I want you to realize that I'm grateful for this. You are a special man, and I appreciate it. Thank you."

"You're welcome. I'd be rude if I didn't give you an opportunity to express that gratitude. Do you want to thank me at my apartment, or yours?"

She shook her head. "Michael, Michael, Michael. What am I going to do with you?"

"I'm glad to hear you ask, because that's exactly what I'm talking about. Now that we're thinking alike, may I make some suggestions as to what you can do with me?"

~ * * * ~

Wearing what in an office would be called business casual, Evelyn and Michael showed up to get married. They were at the mayor's office on a day off. They weren't making any sort of statement or being disrespectful, neither of them owned anything more appropriate. Michael considered, and then rejected, his tuxedo. It would have pressured Evelyn to spend money she couldn't afford to buy an equivalent outfit.

Evelyn and Michael were by themselves. Michael didn't have any family or close friends to invite to the wedding. And Evelyn didn't tell her parents that she was marrying an American, they would realize that she probably wasn't returning to Germany to live.

There was no honeymoon, it didn't seem right. They did agree to spend a week at a Caribbean beach resort if they were still together in six months. Instead, that night they ate dinner alone at Arthur's Tavern in Hoboken, their preferred steak restaurant. They ordered a bottle of Dom Perignon.

Michael felt that life was too important to take seriously. And he enjoyed new experiences. So, while he acknowledged the practical purpose of their marriage, he smiled at the unlikeliness of it.

Evelyn stayed at Michael's apartment often, though she didn't move out of her room at The Mansion's barracks. She didn't experience any further problem with the other Germans. And they were sensible enough to ignore Michael whenever he went there to pick-up Evelyn.

~ * * * ~

If I had a magic wand, I would wave it over Evelyn to be communicative about our relationship. I'm pretty much in the dark about the depth of her feelings, her wants, her needs, her plans for us, or about me. Is knowing that too much to ask?

Michael felt that attempting to understand Evelyn was like staring into murky water while trying desperately to see what lay beneath the surface... and failing. This obstacle prevented his desire to be with Evelyn from reaching its deepest and most intimate levels. Worse, Michael could feel his oldest nightmare and fear, his dread of betrayals, rumbling awake inside of him.

Michael considered personal responsibility and accountability to be two of the better qualities a person could possess. And he lived his life to reflect that. So he looked first to himself as the source of this hollow crater in the middle of his relationship with Evelyn.

I've done everything except beg to alert her of my feelings and wants. I can merely ask and suggest. I can't insist, or make demands. And I wouldn't anyway. I want her to do this out of caring, not as an obligation. Evelyn is smart, funny, and kind-hearted without being syrupy.

We have the same tastes in just about everything. She's beautiful. The sex is outstanding. And she isn't moody. So why am I unsatisfied?

Michael already knew the answer. He didn't want to admit it because he didn't like what it said about him, or his relationship with Evelyn.

He didn't like that his childhood circumstances, or some other cause, created a hunger, a need inside of him for emotional nourishment. And despite trying mightily over the years, he never successfully purged his sensitivity to what he considered betrayal.

Michael knew that betrayal came in different flavors, shapes, and sizes. There was the low-level, rather harmless deception of running into someone you haven't seen for a while, who after chatting briefly, looks at their watch and says, "Got to run. Let's get together sometime."

Michael doubted that they meant it. If they did, they would get specific, "How 'bout lunch on Saturday?" *It's okay to not want to see someone again. But don't lie about it, and give people false expectations.*

One hundred and eighty degrees away slithered the not-so-harmless betrayal of running around behind the back of a loved one, or spouse. Michael believed that if you would lie to, and cheat on that person, you would lie to, and cheat on anyone.

In between those two boundaries lived various degrees of betrayal - and no shortage of willing betrayers.

Michael increasingly felt that Evelyn's stubborn refusal to share her inner-self was an indirect form of betrayal. And it grew bigger and bigger, until it symbolized each of the betrayals from his past.

I've got two choices. I can accept that Evelyn is not going to share her feelings about me, or our relationship. Or move on without her. Hold on. There's the answer. Move on. I'll move. Literally. Physically. Distantly.

Distantly? Is there such a word? There should be. Yeah, I'll move. She's comfortable here. She'll want to stay.

Michael picked-up Evelyn, and said he had something to discuss. She snapped her seatbelt, and turned to him. Michael looked at her. He said, "I'm moving to Boston."

Chapter Seventeen

EVELYN KNEW MICHAEL WAS SETTING her up for a funny comment. She continued to look at him. His eyes whispered regret. Then it hit her. *Maybe he isn't kidding.*

When Michael breathed in, and let it out, without saying anything, Evelyn knew that he was serious. She stared at him, unable to think, or speak. Finally, some words spilled out. "Can I come with you?"

Michael had tormented himself with concern, planning, and regard for any potential zigs and zags. But he was surprised by her request. He wanted for neither of them to be in this uncomfortable situation. That wasn't an option.

Michael possessed personal honor, and respect and affection for Evelyn. Those virtues wouldn't allow Michael to continue like this – in a relationship that had reached the end of its sizzling, short life. Dead from emotional starvation.

Michael wasn't positive that he knew what love in a romantic relationship was. *But I know I'm damn close to it with Evelyn.* It required effort and willpower to hold back from surrendering his heart totally to Evelyn. Her reluctance, no, her refusal, to open her heart prevented it.

This was a slice of what flashed through Michael's head as Evelyn stared at him. Not as complete sentences. Or even fully formed concepts. They were sensations, perceptions, and memories. Betrayal, and its first cousin, abandonment, never strayed far away. They lit up Michael's soul like spotlights shining at a midnight murder scene.

Evelyn hadn't done anything wrong, except by omission. Michael repeatedly asked her to fill his unwanted and detested neediness with a plain and simple confirmation of her feelings toward him. She hadn't. *Why?*

He struggled to come up with the correct answer. Not for himself, for both of them. Michael wanted to balance not hurting Evelyn against his dissatisfaction and frustration with their relationship. *Why do our emotions have to be so damn complicated?* He wondered what Evelyn was thinking about the delay in his response to her question.

"Why do you want to come with me?" he finally asked.

"Because I don't want to lose you."

It isn't working with Evelyn. She's a beautiful and desirable young woman. Just not the right one for me. We'll move to Boston, and I'll gradually start pulling away. She'll begin dating other guys, problem solved.

Michael looked at her hopeful, yet worried face. "Okay."

~ * * * ~

Michael opened the trunk of his car and deposited two grocery store cartons containing the evidence of his thirty years of life. It wasn't a lot. Michael lived light, and traveled light. He'd carefully packed his photo album and mementos of the La Rue family, a small stereo, some meaningful books, a file with difficult to replace documents like his passport, and his DD-214, the discharge form from the Marine Corps.

Evelyn carried the two suitcases that she'd arrived in the United States with. Michael lifted them into the back seat. He glanced at Evelyn. *Nearly a kindred spirit. If only...*

A month earlier, Michael bought the Sunday editions of the two main Boston newspapers from a large bookstore that stocked newspapers from big cities in the U.S., and major foreign capitals. He carried them to a nearby Dunkin Donuts. Armed with a black marking pen, a large coffee, and two French crullers, Michael searched the rental apartments section.

Michael knew Boston well, he'd spent time there after the Marine Corps. A prominent ad, featuring a black and white photo of a building on the corner of Tremont and Boylston, right across the street from the Common, just about jumped off the page.

He let out, "Well, lookee here." Michael glanced around, a bit embarrassed. Either no one heard him, or they didn't care.

The apartment location was in the heart of that stunning city. And they were offering a month's free rent with a one-year lease. Michael put his coffee down, wiped any stray donut from his mouth with a napkin, and found a payphone. He called the building manager, and secured the apartment with a credit card.

Their drive to Boston took about five hours. Michael and Evelyn stopped a couple of times to get out of the car to stretch, use the restrooms, and get coffee. The conversation started as scarce as the midday traffic on route 95 North. Michael wasn't going to be phony, and create artificial talk to fill the silence. He knew Evelyn was the same way. They were aware that this was a tense situation. There was no pretending otherwise. The silence was not awkward.

The radio entertained them with some songs. They searched for new stations as the miles melted like a bowl of half-finished ice cream forgotten on the front porch in the summer sun. And they had their private musings.

Evelyn asked Michael if he wanted her to drive for a while. He declined the offer, but that started a conversation that comfortably continued until they carried their belongings into the door of their sixth floor, one-bedroom apartment.

Evelyn relied on her InterContinental experience, and applied at all the downtown luxury hotels. She accepted a management trainee opening at the Four Seasons on Boylston Street, three blocks from their apartment. `

Michael discovered from the Sunday Boston papers employment section that radiology was in one of its hiring flurries. He arranged interviews at several large hospitals. The pay and benefits were roughly the same at each of them, so Michael went with his gut and chose New England Deaconess Hospital, a major Harvard teaching facility.

One of Michael's employee benefits was a deeply discounted monthly pass on the Boston subway system, called the 'T'. Michael kept his car out of town at a co-worker's house. It wasn't needed, or even practical, while living downtown, even less so with his 'T' pass.

Each morning, Michael walked across the street from their apartment and descended into the Boylston Street 'T' stop. Minutes later, he was at the hospital complex. Evelyn had a three-minute walk to get to work.

Ah, the pleasures of living in the middle of downtown!

When the weather allowed for it, which was often, Michael enjoyed the scenic twenty-five-minute walk home. Fenway Park, a mystical place that transcended baseball, and lived in the soul of Boston, was visible within blocks from his walking route in the condensed center of the city. Michael usually stopped and stared at the beautiful old structure as he passed near it. He always felt a tingle while he listened carefully for any echoes of long dead crowds cheering the ghosts of splendid and legendary ballplayers performing their timeless magic over and over.

Boston is a great walking around city. Maybe the finest one in the U.S. When Michael got home from work, Evelyn was already there. The May weather pleaded with them to come outside and play, and they didn't resist.

Boston was a new experience to Evelyn. Michael escorted her on daily long walks through interesting neighborhoods, and to famous sites. Beacon Hill, the Back Bay, Quincy Market, Faneuil Hall, Copley Square, Boston's Little Italy - the North End, Chinatown, Paul Revere's house, the Freedom Trail, and others were explored, enjoyed, and appreciated.

But, the perfect thing about Boston was not the historical, enjoyable sights, or the activities. No, the number one thing about Boston was that it saved the relationship of Evelyn and Michael. More accurately, it started a new relationship for them.

Chapter Eighteen

New Jersey was not a walking around paradise like Boston. When Michael and Evelyn lived in New Jersey, their dates always involved driving somewhere, often Manhattan. Then doing something there, and driving back. A local date meant a shorter drive. Being in the car, in New Jersey and New York traffic, surrounded by New Jersey and New York drivers, was not exactly relaxing or enjoyable. And, it did not encourage, promote, or stimulate meaningful conversation. In contrast, their walks around Boston provided a daily three-hour oasis.

When their walking voyages started, Evelyn continued to resist sharing herself. Then the peaceful, relaxing, leisurely togetherness worked its magic on her. Evelyn started opening; though gradually, and somewhat guardedly. She was a beautiful flower reluctant to enter full bloom.

Ever since their first date, Michael felt curious to know everything about Evelyn. Now, he was lucky enough to begin to discover it. And nothing was disappointing. He considered one of the many impressive qualities about Evelyn to be her genuineness. You can't spend great amounts of time alone with a person each day and not get to know who they are. The deep, down to the marrow in their bones, human being they really are.

On one of their walks, they stopped for a break and sat outside at one of Boston's irresistible cafes; enjoying the weather, their coffee, the vibe of the neighborhood, and each other.

"Michael, do you like being an x-ray tech again?"

He didn't need to hesitate. "The short answer is 'yes' otherwise, I wouldn't do it. I know that I could be more ambitious." Michael shrugged. "I'm happy doing this. I like meeting the patients, and chatting with them, depending on how busy we are. I've heard some terrific stories from the patients."

Michael raised his cup, and drank from it. Still holding the cup, he said, "And my quest for the ultimate x-ray continues. I try to make every x-ray look like the ones in the text books. Obviously, I'm not always successful. It's a fun challenge. And the patients deserve the highest quality images."

Michael put his cup down, and asked, "Are you happy with your job at the Four Seasons?"

"For now. I'm not sure what I want to do when I grow up. Uh, oh, I'm starting to sound like you."

They smiled. And enjoyed the comfortable, loose-fitting silence.

Michael finally said, "I enjoy being alone. There aren't many people I would prefer to be with over my solitude. Evelyn, you're one of them."

"Thank you. I'm flattered."

After a pause, as if she needed to work up the courage to say it, Evelyn added, "I like being with you, too."

Michael smiled. *OK, this is progress. You don't jump from the first floor to the second. You go up one step at a time.*

Michael had already paid, so he tucked some dollars under his cup, and they continued walking. Evelyn slid her hand into his, which mildly surprised him. They were sensual, intimate lovers in the bedroom. But this public display, even holding hands, was unusual. They held hands until they needed to separate to allow a group of obvious tourists to get by. Then Evelyn reached for Michael again.

He smiled privately. *This relationship sure isn't following the conventional path. First, we became lovers. Now we're getting to know each other and becoming friends. Tight friends. I hope this continues.*

~ * * * ~

In the time that they lived in Boston, Evelyn and Michael ate dinner in their apartment twice. This always astounded them whenever they commented on it to each other. They discovered inexpensive ethnic restaurants all over Boston, and soon collected their top Vietnamese, Thai, Indian, and Chinese places.

These were usually small and family run, with the owner's young children sitting at a table, drawing on paper placemats, or giggling about something.

Evelyn and Michael enrolled in a six-week course, 'Cheap Eats In Boston' at the nearby Adult School on Newbury Street. The instructor was the restaurant critic for the main Boston newspaper. He, and the ten members of the limited size class, met each Monday evening at a different downtown restaurant, and shared satisfying platters of food that they passed around. Evelyn and Michael added those restaurants to their mental list.

Often, Evelyn and Michael would start out walking in one direction, having decided on a certain restaurant. Before they got there, one of them would say, "Let's go somewhere different. I've changed my mind."

Neither minded the fresh air, the exercise, and the promise of extra time together.

Lying in bed at night, they always embraced. The physical closeness, and the growing emotional intimacy, left both fading into sleep with a smile in their minds.

~ * * * ~

Michael loved his job at New England Deaconess and considered it his number one ever. It was an exceptional place to work - world-class professional, and at the same time friendly and low-key.

Being employed at the Deac, pronounced like *teak*, was like a one-way portal in a sci-fi movie - people went in, they didn't come out. One of Michael's friends there, Paul Rhodes, was the manager in the file room. Paul had earned summer money at the Deac as a literature major attending Boston University twenty years before. Paul's affection for the people and the atmosphere at the Deac was too great for him to leave when he graduated from B.U. His diploma was probably stored in a box, or a closet somewhere. Paul was typical of the Deac.

And so was Eli Fritz. Eli was a retired, prominent local sociologist. He volunteered at the Deac several days a week. Eli was Abe Lincoln tall and thin, and as distinguished looking as you would expect from his Bostonian background.

Eli stood in the large, open, and tastefully decorated hospital lobby, and welcomed visitors with an intelligent and caring face, and an eye for those who needed directions within the huge building. Eli's presence raised the already high dignity level of this prominent center of healing.

Michael always smiled and said 'Hello' to Eli whenever he passed through the lobby. He and Eli became friendly, and began eating lunch together on Eli's days there. The hospital cafeteria was run by the Marriott hotel business, and the choices and quality were far above average. But not the prices. Michael was certain that the cafeteria was subsidized by the Deac, the prices were too low not to be.

One day Eli shared a story. "Michael, after my undergraduate studies, I enrolled in a master's program.

In one of my courses, the professor said something that I disagreed with."

Eli enjoyed a forkful of his lunch, and continued. "Now, you must remember, this happened years ago. The academic world was quite rigid about the relationship between the faculty and students. They pontificated, we silently, obediently, listened.

"I raised my hand, which earned me lightning bolts of anger from the professor's for interrupting his lecture. He stopped theatrically striding back and forth in front of the class, and glared on me. Annoyance was the dominant tone of his voice. 'Yes, Mr. Fritz? Do you have something to share? Something so urgent as to rudely rob this class of my knowledge?'

"I politely, tactfully, and respectfully pointed out what I felt was an error in his monologue. The professor scowled at me. 'Mr. Fritz, how many years of post-graduate experience do you have?'

"One,' I responded."

"'That's right,' the professor said. He was king speaking to a peasant in the gutter. 'And *I* have thirty-four years of post-graduate experience. Do you dare, with your one year of experience, to challenge my thirty-four years of experience?'"

"Professor, is it possible that you have one year of experience, repeated thirty-four times?"

Michael nearly choked as he laughed. It wasn't easy to keep his mouth closed, no one wanted to see his food. After he wiped his lips with a napkin, he said, "I love that story. What grade did you get?"

"Dear boy, I withdrew from the class. I had to. After what I'd said, he would have given me a failing grade no matter what I did."

Michael didn't forget that story, and sometimes was reminded of it when he saw an ad for a business that bragged about their years of experience.

Chapter Nineteen

MICHAEL RODE THE 'T' TO work each morning, to save time. He stood, all the seats were already taken. One hand held a strap on the swaying, crowded subway car. Michael closed his eyes, smiling at how satisfying his life was, as the train rumbled under Boston. Then, he felt the heat of being stared at. Michael opened his eyes. He swept his gaze around, and saw the angry looks of fellow riders whose faces accused, "It's six thirty in the morning. You're on your way to work, and you're smiling. I hate you."

~ * * * ~

One warm and sunny day, Michael and Evelyn held hands while walking downtown on Boylston Street, about two blocks from their apartment. An insight burst into Michael's head. It was unannounced, uninvited, and unexpected. *Evelyn is my best friend.*

He stopped in the middle of the sidewalk, nearly yanking Evelyn back and off her feet. She looked at Michael. He stood there, smiling, and unmoving. Then he nodded at the truth of that. *I'd rather be with Evelyn than with anyone I've ever known. This must be serious, I'm not even thinking about sex right now.*

"Michael, is something wrong?"

"Uh, no." He continued smiling, and pulled Evelyn close, ignoring the people walking around them.

"Unless you consider that I just realized you're the most important person in the world to me to be something wrong."

"I am?"

"Yes, you are."

Evelyn joined his smiling. "No, I don't consider that to be wrong."

They continued walking. Evelyn put her arm around Michael's waist.

~ * * * ~

Michael walked into their apartment to see Evelyn standing by the door, waiting. After they hugged and kissed, she said, "My mother called today."

"How is she?"

"She called from a hospital. She fell and broke her hip."

"Ouch. I'm sorry to hear that. Evelyn, as you know, there are different types and degrees of fractures. None of them are good. Hopefully this is one of the lesser ones. Do you have any other information?"

"My mother was taking a basket of laundry into the basement, and slipped on a step and fell."

Michael said, "Do you know what tests they did at the hospital?"

"After they examined her, they x-rayed her, and did either an MRI or a CAT scan, she isn't sure which."

"OK. Then what?"

"They told her it's a minor fracture, like a thin crack running through her bone."

Michael didn't add anything about fractures. It would needlessly divert from the main issue – her mother's health.

Evelyn continued. "They said she could start walking with a cane in a day or two, and maybe go home. My mother needs me to come to help her around the house.

She can't risk showering, or bathing by herself. Or shopping."

"I understand. When are you leaving?"

"Tomorrow."

"I'll miss you. I'll catch up on my reading, and I'll be at the "Y" so often they'll think I'm a new employee. By the time you come back, I'll be widely read and superbly conditioned."

Evelyn smiled.

Michael said, "Speaking of when you come back, any news on that? I don't expect you to know exactly, but is there any rough timetable? Did the doctors mention how long it would take your mom to recover?"

Evelyn shook her head. "I'll know more after I get there, and speak to the doctors myself. I promise to come back as soon as I can."

"The important thing is your mom's health. Take care of her, everything here will be fine. Don't worry, or rush back. I'll go with you to the airport tomorrow. What time do you want to leave?"

"Three o'clock, thank you. Will it be a problem leaving work a little early?"

"Nope."

They rode the 'T' to Logan Airport. Michael carried Evelyn's small suitcase. She didn't need to take many things, a closet full of clothes waited for her at her parents' house.

Evelyn and Michael stopped about twenty feet before the airport security checkpoint. Without a boarding pass, this was as far as he was going. People hurried around them to get into the already long line.

Evelyn and Michael faced each other. Michael said, "I hope you have a safe and pleasant flight, and can get some sleep. I'll call you tomorrow when I get home from work. Is that too late?"

"No, I'll probably be in the kitchen with my father,

trying to figure out how we're going to handle this. He's become so used to my mother doing everything around the house over the years that he's completely lost. I don't think he even knows how to use a can opener. And I'm not exaggerating. If she's unable to limp around and cook for him, he'll starve. I'm going to be the live-in maid, grocery shopper, cook, dishwasher, cleaner-upper, laundry service, and...I'm sure they'll think of more things."

"I envy you. That sounds like fun."

"I don't mind. This will be easier than what lies ahead."

"What's that?"

"In the beginning of my life, they fed me, changed my diaper, and bathed me. It's fair that at the end of their lives I'll be doing the same for them. Compared to that, this will be easy."

Michael laughed, impressed once again at Evelyn's sense of loyalty and responsibility. "When you look at it like that, you're right."

She moved closer and they hugged tightly.

Michael said, "I'm going to miss you."

"I'm going to miss you, too. Now go home, have dinner, read, and go to bed. I'll try to sleep on the flight."

They kissed, and Evelyn left. Michael watched her until she passed through the metal detector. She turned, knowing he would be there watching, and she waved.

Michael rode the 'T' back to the Boylston Street stop and went to Chinatown for some Singapore rice noodles. The restaurant he usually went to for this satisfying meal always added exactly the right amount of curry, and they didn't let him down that night. He walked four blocks back to their apartment, and read for a while before turning out the light.

Michael jumped on the 'T' after work the next day, despite the weather being right for walking home. He was eager to call Evelyn. She picked up before the phone rang twice, her native language announcing, "Hallo?"

"Hey, who else would call at this hour?"

His mock insulted tone made Evelyn laugh. "Sorry, I've been taking calls all day. It's now a habit. My father's sisters called. Nieces, nephews, and cousins from around Germany that I haven't seen since I was in grade school called. My ear is sore from having the phone pressed to it all day."

"It's late, and your ear needs a break, I'll keep this brief. Let's start at the beginning. How was the flight?"

"The flight was too long, the seat was too small, and the plane was too crowded. Other than that, it was sensational. Alright, I'll get serious. We departed on time, we landed on time, and we arrived safely. Anything additional was a bonus. I'm fine, thanks. How are you?"

"Missing you. How's your mom?"

Evelyn made a noise that from Michael's side of the Atlantic sounded like a sigh. "I went to the hospital, and spoke to the doctor. They'll let her come home after one additional day of observation and another x-ray. There's a small line through the bone, it isn't broken apart. The doctor said that the crack is so minor, or hidden so well, that they're having trouble visualizing it. They're relying on how she feels, and their physical examination."

"Ah, clinical evaluation. I was beginning to believe that skill was no longer being taught in medical schools. That it was replaced by a total reliance on imaging, lab work, and test results. I'm glad that this is no worse than that. How's your dad?"

"He's fine, since I'm doing the cooking and cleaning. For all his life, women have been doing everything around the house for him. First his mother, and then his wife. He's a product of his time, and helpless on his own. He's too old to change now."

Michael reminded himself of the six-hour time

difference. "It's late. Let me allow you to get into bed with a book, and unwind from your busy day."

"That sounds like a fine idea. Why don't you crawl through the phone and join me?"

Evelyn couldn't see it as Michael smiled. "I wish I could."

"Me, too. Goodnight, Michael."

"Goodnight."

They hung up. Michael replayed her last words over and over. *Goodnight? That's it? Goodnight? I say 'goodnight' to the cleaning crew at the Deac when I leave. Is that all Evelyn's capable of...a sprinkling of sugar? I know there's much more to Evelyn. But if she keeps it locked up inside of her, it may as well not exist.*

Michael felt bad for Evelyn. *Okay, cut her some slack. She's under a lot of stress. She won't complain about anything, and she's jet-lagged, and time-zone zombied. Taking care of her mother's injury and her father's neediness must be emotionally and physically demanding, and draining.*

Michael hurt for their relationship. He wanted to give Evelyn every bit of leeway that he could, with the new challenges she faced. *However, I can't ignore that although Evelyn has made progress, she remains largely unwilling, for some unknown reason, to open up, and express her feelings.* Her reluctance, or refusal, to do that prevented him from releasing the brakes and restrictions on *his* feelings.

Michael didn't believe in half-measures when it came to commitment. You were either in, or you were out. And he wasn't going to give himself emotionally to Evelyn unless, and until, she gave him a clearer understanding of her position.

I don't deserve, and won't accept, a lopsided relationship. It doesn't have to be precisely fifty-fifty. But seventy-thirty ain't gonna fly.

Michael battled that these feelings long after his conversation with Evelyn. He fiercely wanted their relationship to work. However, Michael wasn't going to surrender his emotional needs, or his principles. *If Evelyn doesn't think our relationship is worth opening up for, well, that's her choice.*

Chapter Twenty

EVELYN WAS LEAVING THE LOCAL bakery with a bag of fresh, still-warm-from-the-oven-rolls, when she saw him. He was walking in the other direction, looking in shop windows. *Don't turn around.*

But her old boyfriend did. And, he approached her. Had he somehow sensed her presence, even from across the street?

"Evelyn, what a delightful surprise," he said in German that informed any listeners of his Sicilian upbringing. Sergio's smile and words displayed more warmth than was merited by seeing the woman who dumped him as if he were a sack of something quite unpleasant.

Sergio continued. "I knew when I got up today that something exceptional would happen. I didn't know it would be this fantastic."

He leaned in for a kiss. Evelyn avoided it by turning her head, not offering a cheek, or bothering to feign discretion.

Sergio pretended that she hadn't done this. "I heard you were living in the U.S."

"I am."

"Are you involved with a man there?"

"Why do want to know?"

"I'm concerned about a friend."

"You were not honorable enough to be my friend."

Sergio smiled. "Have it your way. I'm asking about my lover."

"Ex-lover." It disgusted Evelyn to think of him even that way. "Not that it's any of your business, yes, I am *seriously* involved." She felt that her emphasis should discourage him.

It didn't. It had the opposite effect. *Ah, forbidden fruit. How sweet it tastes.* "Evelyn, we should get together. I'd love to hear all about the U.S."

Evelyn knew what time it was as she bluntly looked at her watch, signifying their chat was over. "I don't think so. I believe in leaving the past where it belongs. In my rear-view mirror."

She started to leave, then said, "If you're so curious about the U.S., go visit it. There are flights leaving every day."

Evelyn walked home, angry about the nerve of Sergio to attempt to somehow sneak back into her life. Evelyn wasn't thinking about her break-up with him, yet the details leaped into her mind anyway.

She and two girlfriends who she didn't see very often were enjoying a warm Saturday afternoon sitting in a local coffeehouse, catching up on their lives. The irresistible subject of boyfriends came up. Twenty-one-year-old Evelyn was asked who she was dating. She mentioned Sergio. Both of her friends were first surprised, and then disgusted, when a few questions revealed that they were all dating the same Sergio, each believing his claims that he was faithful to them.

"We need to be sure it's the same person," one of them said, so they probed each other, suspecting the worst. They were embarrassed, and sickened when they realized that he was using the same phrases and words with each of them. The three girls felt used, and unclean. After they each spilled their anger, a joint decision was made to dump Sergio. They toasted it by clinking coffee cups.

After the coffeehouse, Evelyn went directly to the apartment where Sergio lived with his parents, and sister. Evelyn wasn't there to hear his side of the story with the possibility of working this out. No, that died when the proof of his lying and cheating was exposed. She wanted the pleasure of informing Sergio to his face how she felt about him. Evelyn knew it would have no impact, he was too wrapped up in himself for redemption. She needed the well-deserved pleasure of telling him off in person.

Sergio denied the claims of the other young women, as she knew he would. Both, he said, were jealous of Evelyn and angry at him because he turned them away when they tried to seduce him. "Evelyn, you know that I would not cheat on you. You are the one woman for me."

She nodded. "Well, that explains why they listened in."

For the first time, Sergio's face and voice lost some of its confidence. "Listened to what?"

"The expressions of love you said to me that you swore you never felt with another woman."

Sergio didn't look comfortable.

Evelyn continued, "They must have somehow listened to you saying them to me, and written them down. How else could each of them repeat your words exactly?"

Sergio instantly displayed his fake version of a sincere smile, developed from countless practice viewings in his bedroom mirror. This was the smile that he was sure would soften the hardest of women.

"I confess - I am a man." The volume of his smile increased. "These women made me do this. They would not stop until I gave in. As I said, I am a man."

He paused for emphasis. "A man with needs." He seemed proud when he said, "This is what real men do."

Evelyn wondered, *Does he really believe that garbage? It doesn't matter.*

She said, "No. That's what liars, cheaters, and manipulators do. Our relationship is over. I never want to see you again."

For a long time after that, Evelyn felt shame and embarrassment that she'd been fooled so completely. She later realized that was how life taught you: first you got graded, and then you learned the lesson. And, unfortunately, bad people, or those with bad intentions, didn't come with warning labels: 'I'm a toxic, poisonous person. I can, and will be harmful to your health. Stay away from me.'

Back in the present, Sergio watched Evelyn walk away, the brown paper bag in one hand, and her purse over her shoulder. Her hips swayed, further tightening her snug jeans across that shapely rear. His fantasies about her grew with each step Evelyn took, giving him a warm, satisfying feeling. Sergio's stare was that of a wolf hungrily eyeing a confused and lost lone sheep. He knew his desired outcome with Evelyn. And the steps needed to get there were as natural to him as breathing.

Sergio was cunning. He didn't go to Evelyn's parent's house until later that evening. He wanted any distractions she might have that day to be resolved, or forgotten. And since it was well past dinnertime, she should be relaxed after their earlier, tense encounter.

His plan was to first soothe her with words. Sergio knew that would be a challenge after the afternoon's confrontation. He looked forward to it.

Sergio studied the art of seduction the way a young artist would analyze Da Vinci, Michelangelo, and other geniuses of the canvas. Sergio understood the calming, compliant effect of a hypnotist's tone. And, his hours of listening to, and mimicking them should pay off tonight.

They usually did. When Evelyn and her anger toward him were sufficiently neutralized, his fun would begin.

Sergio would pretend to notice and comment on her tenseness, and surely Evelyn had some. He didn't care if she did or not, this was merely a deception to massage her shoulders. Sergio believed that if a woman would allow him to touch her *anywhere*, she would allow him to touch her *everywhere*. Then, the question that would remain about caressing her body would be how soon, and where to start?

He could already feel the pleasing sensation of waking up tomorrow morning in Evelyn's bed.

Chapter Twenty-One

SERGIO ARRIVED AT EVELYN'S PARENT'S house. Before knocking, he tried on facial gestures until he settled on one that portrayed a blend of innocence, and sorrow. This was what Evelyn saw when she opened the door several inches.

She said, "Didn't I make it clear that I didn't want to see you again?"

"Yes, you made it too clear. That's exactly why I'm here."

Evelyn continued to stare at him, not opening the door any further. Sergio was excited that she didn't slam it, either.

"I was tortured by what you said. I came here to apologize for hurting you."

Her obvious anger dissipated slightly. The tightness in her face relaxed a little.

Sergio opportunistically seized this small success. "All I expect to come of this is the cleansing of my guilty conscience."

"You don't deserve a second chance. And you aren't getting one." Evelyn's tone didn't match her words.

Women are so predictable. And so easily fooled. Over, and over. Thank God.

"That isn't why I came here. I want you to know that despite what you may think, I was in love with you."

He paused, he needed to gauge precisely the way to proceed. Evelyn's response would be a compass pointing him in the right direction. She said nothing. But the door stayed open.

"If you will allow me five minutes of your time, I will offer you the apology that I hope is worthy of you. Then I will leave, knowing that this chapter in my life is over. At least I finally acted like a man."

Evelyn hesitated. *He's a skilled liar, and he's proved that. Maybe he has finally grown up. Should I give him a little time before I toss him out?*

She said, "You can come in for five minutes. Not one second longer."

"Thank you. You are as gracious as you are beautiful. I promise to be quick." *Until I have your clothes off. Then I will be slow. Very slow.*

Evelyn led him into the kitchen. "My parents are asleep, so we must be quiet."

She sat down, pointing to a chair on the opposite side of the table for him. She picked up the cup in front of her. "I was enjoying some chamomile tea. When I'm finished with it, you're leaving."

Sergio was still standing. He lifted his chair, and started to move it around the table, toward Evelyn.

She raised a hand. "Stop. Stay over there. I can hear you from that side of table." *That's not the move of someone who only wants to talk.*

This wasn't going the way Sergio hoped, or planned. He knew from experience that the path to the bedroom sometimes included detours. "Aren't you going to use your excellent manners to offer me a cup of tea?"

"All I'm going to offer you is three more minutes. Speak quickly, or you'll be leaving in the middle of a sentence."

She looked at her watch. "You now have two and a half minutes." *I was foolish to believe him.*

He knew he needed to skip some steps in his plan. Sergio didn't like doing this. He considered each successful step in a seduction to be built on the ones before it. *This bitch won't allow that.*

"Why are you being this way?" Sergio's voice nearly overflowed with an appeal for sympathy, "Will you permit me to speak from the heart, and not make a hurried speech?"

"If you feel the need to confess your sins, there's a church near here. If not, get on with your apology, I'm waiting." *You're stalling for time. Time that I won't give you.*

He sighed loudly. *Think, Sergio, think.*

"Evelyn, do you remember how we enjoyed being with each other when we first met?" *Awakening old, warm sensations always works. This should get her feeling pleasant about me.*

Evelyn smiled. He finally liked the way things were going.

"Yes, I do." Her smile disappeared as if it never existed. "Then I found out what a snake, a rat, and every other disgusting creature you are. I let you in tonight to give you the chance to do exactly what you said you wanted to do – to apologize. Instead, you tried to get close to me physically and emotionally. The Americans have a saying, 'Fool me once, shame on you. Fool me twice, shame on me.'

"I told you that I have a man in the States. He is a real man, not a pretend one like you. You look like a man, and you say the things a man should say. They are the phony lines of an actor imagining to be something he isn't. There is nothing genuine about you except your desire to please yourself."

Evelyn picked up her cup, and swallowed the last of her tea. Then she looked at her watch. "Your time is up. You'll have to save your well-prepared lies for your next victim."

The phone rang. She snatched up the receiver on

the old phone that her parents had not replaced. Evelyn didn't want the ringing to wake them.

This must be Michael. I'll finish throwing Sergio out after this brief call. I'd prefer he wasn't here for my private conversation. But this will add to his well-deserved punishment. "Hello?"

"Ah, you expected me this time. Did I catch you at a bad time? I know it's late."

"No, Michael, this is fine. My parents are asleep. I just finished a cup of tea."

Sergio listened, a captive to her conversation. He was frustrated at going home unsatisfied. Worse, he was angry that he was forced to hear this, and see her face so happy to be talking to her lover. Sergio started to leave. He didn't want to be slapped with this.

And then a better idea crept from under a rock. *If I can't have her tonight, I'll make sure she can't have him. Ever.*

Sergio's English wasn't as handy as his German, though years of admiring American action movies and television shows had taught him enough. He carefully moved as close to the distracted Evelyn as he could silently do, and spoke loudly, in the direction of the phone, "Evelyn, mi amore, come back to bed. We were barely getting started."

Michael heard it as clearly as if Sergio were alongside him. He felt like a lightning bolt had scorched his heart. Then Michael hung up the phone.

Chapter Twenty-Two

Only Evelyn's discipline kept her from yelling. But it did not restrict her anger. "You are even lower than I believed possible. Get out of here right now. Or I will call the police."

Sergio smiled. "You are so emotional. Why don't you let me make this a night you will never forget?"

You've already done that. "You won't get a second warning, you lizard. Get out!"

Evelyn walked behind him to make sure he left. Then she hurried back to the kitchen and called Michael.

Michael stared at the ringing phone. Not picking it up was possibly the hardest thing Michael ever did. He knew it was Evelyn. He also knew that this would be the worst time to speak to her. His mind was dizzy with competing emotions: hurt, confusion, betrayal, and others. Michael wasn't sure what to say, or what might leap out of his mouth. He was afraid of any unknown, irreversible damage those unplanned and emotional words might do.

I'd better keep my mouth shut for now.

He clicked off the answering machine. Hearing Evelyn's voice, and not picking up the phone, would be impossible. He let the phone continue to ring.

Michael wanted desperately to believe that there was an innocent explanation for this. *Maybe there is. But I can't imagine what it would be. And this is far too important a conversation to have the way I feel right now.*

He needed to get control of himself. To lasso his emotions before they went wild and grabbed control.

The phone finally gave up and surrendered. The ringing died a silent death.

The monster inside of Michael, Fear of Betrayals, smiled.

Michael forced in deep breaths and slowly exhaled them. He'd listened and learned well from Marvin La Rue, a compliment to Michael's intelligence and his love and admiration for the man he would always consider his father. One of the wise and practical treasures that Mr. La Rue told him came back at that moment, "You've got to play the hand you're dealt. Not the one you want to be holding."

Michael did everything he could to calm himself and cope with this rationally and intelligently. *I know that things are not always what they appear to be. But...who was that in the background? Why was he in Evelyn's house at night? And what was going on? I mean, really going on?*

Michael loved math, and excelled at using that systematic logic to solve life's mysteries, whenever feasible. Without needing to think about it, Michael reduced every problem, every situation to be conquered, to as short a list of variables as appropriate.

Michael paced around the room as he tried to sort this out. To put some meaning to it that made sense. He knew that using math lessons had limitations. Humans were too complicated to be represented as a series of x's and y's. In some ways, numbers were easier to deal with. When you looked at a number, it was a constant. It never changed. It always had, and always would have, the same characteristics. And, a number never had a bad day, a poor night's sleep, or a grumpy mood.

Numbers were exactly what they appeared to be, with no hidden motives, no secrets, and no pretenses. The same could not be said for many people. Except Evelyn. To Michael, she was as steady, as stable, and as faithful as any number. *I know her well enough to believe that.*

Michael abruptly stopped. He shivered as a warning jolted him with the sudden and startling clarity of cutting a large hole through some thick arctic ice and jumping into the freezing water beneath.

I'm not always sure of my own motives, desires, and secrets. Do we ever really know another person?

Michael's mind was nearly numb. His body broke the spell by resuming walking, randomly, in his living room.

This is going to give me an even worse headache than I have now. I'm not sure what to do. And Evelyn's four thousand miles away. I'll go to 'Y' and take out my frustration, confusion, and anger on the weights, and my muscles. Then, after a hot shower, I'll be able to think clearly. Yeah, that's what I'll do.

Michael forcefully shoved his workout shorts and t-shirt into his small work-out bag, and grabbed his wallet and keys. Twenty minutes later he scanned his ID at the front desk of the 'Y' and said "Hello" to the two older ladies behind the counter.

Michael walked across the small lobby, and opened the glass door to the big workout area. He glanced at the two rows of treadmills to his right. Michael didn't see anyone from the Deac, like he sometimes did.

The weight-lifting section was adjacent to the treadmills and other cardio machines. A large area filled with well-maintained, and expensive exercise machines to isolate, tone, and strengthen each body part invited the 'Y' members to improve their fitness, and appearance. The free weights, and the bars and benches for using them, were arranged and stacked in a large, open room off to the side.

Michael nodded politely to other people in the weight room area. He knew them by sight, not name, and he planned to keep it that way. One of them was a young woman about twenty-five years old. She was a real head-turner, both for her face, and her impressive body.

She didn't advertise or emphasize her physique. She wore ordinary work-out clothes, nothing flashy or up-to-the-minute fashionable. Her shorts and t-shirts looked chosen for comfort and practicality, and the tops were always decorated with a big zone of sweat in the front. She worked-out like a man, but she sure didn't look like one.

She sometimes asked Michael to spot for her as she benched-pressed an impressive amount of iron for her bodyweight, which he estimated at about one hundred and twenty-five pounds on a roughly five feet seven frame.

She was adding steel plates to each side of a barbell when she looked over and saw Michael. She smiled, and made a motion that asked if he would help her.

He put his gym bag against the wall, and walked over.

She said, "Thanks. I hope I'm not holding you up."

"No, I just got here. There's no rush."

"Where's your girlfriend? She's usually with you."

Michael didn't know what to say. *I came here to forget Evelyn for an hour or so while my subconscious figures this out. How do I answer this question? And what is the answer? That I know where Evelyn is, I'm not sure where our relationship is?*

"She's visiting her family in Germany. Evelyn's not my girlfriend, we're married."

"Germany? That's far. You must miss her."

"Uh, sure, yes. Of course, I do."

He stood behind the bench as she moved her body to get into the right position. Then, she reached up and gripped the long barbell at shoulder width. She took in and let out deep breathes, and hoisted the weight off the rack. She pushed it straight up. Then, she lowered the weight to her chest, and repeated the movement. Each up and down movement needed about two seconds.

After about seven repetitions, her upward thrust slowed down, and she nodded to Michael. He used two fingers of each hand to gently add a little to her efforts. She slowly cranked out two additional reps, barely. She lowered the bar to the rack, and dropped her arms, breathing hard with exertion.

She sat up, and smiled. "Thanks," she said between deep breaths.

"You're welcome," he said as she stood up, still panting. Although Michael wasn't particularly looking, he would have been blind not to have seen how the thin and damp t-shirt clung to her. Despite the obvious outline of a skimpy sport bra under it, every contour, every feature, and every detail of her firm breasts was displayed.

Chapter Twenty-Three

After his work-out, Michael was buying some fresh vegetables and fruit at a local specialty store. He paid for his groceries, and heard a friendly female voice. "I thought that was you."

He looked around. The girl from the "Y" walked toward him.

Michael said, "Hi." He didn't want to block the exit area, it was already busy with people pushing carts in and out, and old people moving slowly. He headed toward the door as she walked beside him, carrying a small paper bag.

"We haven't exchanged names. I'm Jill." She moved the small grocery bag to her left hand, and stuck out her right.

"Michael." Jill's hand was lightly calloused from lifting weights. It was still the hand of a woman.

"Hi, Michael. I'm glad I finally know your name. Don't you love this store?"

"Yeah, we particularly like the organic selections."

"Why is your girlfriend, I mean your wife, in Germany?"

"Her mom fell, and hurt her hip. Evelyn is helping around the house."

"That's considerate of her. She's lucky to have such an understanding man."

I don't want to discuss my personal life. Especially with a stranger. "Yes, she is."

They were out on the quiet street. It was early evening. The pedestrian crowds were probably at home getting ready to sit at the dinner table, or maybe already in front of a TV.

Jill stopped walking, and Michael did too, out of politeness.

She moved in a little closer. "I'm glad I ran into you."

Michael wasn't sure how to respond. He didn't want to encourage her, so he said nothing.

Jill smiled. "Aren't you going to ask why?"

Let's keep this light. And brief. He looked at the small bag she held. "You needed help carrying your groceries?"

She laughed, and moved closer. "No, that's not it. I've seen you looking at me at the 'Y'."

Michael shook his head. "I wasn't looking. I noticed you. There's a big difference."

Jill smiled. "Okay. Did you like what you noticed?"

Michael felt some blushing creep onto his face. "You're an attractive woman. You don't need me to tell you that."

"Thank you. I think you're a handsome man. A handsome man who is currently all alone."

Jill moved in a little closer. Inches separated them. Michael could feel heat radiating from her.

She said, "Why don't you walk me back to my apartment, and let me cook you a healthy dinner?"

Yes, I am currently alone. And if I took you up your offer, and Evelyn and I somehow get back together, she would never know about this. But I would. That flashed through Michael's synapses in a burst of time no stopwatch could measure. He didn't need to articulate his feelings about certain things. They were a natural part of him, and didn't need to be elaborated on. When you were in a committed relationship, you didn't cheat. If the relationship blundered off in the wrong direction, with no way to avoid a cliff, you bailed out. Until you did, you stayed faithful. No matter what happened, or how tempting things seemed. *You either are a person of honor, or you aren't. There is no in-between.*

And, you were faithful not when you felt like it. Or, when it was convenient. Or, because you might get caught. But, always. That was part of what Semper Fidelis meant. Michael paused. *I hope Evelyn feels that way.*

Michael knew exactly what Jill was inviting him for. He pretended he didn't, to spare her any embarrassment. "As innocent as dinner is, I wouldn't feel right taking you up on your offer."

Jill flashed an exaggerated, humorous, and cute pout. "Are you sure? We can exchange workout secrets?"

Michael laughed. He shook his head. "Thanks, I'll pass."

She nodded. "I can accept that."

Jill placed her right hand tenderly on his face. "The offer remains if you change your mind. Or your situation."

Her hand lingered before she withdrew it.

Michael walked home, cooked a simple meal, and went to bed. He looked at the alarm clock on his night table. It wasn't necessary. He knew it was too late to call Evelyn. Even if it weren't, Michael hadn't figured out how to handle his long-distance problem. The problem that was made worse, maybe unsolvable, because of Evelyn's reluctance to let her deeper feelings and emotions out. She barely revealed even any tip-of-the-iceberg glimpses into her soul and heart, preventing a more meaningful, and emotionally pleasurable relationship.

Michael woke up, sweating, and startled. Dreaming about Evelyn. Or had it been a nightmare?

Chapter Twenty-Four

BANG!

Evelyn wasn't sure why the realization exploded into her mind. It was uninvited, yet not unwelcome. She'd been trying to figure out how to get in touch with Michael since he wasn't taking her calls. Those efforts were shoved aside by the awareness. Evelyn said out loud to herself, "Now after all this time, I finally understand."

Evelyn paced in large circles in her parent's living room. She wasn't going anywhere, she was thoroughly overwhelmed and could not sit, or stand still.

She stopped suddenly. Evelyn became a statue. Insights bounced around in her head, while hazy perceptions solidified into clear understandings.

Why didn't I think of this sooner? I've been afraid to completely commit to a relationship because I worried that I would lose my identity. I feared that becoming half of a couple would somehow diminish who I am. As if that merging would rob me of something essential. Something that I wouldn't ever get back. And to make it worse, I've been foolish and stubborn not to admit this to myself.

She resumed making circles inside the large room. Her intensity burned as a light layer of sweat seeped from her forehead. Evelyn's awareness leaped from one new recognition to another.

The inner monologue continued. *This nonsense kept me from telling Michael how I feel about him. I can't believe how this has prevented me from fully savoring our relationship. And, our love for each other. Yes, love. I've hurt myself and Michael. I've been my own worst enemy.*

Evelyn couldn't decide if she was more angry, or embarrassed. *This is going to stop. Right now!*

Evelyn called Michael again. All she heard was her own voice on their answering machine.

I'm not going to sit around and hope he changes his mind. I'm going to go home and change it for him.

~ * * * ~

Evelyn waited until after dinner to tell her parents that she was leaving.

Her mother pleaded, "Why do you have to leave tomorrow?"

"I'm sorry. I know its last minute. I must do this. I called your doctor this afternoon. You're cleared to walk short distances. He said you should get some exercise, to strengthen the muscles that hold the hip joint together. I asked the people across the street if their son would do the shopping for you until you feel up to it. They said it would be fine. I'll miss you both. But I need to get back to the U.S."

~ * * * ~

Evelyn opened her paperback novel to the pages with the napkin between them. Then, she changed her mind. Evelyn closed the book, and placed it on her lap. She hadn't slept well the night before, and hoped she might make up for it on the nearly nine-hour flight. She looked out of the small window to her right in the full coach cabin of the earliest United Airlines flight out of Frankfurt that day. Evelyn closed her eyes, and tried relaxation breathing exercises. She knew they wouldn't work. The inner peace needed for sleep remained as distant as the ground that rolled by 37,000 feet below.

Evelyn knew what to expect at Immigration and Customs when the plane landed. But, she possessed no clue what waited for her at the apartment that she shared with Michael.

The twenty minute 'T' ride from the airport to their apartment somehow seemed both longer than the flight from Germany, and shorter than a politician's promise. Evelyn was not inclined toward optimism, so doubts about the wisdom and outcome of confronting Michael grew as the distance shrank.

She exited at Boylston Street and crossed to their building. In the elevator, Evelyn closed her eyes for a moment. *I would give anything for a time machine and a second chance.*

Evelyn walked down the hallway to their apartment hesitantly. Evelyn stood in front of the door and raised her arm. Her hand stopped. Then, she knocked.

Michael opened the door. After two long seconds he said, "This is a surprise."

"I'm sure it is."

He didn't move, as he tried to sort this out.

Evelyn said, "Aren't you going to invite me in? I do live here, don't I?" *At least for now.*

He moved aside. Evelyn picked up her suitcase, and entered the living room. "Michael, I don't want this to be a battle. I have a lot I want to say, and I hope that you'll be the excellent listener you've always been."

He needed a moment to recover from seeing Evelyn. Michael nodded. "I'll listen."

"That's all I expect." *Or deserve.* Evelyn wasn't going to damage her chances by saying that.

Michael was hurt, confused, and angry. Yet, he was still Michael. And she was still Evelyn. "You look tired. Can I get you anything?"

Before she could answer, Michael moved in and hugged her.

The embrace was awkward, stiff, and tentative. Neither of them was sure where to put their arms, or how hard to hold each other. That lasted about three heartbeats, maybe less. Then their feelings took over, and they held each other without inhibitions.

Michael said, "Damn it, Evelyn, I'm mad at you." His tone was that of a wounded lover, not an adversary eager for a fight.

Evelyn smiled inside. *Thank you, God. And, please hold off on the time machine. At least for now.* She said, "You don't need to be. I'm mad enough at myself for both of us. I finally figured out the answers to some problems."

She paused. "If you'll make me a cup of coffee, I've got a story to tell you."

Chapter Twenty-Five

MICHAEL'S MIND STRUGGLED TO STAY balanced. *Someone once said that our eyes are windows to the soul. Even if that's not true, they are lie detectors. I don't think Evelyn cheated on me. I need to be sure. If I can't trust her, then we have nothing to say to each other. Not now, not ever.*

He believed that only an experienced and skilled liar could fake telling the truth about something important without their eyes betraying them. Michael felt that if Evelyn didn't look him in the eye, or perhaps nervously glanced around, maybe repeating a question to stall for time to create a lie - he would know she wasn't telling the truth. And then he would get up and leave. And never come back.

"Evelyn, I need to be absolutely certain of something before we go any further. Please don't take this the wrong way. This is a question, not an accusation. Did you have sex with whoever was with you at your parent's house?"

"Absolutely not!" Her answer was immediate and forceful.

Michael's brown eyes interrogated Evelyn. She probably didn't realize it, but her blue eyes would either convince Michael of her innocence, or sign a confession. Not blinking, Evelyn stared back at him.

"Did you kiss him?"

"Absolutely not!"

Michael stared at her. He went to Evelyn and hugged

her tighter than she'd ever been hugged before. She returned his embrace, trying to merge, to fuse her body with his.

"That's what I thought." He paused. "I had to be certain." They stayed like that for a long time.

Michael released Evelyn, and pulled back a little. "I'm glad I was right about you. For me to even have the smallest doubt means that I don't know you as well as I should." He paused. "This brings me to the next problem."

"Before we go further," Evelyn said, "I want to tell you something. You know what did *not* happen with Sergio, I want you to know what *did* happen. This is important, because I realize that I love you, Michael. I'll say it again. I love you. I don't want any questions to remain about that incident. You may be an exception to this, but, it's a human trait for our minds to take a morsel of information, even if it's incorrect, and make an entire meal, maybe a poisonous one, from it."

Michael nodded.

"Sergio is an old boyfriend. We weren't in the bedroom. It was the kitchen. You've been to my parent's house. It's old, and there isn't a phone outlet in the bedrooms. Besides, I would never permit him anywhere in my parent's house except the kitchen. I allowed that only because he begged me to let him apologize for being a liar and a cheat when I dumped him. He said he changed, and wanted to cleanse his conscience so that he could move on.

"I told him that you were my man. His stubborn Italian pride could not accept that I broke up with him, and didn't want him back. Right before you called, I told him to leave. Then, the phone rang. Sergio knew that it was you from my end of the conversation. He said the garbage that you heard in English so you would understand it, and be insulted, or hurt enough to hang up. It worked."

Michael sighed. "Yes, it did. And, that's not a compliment to me."

"No, it's my fault. If I'd been open, and let you in, you would have known me well enough not to wonder."

Michael nodded again. "As I said, there is one more thing."

"May I say something first?"

"Sure."

"You and I nearly broke up before I realized how lucky I was to find you. I'm embarrassed to admit this, I allowed myself to become spoiled by your attention. I became careless, and didn't give back what you gave me. It wasn't a decision that I consciously made. It was a laziness that I slid into. You're the most generous person I've ever known. You give all of yourself, and ask so little."

Evelyn breathed in and slowly let it out. This was near the top of the difficult things she had ever done. No, this was number one on that list.

"Like I said, I'm not proud of this. I behaved stupidly, letting you make me feel like a princess while I provided you nearly no emotional support." She paused, needing a brief break from this purging.

After a couple of deep breaths, Evelyn continued. "I learned my lesson. I hope that it isn't too late." Her eyes pleaded with Michael. "If you'll forgive me, and take me back, I promise I'll be everything you want me to be. Everything that you deserve."

Michael looked at Evelyn. Silent. Thinking. Deciding.

"I've never begged for anything in my life before," she said. "Nothing was ever that important. And I was always stubborn. I'll beg now, if it will help. You mean that much to me."

Michael said nothing while he considered her words.

He knew this would be the biggest decision of his life so far. Maybe even for the rest of it - his feelings about Evelyn were that powerful. And he knew that he'd been impossibly lucky to find Evelyn out of billions of women in the world.

He reminded himself, however, that that wasn't enough. Successful relationships were woven from many strands. And primary among them were mutual sharing and caring. Evelyn was an exceptional person, but Michael felt she'd consistently left him emotionally hungry. Michael didn't want to accept that. He wouldn't go through life that way. *I don't deserve it. No one should be in a lopsided relationship, with emotional give, and no nourishing take. I don't ask for a lot, and it was important to me. Why didn't Evelyn see that?*

Michael knew that Evelyn wouldn't say anything she didn't mean. And although he trusted her intentions to be genuine, would she be able to make this big a change in her behavior? In her way of thinking? Or would she be like the alcoholic who sincerely promises to stay dry, yet can't do it?

He would rather be alone than with a woman he was gradually growing to resent, no matter how desirable she might be. And he and Evelyn both deserved an honest resolution to this, not a giving-in-to-the-moment one. Michael felt no pressure to answer quickly, and he was not uncomfortable with the silence while he decided.

While Michael weighed things, Evelyn sat so motionless that she might have been a marble carving in a museum. She knew that her future, one way or the other, would be decided by Michael's words.

Evelyn felt like being on trial, waiting for the jury to announce their verdict. She wasn't sure she was even breathing, maybe totally paralyzed by both hope and doubt. Evelyn couldn't look at Michael. She was afraid that his face might reveal a clue, a trace, a hint of what she didn't want to hear.

She bowed her head, and lowered her eyes to the floor. Evelyn felt shame take over her body and her mind. Shame that she'd been so foolish to hold back her feelings. Shame that she'd hurt the one man who loved her without restrictions, without limits, without hesitations. And, shame that she'd neglected, and maybe lost, the biggest chance at happiness she might ever have.

Michael continued his silence. His mind stayed surprisingly calm as he examined this. *I want to make sure that I do this right the first time. I don't want to ever go through this again. Not with Evelyn, or anyone. Once is more than enough.*

So he didn't rush - no hurrying to make a quick, possibly wrong decision. *I'm determined to do what is honorable for Evelyn, and for me. She deserves that. I won't take her back, giving her hope for the future unless I honestly feel that we have one... a long one.*

Michael breathed in deeply. He held it, and let it out. Then he spoke. "Evelyn, no matter what we decide, I want to clear the air between us. I *need* to clear the air. Whether we continue as a couple or not, I want it to be for the right reasons. With no misunderstandings.

"It would be dishonest and cowardly of me if I didn't tell you something that's been bothering me since early in our relationship. I'm not saying this to hurt you, or because I've been holding a grudge. This needs to be said. I've tried to get over it, to forget it...I can't."

Michael felt that what he was about to bring up was like a lump, a growth on his skin that wouldn't go away. One that was painful, annoying, and while not growing larger, would not go away.

He managed a small smile "Okay, maybe there is some element of holding a grudge. Hey, I'm human."

Evelyn couldn't smile, not even nervously. Confusion and worry dominated her mind. Things were already damning enough for her. Now this bomb, whatever it might be, was about to explode. And right in her face.

Evelyn had already resigned herself to the possibility of life without Michael. Now that possibility had turned into a probability. She was embarrassed, hurt, and fearful of what was coming to even look up.

She weakly said, "What is it?"

Michael's voice was a mix of hurt and accusation. "Do you remember what you did for my thirtieth birthday?"

Staring at the floor, Evelyn knew the answer. Her voice shrank even smaller, barely audible. "I didn't do anything for you. Nothing at all."

Her eyes moist, Evelyn looked up into Michael's face. "You said that your birthday wasn't a big deal to you."

"What did you expect me to say? That I wanted a parade?" Michael heard some notes of anger that had unintentionally snuck into his voice. He tried to remove them as he continued. "If I have to ask you to do something for me, I feel like you're doing it as an obligation, not from your heart. My birthday wasn't important to me. But it should have been important to you."

Evelyn fought the impulse to cry, not wanting to seem weak to herself or to Michael. And she needed to avoid having him think that she was somehow crying as a phony gesture, or a pitiful attempt for forgiveness. The tears flowed anyway.

She looked around for the tissue box. He handed it to her, Evelyn wiped her eyes. It tormented Michael to see Evelyn in pain, but, he resisted his instinct to hold her. He knew that if he did, they would be right back where they started. That this agonizing discussion, with its difficult decisions, would be over. But nothing would have been resolved. Michael wouldn't back-down from his responsibility to Evelyn, and himself, to nurture their relationship back to health. Or give it a mercy killing.

Evelyn was certain that this new wound was a fatal one. *Why would he want to be with a selfish bitch? I'm not one, even if that's how I must seem.* Then Evelyn's entire body burned with a new humiliation. *Maybe I am a selfish bitch.*

Evelyn wasn't sure that she could speak without her voice breaking. She tried. "I know I'm repeating myself, please forgive me." She dabbed at her eyes again. "You're right. Your birthday should have been important to me, because you are. You're the greatest thing in the world to me. I hope this doesn't sound like an excuse, there isn't one for my behavior. In some ways, I'm a prisoner of my upbringing. Like I said, that isn't an excuse, it's an explanation. I'll be glad to tell you more about that later.

"I want to make sure that you fully realize how sorry I am, and how thoroughly I've learned my lesson." Evelyn held her breath and continued. "If you give me a second chance, I promise I won't let you – or us – down."

Michael urgently wanted to believe this. This was probably the most severely challenging and stressful episode in his life. He sensed that it was nearly over. One way or the other.

My father advised me that small decisions are made with the brain. The large ones should be handled by the heart. He never steered me wrong. Michael didn't have any words ready, and he wasn't even quite sure of which way he would choose. He opened his mouth to let his heart speak, curious and eager to hear what it might say.

"Evelyn, I know how unique you are. And I didn't expect that you'd be the first person who didn't make a mistake."

As soon as he said those words, Evelyn knew. *Here*

it is. The opening words to the gentle breakup. The quick kiss. Then the kick in the butt out the door.

Michael continued. “You’re not only special, you’re the finest person I’ve ever known. And the all-time number one thing that ever happened to me. I know I’d never get over it if I lost you.” He involuntarily nodded. His brain was in complete agreement with his heart.

Evelyn just about leaped to Michael, and hugged him so tightly she was afraid she might loosen a few of his ribs. She said, “To borrow something I’ve heard you say, ‘No one can go back and make a new beginning. But starting right now, they can make a new ending.’”

Somewhere deep inside of Michael, where for years it mocked and tormented him while it eluded capture, the monster named Fear of Betrayals died.

Michael forced his emotions aside. He believed that humor was an effective way to relieve tension. And there was plenty of tension surrounding them waiting to be relieved. He knew he should try to lighten things up. “Now that we’re back together, shouldn’t we celebrate with something more meaningful than a hug?”

Chapter Twenty-Six

TWO DOORS TO THE LEFT of Evelyn and Michael's six story apartment building in Boston was a Vietnamese restaurant. It was small, and nearly hidden. No sign, no painted name, not even a menu taped on the inside of the glass front. No awning with lettering, nothing. Michael hurried past it frequently without realizing that it even existed.

Evelyn suggested they go in there one night. She said she had not noticed it until recently, when she stopped and looked in the window to see happy faces on the couples in there. She said to Michael, "If those faces were any indication of the food, they're doing something tight."

They sat at one of the handful of tables, looking at a menu that was a sheet of paper with about ten items printed on it from a home computer. The menu choices and descriptions were in Vietnamese followed by English. Michael said, "I guess the order of the languages tells us who they anticipated their customers would be." The English spellings were not all correct, Evelyn and Michael thought that added to the atmosphere.

Evelyn ordered vermicelli noodles with shredded vegetables and grilled shrimp. Michael asked for the same dish, but with grilled pork. It was number seven on the menu. The middle-aged and tired looking Vietnamese waitress came through the swinging door of the kitchen about five minutes later with two large, steaming bowls.

The waitress smoothly glided between the half dozen or so tables crunched together in the cramped dining area, and placed the correct bowls in front of them. Evelyn and Michael both ignored the forks wrapped in a paper napkin, and picked up the bamboo chopsticks that were in front of them.

After tasting their meals, they looked at each other with satisfied faces.

"This is delicious," said Evelyn.

Michael nodded, and was already chewing on his second mouthful of bacon sized slices of grilled pork. He offered the clear plastic squeeze bottle of red Vietnamese hot garlic sauce to Evelyn. She declined. Then, she changed her mind and squeezed a little onto a chunk of the chicken. Evelyn raised her chopsticks, and placed the chicken into her mouth. She closed her eyes while she chewed, concentrating her senses on the taste. She opened her eyes, and looked at Michael. "Mmmm. That makes me want to use one of my favorite English words. What a scrumptious combination of tastes."

Michael smiled.

They finished eating, and passed on the two dessert choices: fried plantains or mung beans in sweet syrup. Instead, they lingered, drinking tea poured from a porcelain white teapot decorated with Oriental scenes.

Evelyn said, "That was fabulous."

"Yeah, it's a shame it was so expensive."

She laughed. Each bowl cost four dollars.

The unbeatable combination of tasty home-cooked meals, closeness to their apartment, and low prices motivated Evelyn and Michael to eat there at least twice a week, often three times. They didn't know the name of this tiny place, or if it even had one. They referred to it as Next Door, which while not quite accurate, rolled out of their mouths smoother than Two Doors Away.

They always ate the number seven. They settled into

a pattern with the meats, grilled shrimp for Evelyn, grilled pork for Michael. They were never disappointed.

After more of their frequent visits, the waitress - Evelyn and Michael figured she was married to the cook - would approach their table with menus tucked under her arm and ask, "Number seven?"

When about two more weeks passed, the waitress didn't bother to even go up to them. She would look at Evelyn and Michael questioningly as they entered. They would nod, and sit at one of the small tables.

Some short time after that, the waitress dropped getting even visual confirmation. Instead, after Evelyn and Michael picked a table and got comfortable, she emerged from the kitchen with two bowls of number seven, one with grilled shrimp, including an extra skewer of shrimp, the other with pork. The grill marks on the shrimp and pork nudged them even higher in desirability.

One night, Evelyn ate her noodles and used her chopsticks to move the shrimp to the edge of the large bowl. Michael said, "You should enjoy the shrimp while they're hot, or at least warm."

Evelyn continued with her noodles, ignoring the shrimp, and said, "I save the best for last."

"Of course, you do. That's why you're married to me."

Then, the cook blasted out of the kitchen like a torpedo fired from a submarine. His target was their table. *What's this about?* Michael wondered. Evelyn seemed startled, Michael calmly watched the cook get closer and closer.

The middle-aged Vietnamese man with thinning hair was dressed in a typical kitchen uniform: a short sleeved white shirt, white trousers, and white apron, each splattered with stains. His shoes were glazed with grease from long hours of cooking.

The man's body language was screaming 'I'm not

happy.' Michael remained sitting. He stood six feet one inch and didn't want to risk embarrassing the smaller man. The cook stopped at their table and stretched up to his full height, about 5'6", reminding Michael of a rooster puffing out its chest for effect. He glared at Michael, and nearly shouted. "Why you order same thing all the time? Not good eat same thing every day. Why you not try something different?"

Michael looked at Evelyn, whose mouth moved a bit as she struggled not to laugh. As quickly as the cook sped to confront them, he punctuated his remarks with a warning scowl, and raced back into the kitchen. He shoved the swinging door so hard that it flapped back and forth squeakily before staying closed.

After that, when they ate leftovers, Michael would sometimes suddenly spring up, and nearly shout with a Vietnamese accent to a laughing Evelyn, "Why you serve same thing all the time? Not good eat same thing every day. Why you not give me something different?"

~ * * * ~

Evelyn and Michael sat at the small kitchen table in their apartment. They'd been out to dinner and were back home, sipping a liqueur, ending the evening exactly the way they preferred, quietly, and alone with each other.

Michael said, "One of my friends at the hospital told me he was thinking of marrying a woman I knew. He asked did I think they would have problems. I told him of course they would. All relationships have problems. I added that isn't what will determine the success or failure of his marriage."

"What will?"

"How they deal with those problems."

Evelyn nodded. "That makes sense." She paused, and

then smiled slyly. "So, every relationship has problems? What are ours?"

"Ah, an inquisitive mind. I admire that. It's a sign of advanced intelligence."

"I'm flattered. Now, perhaps you'll answer my question."

"Well, our relationship is somewhat different..."

Evelyn started to interrupt, Michael held up his hand. "Hold on, please let me continue. Yes, despite our seeming perfection, there are problems. As I started to say, we're different, in that all of the problems seem to be with me."

Evelyn said, "What might those problems be?"

"For starters, when we're apart, I seem to have a problem keeping you out of my mind. When we're together, I have a problem keeping my eyes off you. And when you're near me, I have a problem keeping my hands off you. Sort of like this." He got up, went behind Evelyn, placed both hands on her shoulders and gently massaged them.

Evelyn's shoulders first tensed with the mild pressure of his fingers, and then relaxed. Her head bent toward her chest as she tried to present more of her upper back to him. Michael's fingers became pleasure sensors that helped him maintain exactly the right pressure to induce Evelyn to relax.

He continued this. Michael could feel her upper body surrender. Evelyn's breathing slowed down, and she was so content that Michael expected her to purr. He gently kneaded the muscles on the tops of her shoulders. His fingers explored forward and then south until they were enjoying the upper curve of her breasts.

Evelyn sighed softly. When she spoke, her voice was breathy with desire. "I can imagine that these problems you mentioned would lead to others."

"Problems like deciding on the bed or a blanket on the floor?"

Her eyes stayed shut as Michael continued caressing her. "Yes. Major problems like that."

~ * * * ~

Michael was pleased with the effort that Evelyn was making to open up about her feelings. *I know this isn't easy for her. Not with the family background information she shared. I'm sorry that our relationship needed a near-death experience for this to happen. If things work out, it was worth it. And it could be my imagination, I could swear that our sex is even hotter, more passionate, and more intimate. I didn't think that could get any better, it sure seems like it has! I hope this lasts.*

Michael smiled, thinking about how each night, after they turned the light out in their bedroom, Evelyn turned onto her right side, and he put his left arm around her. She held his hand, and in the darkness said, "Michael, I love you."

~ * * * ~

That summer Michael played softball on the Deaconess team in a hospital league. Although Evelyn never saw baseball being played before, and didn't like it, she came to every game. Evelyn cheered for Michael whenever he got a hit, or made a play at third base. She didn't fully understand the meaning of either, but knew they were good.

Evelyn decided to visit him at the Deaconess one day. When she entered the x-ray department, Michael was chatting with an older, and nearly bald Hispanic man wearing a custodian's uniform. Evelyn couldn't be sure of his age - it could have been forty or sixty. Years of physical labor, maybe in the sun, will do that.

Michael and the other man were too far away for Evelyn to hear the words. She could tell by their smiling faces, and body language, that they were joking around. The older man laughed at something Michael said, and patted him on the arm. They shook hands, and Michael turned around, seeing Evelyn for the first time. "Hey, what a super surprise."

She graced Michael with that smile. It didn't matter how often Michael felt its magic, he always wondered, *How does she do that?* It wasn't a well-rehearsed, ready to be summoned as needed, mega-voltage smile that no real person used to look at someone. That level of phony smile would probably make your face would fall off from either exertion or fatigue. You usually saw those fake poses on an actress or a politician whenever a camera was nearby. This was the opposite of those. Evelyn's smile was a 'My heart is happy to be with you' smile.

Evelyn said, "I was in the neighborhood, and decided to drop in."

"In the neighborhood? Nice try. There's nothing around here except hospitals and medical offices."

"I was shopping and got off the 'T' at the wrong stop?"

"Not likely."

"OK, you caught me. I missed you, and came here so we could walk home together. The weather is too splendid to be underground."

Michael moved closer, and gave Evelyn a quick hug. "Thank you."

"My pleasure. Who was that you were talking to?"

"Felipe. He's on the maintenance staff. He was telling me about the academic scholarship that his daughter got to Boston College."

"Michael, only you would even notice him, or have a conversation about his family. I'll bet no one else in the department even knows his name."

Michael considered that, trying to disprove it.

Evelyn said, “What’s the name of the CEO of this hospital?”

“Mr. Big Shot?”

“Uh-huh. As I expected. But you know the name of the cleaning man. And I’ll bet you know his daughter’s name, don’t you?”

Michael smiled.

Evelyn said, “Ladies and gentlemen of the jury, I rest my case.”

“I see Felipe every day. I’ve never seen the CEO.”

“True. Everyone sees Felipe every day. They’re not being rude, I’m sure he’s invisible to them. They don’t notice him. And how many people do you think care enough to make the effort to let him know he’s appreciated?”

“I’m sure there are a lot.”

“And *I’m* sure that you’re mistaken. Michael, you’re a special man.”

He started to protest.

“Ssh. Not another word. Or, I won’t let you take me to dinner tonight.”

“How did I get so lucky? I get to walk around a world-class city with a beautiful woman. Or, is that a beautiful city with a world-class woman? *And* I get to have dinner with her. I wonder if my enchanted evening will continue after the meal?”

Chapter Twenty-Seven

Evelyn and Michael were sitting at an outside table on nearby Newbury Street, having their usual afternoon coffee. It was the kind of day you would order from Weather Central if you could. Clear beautiful blue sky, mid 70s, enough Saturday tourists for enjoyable people watching, not so many that the streets were crowded or noisy.

Evelyn put down her cup, touched her lips with the napkin, and said, "Did I ever tell you that I always wanted to be a flight attendant?"

"Yes. Didn't you apply at Lufthansa in Germany? They turned you down?"

"They did. My English wasn't up to their standards then. You needed to speak it fluently."

"Thanks to me, you certainly are fluent now."

Evelyn's eyebrows rose up. "You taught me English? My memory must be fading. I could have sworn I spoke it when I came to the U.S."

"Nope. Not a word."

She smiled. "Well, then I was incredibly lucky to meet you. And what a skilled teacher you've been, I barely have an accent. I won't be rude and ask how we communicated, since you don't speak German."

"Please don't."

"The reason I bring this up is that United Airlines is hiring flight attendants." Evelyn stopped; nervous, and reluctant to continue.

"That's great news." Michael saw that Evelyn's facial expression didn't match his enthusiasm. He said, "And the bad news is..."

"United doesn't have a base in Boston." She paused. "Nobody does."

Michael considered that. "I get it. Where does United have bases?"

Evelyn didn't want to say the words. She knew Michael loved working at the Deac and living in Boston. "Newark, Chicago, Los Angeles, Philadelphia, Washington, D.C., and San Francisco."

Michael chewed on this with Evelyn as his anxious audience. Then he said, "I grew up in Newark, don't really need to go back. Chicago is too cold in the winter, it isn't called the Windy City for nothing. L.A.? Easy on the eyes, hard for the brain. Your IQ drops one point every month you spend there, and I can't afford for mine to dip any lower. Los Angeles worships money, power, and looks. Not always in that order. L.A. might be the one place in the world that considers 'superficial' to be a compliment. D.C.? It's the B.S. center of the universe. San Francisco? Tony Bennett was right. And it's near Napa Valley. We're a little late for the Gold Rush, but, let's start packing when the time is right."

Evelyn was stunned. "I-I-I don't know what to say. I didn't expect that. You love everything about this city. I'm thrilled. Michael, are you sure? This is a big decision. Don't you want to give it some time? At least sleep on it? I don't want you to regret this quick decision later. When it's too late."

Michael put his forearms on the table as he leaned across it. "Evelyn, here's how I see it. I like being an x-ray tech. I like it a lot. But, it's a job, not a calling. Besides, there are hospitals in every city. Can you say that about airline bases?"

Evelyn smiled back, and shook her head.

"I didn't think so. Hey, I like to look on the bright side. Maybe I'll find San Francisco's version of the Deac. So, here's the deal: after we move, you owe me big-time. And not just sex. Though that's a dandy starting point. San Francisco has a first-rate Chinatown. I can already taste the dumplings and dim sum. Any questions?"

Evelyn's mouth moved a little, like she was about to say something. Nothing came out. That wasn't the case with her eyes. She dabbed at them with her napkin, coughed to clear her throat, and found her voice. "No one has ever done anything like this for me before. I---"

Michael held up his hands, the palms toward Evelyn. "Whoa, whoa, whoa. Who said anything about doing this for you? I'm already planning my first free trip. They do offer that as an employee benefit, don't they?"

Those words opened the water valves. She left her seat and straddled his lap, facing him. Her arms tightly circled his waist as he pulled her in closer. Evelyn's face was getting the front of his shirt wet, he didn't care. She lightly sobbed for a while, then, lifted her head and kissed him, sharing her tears with his dry face. "Michael, no one except you would do this."

~ * * * ~

Evelyn and Michael decided to move back to the Newark, New Jersey area. With three major airports, Evelyn would have choices of airlines to apply to in case United didn't work out.

Michael informed his supervisor at the Deaconess right away. They were sorry to see him go; and he was sorry to leave. He knew he probably wouldn't ever work at any place like the Deaconess. He never indicated this to Evelyn.

Michael employed the same technique to get an apartment back in New Jersey that he'd successfully used for Boston. On Sunday morning, Michael went to a local bookstore that sold newspapers from around the United States. He bought the thick Newark Star-Ledger Sunday paper, and sat at their kitchen table with it. He found the ads for apartments to rent, and five phone calls later, he looked at Evelyn and said, "Back to Joisey."

Then, he thought, *OK, now that we've got a place to sleep, how 'bout I line up a job to pay for it.* Michael turned to the employment section and wrote down the names and phone numbers of hospitals that needed x-ray techs.

The German managers at The Mansion was delighted about having Evelyn back. Michael showed up at the first hospital on his job list. He handed his letter of recommendation from the Deaconess, the letterhead proudly announced it as a major Harvard teaching hospital, to the interviewer. After reading the letter, his one question was, "When can you start?"

In the morning of their second day of being back in New Jersey, Michael opened the yellow pages of the phone book, and was impressed by one of the ads for a resume service. He made an appointment for the following afternoon.

Jake, the owner of the one-person business went over the features, benefits, and prices. Evelyn gave him her old InterContinental resume, and told him about the Four Seasons Hotel in Boston. Then, she answered Jake's questions while he jotted notes.

After Jake finished getting updated info from Evelyn, Michael extracted a credit card from his wallet, and paid the deposit. He asked Jake if he could rush this - United Airlines scheduled a hiring fair the following week. Jake agreed, and Michael picked up Evelyn's revised and polished resume four days later.

On Saturday, Michael drove Evelyn twenty minutes to a major chain hotel adjacent to Newark Airport for what was referred to as a cattle call. He sat in the lobby of the hotel with a book, while she followed the printed signs that directed interviewees to the correct conference room.

This was a mass hiring opportunity. Hundreds of people showed up. They filled out applications and were herded to lines in front of airline representatives waiting at tables for brief initial screenings.

Those who passed the first round went for a second filtering interview. This one was more detailed and lengthier than the first. Everyone who showed up was thanked for attending, and told that they would be notified of their status by mail within a week.

Michael tried to concentrate on his book, he couldn't. Endless people and a symphony of conversations flowed past him. He closed the book, and enjoyed watching the passing parade. *I can't believe how some of these people are dressed. Don't they have a mirror at home? Maybe they don't have any idea of how to dress for a professional interview. Do they live in caves? Have they never seen a movie or TV show that depicted what to wear? Or, for some of these people, what not to wear?*

After about one hour from the time she went in, Evelyn walked up to him. Michael didn't need to ask, her lack of a giant, satisfied smile told him. He didn't say anything. He tossed her a questioning look.

Evelyn shook her head. "I don't have a good feeling about it."

"You're being modestly pessimistic. I'll bet their eyes popped out at your service industry background with two big name hotels. You're beautiful, have first-class people skills, and speak three languages. What more could they want?"

"I wish you had interviewed me. As you would say, 'aargh'. Here's what happened." Evelyn apparently did well in the initial screening, she qualified to advance. "That's when the trouble started. The witch who interviewed me didn't ask a single question. All she did was brag about herself. How important she was, and all the travelling she does. That she loves to fly from her home in Chicago to Paris to buy scarves, they're the best in the world. And, on, and, on. She barely looked at my resume, she was busy patting herself on the back."

Evelyn shook her head again. "I doubt if I got the job."

Michael said, "Sometimes we want to be wrong. This is one of those moments."

He drove Evelyn to their old steakhouse, Arthur's Tavern in Hoboken, hoping to replace her doubts with better things. Or, drown them with a bottle of Dom.

A few days later, Evelyn received what Michael considered to be the worst letter he'd ever seen from a professional source. Evelyn didn't get hired. The problem wasn't what they said, it was how they said it.

The letter could have read, "Thank you for applying to United Airlines. We regret to inform you that right now we don't have a position to offer you." Or some other variation of a gentle and vague turndown.

But, that wasn't the letter Evelyn received. Evelyn's letter was not a smooth or gentle landing. Instead, it dragged her to a cliff, and without any hesitation, threw her onto the rocks below by stating, "After reviewing your application, we've decided to hire a more suitable candidate."

Evelyn handled it better than Michael. That didn't surprise him; she'd been expecting this. He resisted the strong impulse to rip up the letter, and instead inserted it into the 'Evelyn' file in the four drawers, second hand metal filing cabinet with chipped black paint, that he recently purchased.

About two months later, Evelyn showed Michael a new full page United Airlines newspaper ad promoting a hiring fair at the same hotel, for that upcoming Sunday afternoon.

Michael said, "Maybe they think they'll get more, or better, people on a Sunday instead of a Saturday."

She looked at him the way a stern librarian looks at a noisy child. "You aren't suggesting that I go, are you?"

Michael smiled.

"What if the same witch is there?"

"That's like the odds of being struck by lightning twice. Okay, she may be there. But, that's a huge conference room, with hundreds of people. It's highly unlikely that you would even see her. Or, be in her queue. Let's say that you are assigned to the witch. Self-centered people like her are aware of no one except themselves. She'll never remember you. She was too dazzled and blinded by her own radiance."

"I'd like to believe that's accurate." Evelyn sighed. "Michael, the airline has my application on file. They know I wasn't hired."

"Evelyn, Evelyn, Evelyn. I have so much to teach you. This isn't Germany. I love my country. Not that it's an international contest, but we do a lot of things better than other countries. Record keeping isn't one of them. Nearly every month the newspapers print a story about a person who's been dead for twenty years and still receives Social Security checks. Or, the IRS pursuing what turns out to be a ten-year-old over earnings from a business that the IRS didn't know was a lemonade stand in her front yard. Yes, I know those are bloated government agencies. I'm not convinced that large private businesses are any better."

Evelyn's face glowed with optimism. She liked where this was going. "What about the turn-down letter I received?"

"Close your eyes, and picture the corporate

headquarters building of a giant company." He paused, letting her imagine one. "Do you have it?"

"Yes."

"Okay. The letters of acceptance go out from the sixth floor. That ugly form letter that you got was sent from the ninth floor. I'm making these numbers up. You get the idea."

Evelyn opened her eyes, and smiled. "Do you think so?"

Michael grinned, and nodded.

She weighed that for a moment. "Should I go to this?"

"You'll regret it if you don't. You'll always wonder, 'What if?' You don't want to go through the rest of your life with that haunting you, do you?"

Evelyn shook her head. "No."

"Okay. Now go try on the clothes you want to wear for the interview. I'll come in, and watch. To make sure they match, of course."

On Sunday, Michael drove Evelyn back to the same hotel, and again waited in the hotel lobby, with a new book. He tried to concentrate on his novel. Michael couldn't. He didn't want to see Evelyn come out soon; that would mean bad news. About an hour later Evelyn walked over. This time she was smiling.

Michael jumped up soon as he saw her. He smiled back. "Well?"

"I don't want to count my ducks until they're hatched." Evelyn's smile grew bigger, and brighter. "It looks hopeful."

"It's chickens that you shouldn't count. Ducks get lined up."

"What?"

"Never mind. The birds aren't important, you are. Tell me all about it."

Evelyn held her breath. Michael was reminded of how stressful this must have been for her. No one wants to have their future decided by someone else. And with a rushed, 'You're one of hundreds. You have thirty seconds to tell me why I should hire you' tone. And, taking place in a noisy, crowded, chaotic setting.

Evelyn said, "You were right. I didn't even see that evil witch from the last time."

"Perhaps her broomstick is in the shop."

Evelyn laughed. The needed release was welcome. "I got a normal person this time. She looked at my resume, instead of bragging about herself. She asked about what I do to provide excellent service. Then, questions about how I've handled difficult customers. She jotted some notes, and then stuck out her hand and said, 'This isn't official, but I think you can safely start thinking about your new career.'"

Michael hugged Evelyn tightly. "We need to celebrate. Arthur's and a bottle of Dom sounds about right. After dinner, I'll let you demonstrate some of that excellent service."

~ * * * ~

About five years later, Michael was sitting in the front section of a 747 returning alone, from visiting Evelyn's family in Moerfelden, Germany. They had gone there together, Michael stayed one week. He was saving time off for a future trip. Evelyn was enjoying five extra days with her parents.

Michael sat in a comfortable first-class window seat. To his right was a middle-aged man wearing an expensive looking suit, and highly polished shoes. Michael opened his book after the safety demonstration, looking forward to a relaxing eight hours of reading, eating, and napping over Europe and the Atlantic. He could feel the man to his right glancing at him. *Take the high road. Five minutes of politeness won't kill you.*

Michael used the small cocktail napkin from his glass

of champagne to hold his place, and shut the book. He turned. "How was your visit to Germany?"

The stranger looked relieved to be able to chat. "The usual. I go once a month, on business. The same for you?"

Michael shook his head. "No, I was visiting my wife's family. She works for United, so we're lucky to go over fairly frequently."

"What does she do?"

"She's a flight attendant."

"My ex-wife works for United."

"Ex-wife? I'm sorry to hear that. Going through a divorce must have been brutal."

"It was worth it to be rid of her. She works as a recruiter, travelling around the country to hiring fairs. She loves the travel perks. She loves to fly to Paris for scarves. She claims they're unrivaled."

Michael worked to keep his face blank. *It couldn't be. No, I'll bet it is. How many interviewers could they possibly have who fit this description. I wonder if she lives in Chicago?*

The stranger continued. "Anyway, I came back a day early from a trip to Germany and wanted to surprise her. I didn't call before I went home."

"Where's home?"

"Chicago. I quietly unlocked the door to our condo overlooking Lake Michigan. I don't know who was more surprised, her, or the man she was in bed with." He swallowed from the drink in front of him. "Obviously, I divorced her. Therapy or counseling was not considered. I could never trust anyone who cheated on me like that."

When Michael told Evelyn this story, her wicked smile lingered for a while.

Chapter Twenty-Eight

EVERY DAY AFTER HER INTERVIEW in Newark, Evelyn could barely endure until she got home to check the mail. Michael smiled at her enthusiasm and excitement. Five days later, a magazine-sized package from United Airlines arrived. Evelyn waited until Michael got home so they could share it together.

Evelyn used a dinner knife to open it, and removed three items. First, they read the airline's letter of congratulations, which informed her of the training start date. Then, a voucher for a coach class ticket to get to Chicago, home of United's main hub, its corporate headquarters, and training facilities. A booklet of rules, regulations, and helpful tips regarding her training was the final item.

Michael admired that Evelyn was one of the most disciplined and hardest working people he'd ever known. He was certain that within twenty-four hours she would have read, and re-read every word in that pamphlet. Maybe even for a third time. This would instantly zoom to the top of her priority list.

Evelyn again gave two weeks' notice at The Mansion and planned what clothes to take for her nine-week training class. That weekend she packed and emptied her two suitcases until she was satisfied with everything that fit into them. She wasn't leaving for a week, so the suitcases sat patiently alongside their front door, like two guards at the palace entrance. Evelyn never let anything go until the last minute. If she had a task to do, she did it immediately, regardless of how long she had to complete it. When Michael complimented her willingness to do this, she always answered, "I won't be able to relax knowing that I have this waiting for me."

Departure day finally arrived. Michael drove Evelyn to Newark airport. He carried her suitcase, and walked with her as far as he was allowed. They embraced, and Evelyn promised to call when she arrived at the training center.

At the gate, Evelyn sat, and tried hard not to be nervous about the changes in her life, and all that it would mean. She was about fifty percent successful. Finally, she heard an announcement that her flight was boarding. Evelyn let everyone go first, and then stopped briefly at the retractable tunnel connecting the gate to the plane. *Okay, I've got the man I want, and now the career I want. Let's go.*

Evelyn boarded the plane.

Michael looked out of the big windows closest to the gate until he saw a jet being pushed back. It slowly taxied out of sight toward the runway. He couldn't be sure it was Evelyn's plane, though the timing was right.

Michael waited a few minutes, and then asked a nearby gate agent about Evelyn's flight. He checked his computer, and assured Michael that Evelyn's plane was airborne, not stuck out there with a last-minute mechanical problem. Michael thanked him, and left the airport, smiling for Evelyn.

He drove back to their apartment, thinking about the contrast in their relationship between this trip and when Evelyn flew home to help her mom. Michael remembered some wisdom that his father gave him, "There are two kinds of problems in the world, little ones and big ones. We can absorb the little problems. The big problems absorb us." *Thanks, Dad.*

That caused Michael to think about his parents, and their influence on him. He was reasonably content with the man he'd become. Michael knew that a large part of that was due to the love and upbringing the La Rues provided for the first twelve years of his life.

They patiently gave him a strong foundation to build on. Michael sometimes wondered how he might have turned out if their lessons and examples could have continued, and not been stolen by the drunk driver. Michael wasn't feeling sorry for himself, this was harmless curiosity. He considered himself supremely lucky that when his birth mother abandoned him, the La Rues had enough love in their hearts to take him in.

Michael was reading a murder mystery when Evelyn called from the training center where she was roomed with three other future flight attendants. Evelyn expected roommates, a private room was too much to ask for. As always, she made the best of it. "They can help me study."

She told Michael about her flight, and that there was an orientation for the new arrivals that evening with snacks and refreshments. "That's all I know for now. I'll call you later tonight when I know about my schedule."

"I look forward to it."

"Michael?"

"Yes?"

"I want to thank you again for everything you've done to make this happen."

"What are you talking about? All I did was chauffeur you to the Holiday Inn at the airport for the interviews. And that wasn't difficult, I already knew where it was. You did all the rest."

"That's quite efficient. You just displayed two of your better qualities in several short sentences: being modest, and a smart-ass. You know what I mean. Leaving the Deac, helping me update my resume, coaching me for the interviews, and just about dragging me back a second time after that that first disaster."

"You deserved all of it, and you're welcome."

"I need to go now. I'll call later. I love you, Michael."

"I love you, too, Evelyn."

~ * * * ~

When Evelyn called, she shared details of her training. A stranger listening might have described her as aloof. Michael clearly heard and enjoyed the enthusiasm in her voice. Evelyn was excited about her new career and the travel opportunities.

Michael was happy for her, and himself. Evelyn and he both loved travel, and had already vacationed in Mexico, London, and Jamaica three times. That didn't count their trips visit Evelyn's family. Now, their future travel plans would be decided by the boundaries of their dreams, not the size of their bank account.

Michael considered Evelyn to be quite intelligent. He knew she was smarter than he was, though her modesty prevented awareness of this. He wasn't surprised when she expressed some concern, bordering on worry, about the frequent tests they needed to pass. These would be written exams, and demonstrations of their proficiency with relevant and essential aircraft equipment, such as safety and first-aid gear. Michael hoped that he'd been successful in boosting Evelyn's confidence with his daily verbal injection of 'you can do it' vitamins. In case she was roomed with people who might nibble away at her positive attitude, Michael reminded himself to occasionally, and discreetly, blend in a short motivational pep talk.

Evelyn called every night from her room at the end of her jam-packed day. There were sometimes evening classes, or late training sessions on airplanes that were used during the day. Evelyn ended each conversation by telling Michael she loved him. And she never felt any embarrassment, or the need to lower her voice, and whisper those words because her roommates were there.

Michael always listened with honest interest, and kept his contribution to a minimum. He knew Evelyn needed to unwind, maybe vent, and then get ready for another jam-packed, hectic, and stressful day.

The weeks roared by nearly as fast as one of United's huge jets accelerating down the runway. Evelyn was relieved, and Michael was delighted for her, when the days left could be counted on one hand, and her graduation was a certainty. The airline mailed Michael a coach ticket to attend the ceremony. Return tickets for them were waiting at the training center.

The day before Evelyn's graduation, Michael flew in, and took a taxi to the room he had booked at one of the plentiful hotels surrounding the airport, near United's training facility. When Evelyn finished the final class of her flight attendant training, she grabbed the two suitcases she'd packed days earlier, put her last-minute items in them, and left a greater than adequate amount of money for the maid. She hugged her roommates, and went outside to the waiting cab.

Michael sat in the lobby of his hotel, with a view of the two sliding glass front doors. He was comfortably plopped in a big chair that looked like it wanted to wrap itself around him like a Venus fly trap. He looked up from his book frequently. Whenever a car, shuttle van, or taxi pulled up, his heart jumped like it was on a trampoline. *Damn. The next one will be her.*

After some misses, Michael was right.

He escaped from the chair before it decided it was hungry, and rushed to greet Evelyn. The doors hissed open, and the woman he loved, the woman he hadn't seen in nine weeks, stepped inside, and dropped her suitcases.

The hug was long, tight, and conveyed what words could never express.

Evelyn said, “Michael, it’s wonderful to see you.”

“It’s wonderful to be seen.”

She laughed.

He grabbed the suitcases. “C’mon, we’re in room 812. I want to hear all about everything.” Michael moved closer, and lowered his voice. “Then we can discuss some way for you to repay me for the outrageous phone bills of the past two months.”

“That’s not a problem. I have my checkbook with me.”

Michael shook his head. “I’m sorry, we’re not in New Jersey. I don’t accept out-of-state checks. Or out-of-state cash. And don’t even think about credit cards.”

Evelyn looked pensive. “I don’t like to have unpaid obligations. Are you familiar with the barter system?”

Chapter Twenty-Nine

LATER, THEY WALKED TO ONE of the plentiful restaurants nearby; many of the major chains wanted the airport business. Evelyn chose a wood-sided building that looked like it wanted you to think of the Old West. Its specialty was steaks and ribs. Of the various American foods that Evelyn happily enjoyed, barbecued ribs were near or at the top. They asked for a remote booth, scanned the menu, and ordered.

Evelyn's rib platter was large, tender, enjoyable, and worth every penny. Michael's steak wasn't Arthur's, yet didn't disappoint. When they were done eating, the waitress cleared away a small mountain of crumbled napkins. Evelyn had used her fingers to eat the ribs.

They shared a chocolate dessert that was Texas-sized. Because the menu described it as served warm, Michael insisted that a scoop of vanilla ice cream would look, and taste luscious with it. Evelyn protested, but not with enough conviction for him to believe her.

Then, Evelyn and Michael walked around outside for nearly an hour, holding hands, as Evelyn told of the past nine weeks. She included opinions, and observations that she'd left out of their nightly conversations, details that were better in person.

Back in their room, while Evelyn brushed her teeth, Michael secretly filled out the room service card, and hung it on the outside doorknob, then, silently shut the door.

The sun gently spilled over the top of dark window curtains in their room. Gentle taps on their door woke Evelyn. Then she heard a muffled, "Room service." She looked at Michael, her eyes were question marks.

He got up, and put a towel around his waist. He snatched the extravagant tip he'd placed in the book he'd been reading when they turned out the light, and opened the door.

"Good morning," he said to the room service waiter. "Thank you for bringing this to us."

The waiter gladly exchanged the tray in his hands for what Michael held in his hand. The door shut, and Michael approached the bed as Evelyn was placing two big pillows behind her.

He said, "It's a La Rue tradition. When someone is about to graduate into a new career, they get room service breakfast in bed."

Evelyn covered her yawn with a hand, and smiled.

Michael looked at the clock radio on the night table. "If we don't eat slowly, we'll have time for the rest of the custom."

~ * * * ~

Evelyn showered, worked on her hair, and put on her United Airlines flight attendant uniform for the first time since she was fitted for it. She looked smashing, and Michael told her. He snapped some pictures, including both of them together through the large mirror on the wall. Michael needed to take them from different angles so that the flash didn't go off. Then they went downstairs to wait for the taxi.

The graduation took place in a conference room of the training facility. The large area filled quickly with family members, spouses, boyfriends, girlfriends, and conversations. Michael smiled at all the well-deserved delight that dominated. The look of pride on the faces of the guests, particularly the parents, was moving. Michael overlooked that he didn't like crowds, and enjoyed himself.

Evelyn was standing on a platform stage with the other about-to-be graduates, listening to last minute instructions. Then, a middle-aged woman in a flight attendant uniform walked up to a microphone and tapped on it lightly. Mild thunder boomed from hidden speakers. Somebody adjusted the volume, and she said, "Good morning, ladies and gentlemen, family members, and guests. Thank you for traveling here for the graduation of our newest class of United Airlines flight attendants."

She paused, knowing from experience that applause, whistles, and happy shouting always burst apart the nervous silence here. She smiled, and waited for the enthusiastic crowd to quiet.

"After I say each graduate's name, I'll mention their first duty station, the one they'll be flying out of to start. Don't worry, they can put in for a transfer after six months if they want." She looked down at the paper in front of her, and started with the A's.

After the last name was spoken, the graduates were dismissed to join their visitors. The room echoed with excited voices. Michael believed there was enough energy in that room to light up the training facility.

Evelyn found Michael and embraced him again. Then, she introduced him to some of her classmates, who were wandering around, hugging their new airline friends.

Michael tried to stay in the background so Evelyn could concentrate on the people she'd gone through training with. Soon, with a collection of names and phone numbers on scraps of paper and small napkins, Evelyn gave Michael the 'it's-time-to-go' look.

That night, they joined a couple of her friends and

their guests for dinner. Then, Evelyn slept as in a coma, finally able to totally relax, without the pressure of more tests to pass.

In the morning, they flew back to Newark. Evelyn began a rookie's domestic flying schedule. Michael remembered a phrase from a book that he'd read years before, and prior to each of Evelyn's flights, he always said, "Vaya con Dios," before kissing her good-bye. Michael wasn't superstitious, but considered it a lucky charm. He never failed to say it to Evelyn.

Evelyn flew the mandatory domestic routes for her first six months. One weekend she had a Friday flight to Los Angeles, with a layover there after a stop in Denver first. Michael went with her. In Denver, there was a one hour wait while some passengers exited the plane, and new ones got on. Evelyn suggested that Michael leave the crowded and cramped plane, and relax in the adjacent, open gate area.

He was sitting there, reading his book when Evelyn came over and said they'd be boarding in about five minutes. She gave Michael a quick kiss. After Evelyn went through the ramp back to the aircraft, a man about five feet from Michael said, "Do you know her?"

"Yes. That's my wife."

The man smiled. "I wondered about that. I know that United's motto is 'Fly the Friendly Skies.' I didn't know they were that friendly."

~ * * * ~

When her domestic flying requirement was over, and relieved of her probationary status, Evelyn transferred to Dulles Airport near Washington, D.C. She entered the German speaker program as a translator on flights to Germany and Switzerland. The drive from Newark to Dulles was long. Evelyn didn't mind, it was only once a week. And, since her check-in was at around 3:30

in the afternoon, she slept-in, and left after breakfast, avoiding rush hour traffic.

Evelyn flew four or five three-day trips per month. The first day was the 5:25 PM flight to Frankfurt or Munich in Germany; or to Zurich, Switzerland. Day two was an early morning arrival and a layover there with a private room in a pleasing hotel. Day three meant a return to the U.S., arriving around 3 PM.

"Why don't we move closer to Dulles airport?" Evelyn made that suggestion two months later. "Neither of us has family to keep us here, and the shorter commute will give us more time together."

"That makes sense." Then, Michael said, "I'm mad at myself."

"Why?"

"Because a blonde flight attendant thought of something that I should have."

"Very funny. You're lucky, I'm quite forgiving. I'll give you a second chance to show your genius. All you need to do is figure out where to move to."

"You're letting me off easily. Let me think about this for a minute." He did. "Okay, here's what we'll do. We'll get a map of northern Virginia, draw a circle around the airport that goes out, oh, fifty miles should be plenty. Then we do some fun homework, which is to visit the chosen locations and decide which lucky candidate wins our presence. Once that's done, if I think there's something in it for me, I'll even help you with the packing."

"Your generosity is overwhelming."

Michael went to their bookshelf, pulled down a road atlas of the United States, and opened it to Virginia. While Evelyn watched, he used the legend on it to measure out the fifty miles. They both wanted to live in, or close to a city with at least one notable bookstore, and the other shops and qualities that they deemed essential: multiple grocery stores - competition would keep each of them sharp, and well-stocked - a public library, and an enjoyable, friendly downtown area.

Evelyn looked at the map and wrote down the names of four adequate sized cities that fell within commuting distance. Front Royal, they both loved that name. Manassas, Evelyn never heard of it; Michael knew it, of course, from U.S. history classes. He loved the sound of saying it, and made up suggestive limericks around it. The cities of Winchester and Fredericksburg were added to their list.

Evelyn and Michael knew nearly nothing about any of four candidates. The following Saturday morning they put two small suitcases in the trunk of Michael's Civic and drove to Virginia in search of their next apartment.

They spent about an hour driving and walking around each of the first three destinations. They commented on the overall appearance, and the feel they got after walking around the main part of downtown, and looking in store windows. Each city had a hospital, and since the field of x-ray was in one if it's hiring cycles, Michael wasn't worried about finding a new job. Evelyn jotted brief notes of their observations in a folder. With four cities to look at, she didn't want their impressions to get confused or forgotten.

Fredericksburg was the last place on their list. This wasn't planned, it was by chance. Michael turned his car onto one-way Caroline Street, and they slowly drove through downtown, looking left and right at the people, and the stores. After about six blocks, Evelyn turned to Michael. She didn't need to say anything. He agreed. They were home. For Evelyn and Michael, it was love at first sight with Fredericksburg. Once they saw it, they couldn't imagine living anywhere else.

They carefully coordinated leaving his job, and their apartment, for new ones in Fredericksburg. Michael interviewed at the one local hospital, Mary Washington. They offered him a job at their outpatient facility. It was an easy decision.

The move went smoothly. On Saturday, December 1, Michael loaded the truck they'd rented. This didn't take too long, Evelyn and Michael lived simply, with basic possessions. He hitched his Civic to the back of it of the small truck, Evelyn followed in her Accord.

The temperature in Fredericksburg was 74 degrees. They considered the unusual and welcome December weather to be an omen that they'd chosen the right place. After they checked in at the office of their new apartment, Michael unloaded the truck.

Evelyn and Michael celebrated their first night in Fredericksburg at a local Chinese restaurant. The menu choices covered all the usual items expected at a Chinese restaurant in Virginia. Michael considered that as a description, not a critique, or criticism. The food was more than acceptable. Nothing to rave about, nothing to complain about, either. It did not inspire any flashbacks to Chinatown in New York for Michael, but none of the mess hall in the Marine Corps either.

The next day, Sunday, Evelyn and Michael unpacked boxes, and went food shopping. Over dinner, Michael said, "We've both done a lot of traveling, and I get a warm feeling being downtown in Fredericksburg."

"I feel the same way."

As they got to know Fredericksburg, they loved it. And the friendly, courteous people. After living and working there for a few weeks, Michael said to Evelyn, "Although we've been here in Fredericksburg only a short time, I feel right at home. Like this is where I belong. How 'bout you?"

"Me, too. This seems like a great place to raise a family."

Chapter Thirty

EVELYN AND MICHAEL ENJOYED LONG, lazy, sightseeing walks around delightful Old Town Fredericksburg with its colonial and Civil War history, terrific shops, and down-to-earth people. One evening Michael saw a bumper sticker on a car that summed up his feelings: 'I wasn't born in the South, but I got here as soon as I could.'

They sampled every restaurant in, and around town. Some were better than others, as expected. None were so disappointing that they were sorry they ate there. Driving through downtown was not the quickest, or direct way for Michael to get home in the afternoon, he often did it anyway. This was his favorite Fredericksburg experience. He always hoped to see lots of pedestrians; Michael wanted all the local businesses to do well.

Evelyn and Michael visited the main branch of the library nearly every weekend, it was downtown on Caroline Street. The helpful staff there put a lot of effort into displaying books nearly everywhere, making browsing something to look forward to. This was better than wandering past row after row of tightly packed shelves. Evelyn and Michael usually had some books on hold that they'd requested online. It didn't take long before either of them would walk up to the library check-out counter, been already recognized, and had their books pulled from the reserved section and waiting for them.

Sunday drives served as a scouting mission for where Evelyn and Michael wanted to buy a house and settle in. They decided not to purchase anything until six months of exploration had gone by. They wanted to discover the right section of town for them. It needed to be convenient for both of their jobs, and near the delightful downtown. Yet, not too close to the river of traffic that flowed north to work in Washington, D.C. each morning, and back again in the late afternoon.

Before their target date arrived, Michael happened to drive past a model home that caught his eye on a Wednesday. He went in, and was impressed right away with the layout, features, and price. The salesman showed him a diagram of the development they were starting soon, it was nearby.

When Evelyn returned from a trip two days later, Michael waited for her outside of their apartment. Without giving her a chance to change out of her uniform, he drove her to the model home and let the salesman take over. That was on Friday.

On Saturday, they went back to the model, chose the lot they wanted from his development map, and put a deposit on the property. Their new home would be the last one on the right in a future cul-de-sac, without traffic, where their hoped-for children would play outside.

Over dinner that night, they enjoyed talking about their future first home. Michael said, “Why is it called a cul-de-sac? What do those words mean? And why do we use a fancy French phrase? C’mon, it’s a dead-end street!”

Their wooded lot had a stream running through the back of it that was part of the protected Chesapeake Basin. This meant that no one could build behind them. Their future neighbors back there would be the families of chattering and playful squirrels running around the countless trees, and of course, colorful birds. They later found out that at least one family of deer passed through there each mid-morning, enjoying a roving picnic.

Evelyn and Michael had picked out the lot, now there were various styles of homes to choose from. Evelyn preferred the colonial with three bedrooms, two and half baths, and an attached two car garage. Michael said, "I don't have a preference. And I trust your taste and judgment more than I trust mine. Now that we've decided that, let's pick out colors."

They put a large down payment on the home to keep the mortgage payment as small as possible. The airline industry was volatile, and they wanted Michael to be able to afford the house with his pay alone, if needed. The mortgage broker tried repeatedly to get them to purchase a pricier home, "Your combined income qualifies you for added luxury, extra goodies, and increased space."

"No, thank you," was their consistent reply.

Every Sunday, they drove past their home-site to enjoy the progress. They made sure to photograph the new work that was completed during the week. First, it was a wooded lot. As the weeks unrolled, the lot was cleared, the ground leveled, the basement dug out, and the concrete poured. Evelyn said, "These photos will be to remember this project, and show our children."

When the frame of the home went up, they walked through it, planning which first floor room would be their first child's playroom.

"Michael, we haven't discussed this in detail before, how many children do you want?"

"I like small families. No more than a dozen."

Evelyn laughed. "If you don't show me yours, I won't show you mine."

"Since you put it like that, two or three? I'm open to suggestions. Okay, your turn."

Evelyn nodded. "Two or three sounds right."

Michael held out his hand. "Let's go back to our apartment and get started on the first one."

~ * * * ~

The house moved along, and so did their lives. Evelyn continued her once a week flights, usually to Frankfurt. It couldn't have been better. Her father picked her up at the airport on the morning she arrived. She spent her layover with her parents, sleeping in her old room, eating home cooked meals. And she got paid for it.

Michael enjoyed going to work each day. He liked the people he x-rayed, and the ones he worked with, especially the radiologists.

~ * * * ~

Evelyn sat at their kitchen table updating her flight attendant manual. Federal Aviation Administration requirements insisted that she have it accessible whenever she flew, and that it stay current with the frequent changes and amendments issued. The thick, dark blue binder in front of her was kept company by two small stacks of papers to the right of it. Evelyn removed pages from the binder and deposited them in one pile, then replaced them in the binder with pages from the other bundle.

Michael stood there watching her for a moment, and said, "Let's go upstairs. You can put your uniform on, and be the naughty flight attendant."

"I'm in the middle of something important."

"I'm the birthday boy. You can't refuse me."

"We already celebrated your birthday."

"If I'd been born a little late, today might be my birthday."

"Michael, your birthday was six months ago."

"Oh." He moved on to one of their prime topics,

travel. They talked about their list of places to visit, and savored some exceptional moments from past vacations. They knew how fortunate they were to have enjoyed experiences, restaurants, and coffee houses from around the world. For an hour, their chat drove through the conversational countryside covering a lot of territory, like a high-end German car cruising the autobahn.

And then something rare happened. Evelyn and Michael were not in complete agreement. The object of contention wasn't a big deal, but, both were convinced that they were right. Neither used the word 'wrong' as the issue bounced back and forth between them like a tennis ball being whacked by two determined competitors. Soon, they leaned across the table and kissed.

Michael asked, "How did you do that?"

"Do what?"

"Get me to see that you were right."

"It's easy. I determined what factors would influence you to change your mind for reasons that make sense to you, not ones that make sense to me. Despite our similar tastes and traits, we're different people, with different backgrounds and influences."

Evelyn paused. "Aren't you likely to respond to stimuli that motivate you, not ones that motivate me?"

"Stimuli that motivate me? Am I a lab animal? Perhaps a rat?"

"No, of course not. Lab animals are domesticated, and cooperative."

Chapter Thirty-One

United Airlines, and its employees, performed something impressively compassionate for terminally ill children every December. It was called the Fantasy Flight. About two weeks before Christmas, United closed two of their departure/arrival gates at airports around the country for a Friday and Saturday. Volunteer flight attendants decorated the gates in their time off. This was not a small sacrifice for the employees. A couple of them lived within a short drive of the airports, the majority were at least an hour away, where home prices were more affordable. These volunteers did this on Friday, giving up sleeping in on a day off, and time with their families. Late that afternoon, they were replaced by different crew members who finished the decorations.

At six in the morning on Saturday, a new crew of flight attendants arrived in pre-dawn December darkness for last minute modifications, and to get ready to greet the children. Evelyn was one of them of those volunteers. Michael drove her to Dulles Airport, deflecting her suggestion that he sleep in, and not get up at 4:00 with her. "The queen of the house doesn't drive herself. That's why she has lackeys. Besides, I wouldn't miss this."

The children, some were bald from chemotherapy, several were confined to wheelchairs, began to arrive at the first of the two gates. This was designated as the departure gate. A few of the wheelchairs had attached IV poles with plastic bags of clear fluid flowing thru tubing into the children's arms.

At that departure gate, folding tables were covered with Christmas tablecloths, donated breakfast items, and bottles of juice, milk, and water from local restaurants. Christmas music floated down from overhead speakers that usually announced flight information as the steady flow of parents and their children entered the festive gate area. The children giggled, laughed, and seemed nearly dizzy with excitement.

Ronald McDonald entertained with vaudeville worthy antics, and well-received corny jokes, carefully chosen for the young audience. Uniformed volunteer flight attendants fussed over the enchanted children, which was easy to do. The hard part was holding back tears of sadness for the diseases and the bravery of the kids stricken with them.

The airport wasn't shoulder-to-shoulder crowded as it would be by mid-morning, but it wasn't empty either. Passengers rushed by, anxious to catch a flight, or eager to go home. Some of them stopped to see what all the activity was about. This wasn't what they were used to seeing at an airport departure gate. Michael watched their faces journey from confusion, to understanding, to a blend of sorrow and joy. , they looked at their watches, maybe out of necessity, maybe as an excuse, and hurried on, tugging their rolling suitcases.

After ample time at that gate for the children to enjoy the snacks and attention, the overhead speakers announced that the flight to Santa's workshop at the North Pole was now boarding. Evelyn and Michael commented earlier that all the departure boards they'd passed listed a 9 AM flight leaving for the North Pole. They wondered if the people stopping to check on their flights and gate numbers noticed this.

Flight attendants wheeled and escorted the children

into the plane decorated with Christmas ornaments and trimmings, and seated them. Michael watched Evelyn take her turn boarding the children. *Maybe it's my imagination, Evelyn seems highly radiant helping them. She'll be an outstanding mother when we have children.*

He noticed Evelyn chat with one of the gate agents, and then she approached Michael. She whispered, "Would you like to go on the flight?"

Michael didn't hesitate. "I'd love to."

"Hurry, they're about to shut the aircraft door."

He followed Evelyn into the plane, she looked for an empty seat for him in the nearly full aircraft. She found one, and Michael quickly slid into an aisle seat over the right wing. He pulled the seat belt around his body, and snapped it in place. The flight attendants patrolled up and down the aisles of the large four engine plane while handing out candy canes and other Christmas candies to ecstatic children.

Crew members stood in front of the cabin for the mandatory safety demonstration. A voice over the public-address system read an amusing version of "The Night Before Christmas" with appropriate flight safety rhymes that accompanied the flight attendant's gestures.

When that was finished, flight attendants scurried through each aisle, heads swiveling left and right, making sure everyone was strapped in. The plane filled with a friendly voice. "Good morning. This is your pilot, Captain Bob. Welcome aboard Sleigh Ride One. We'll be departing for the North Pole as soon as we get clearance from the tower. I'm going to leave this on, you can listen to our conversations."

Then, as planned, the control tower came on. "Sleigh Ride One, this is the tower. You're cleared to taxi to runway three for takeoff to the North Pole."

"Tower, this is Sleigh Ride One, roger that. We're

backing out of the gate now, starting our taxi to runway three."

The communications went like that, and then the plane sped down the runway. The acceleration gently pushed everyone backward into their seats. The front wheels left the ground as the plane tilted up. The speeding silver ship flew higher and higher, faster and faster.

"This is Captain Bob again. Please make sure that your window shades are in the down position. We're going to use supersonic thrusters to get us to the North Pole in about fifteen minutes, and we don't want you to get dizzy from watching the ground zoom by that quickly."

Michael smiled at that creative way to prevent the children from realizing that they were flying around northern Virginia, and landing back at Dulles Airport.

Captain Bob made brief announcements about the flight, and then they heard, "Sleigh Ride One, this is the North Pole control tower. You're cleared for final approach to our airport. Please watch out for a big, red sleigh. It has reindeer power, not four huge engines."

"North Pole control, this is Sleigh Ride One, roger that. We're beginning our final approach."

Minutes later, "Sleigh Ride One, this is North Pole control again. You're cleared to land, and welcome to the North Pole. After you land, please taxi to the gate. We're waiting for your important passengers."

"Roger that."

As soon as they landed, taxied, and stopped at the arrival gate, everyone on the plane started clapping in thanks, and anticipation. Michael looked around at the pure and total joy on the faces of the children. Everyone rose, patiently lined up in the aisles, and waited, chatting excitedly as the plane emptied. Some parents carried their children, including those waiting for wheelchairs at the gate.

Evelyn volunteered for the Fantasy Flight every year, so Michael had experienced this before, but not as a passenger. This perspective was completely different. In the past, Michael respectfully remained at the arrival gate, at the back of the crowd. He had been a spectator, not a participant.

Now, as he and Evelyn walked off the plane, he saw things as the children did. Two rows of well-dressed students from a local high school formed a passageway that began immediately after exiting the covered ramp from the plane. As the children left the ramp, and entered the tunnel of students, the applause at the gate started. The cheering zoomed to maximum volume as the children walked, or were wheeled, between the twin lines of students.

The passengers emerged into a large gate area decorated as if it were Santa's workshop. Costumed elves strolled around handing out small shopping bags with toys in them. A choir of about a dozen Christmas carol singers in costumes that made them look like they stepped out of a Charles Dickens novel, entertained in one corner, as children were tempted by tables of snacks, donuts, hamburgers, child-sized fried chicken sandwiches, small bottles of juice, water, and regular and chocolate milk. Various cookies, the size of a coffee cup saucer, beckoned: sugar cookies, chocolate chip cookies, and cookies with multi-colored M & M's poking out of them. The food was donated by local franchised restaurants, and served by their employees whose hearts, and not their paychecks, brought them there. The children were given as much of anything as they wanted, and were treated like visiting nobility, as they deserved.

After all the children had a chance to wander around

and sample things, the fun started. Face painting was popular, though a distant second to sitting on Santa's lap. Evelyn was certain that these children believed in Santa, or wanted to. And everyone who watched them look up into Santa's bearded face as they confided their wishes and hopes, needed to wipe their eyes. Evelyn looked at Michael, and knew that he was tortured by the same question that she was: Were the children asking Santa to take away their disease so they could live to see more Christmases?

On their way home, Evelyn said, "This is the most heart-breaking, and the most rewarding thing I've ever done."

Evelyn volunteered for the Fantasy Flight every year.

Chapter Thirty-Two

Evelyn called Michael from her car, which was part of their ritual, as she was about to enter their street, home from a three-day flight. He put on shoes and went outside to open the door to their two-car garage, and he waited in the rear of it. While Evelyn drove down the driveway, Michael waved his arms, mimicking the airport flight line crew who guided the giant planes to the jet way, as he signaled how far forward to park

After they kissed, and hugged, Michael carried Evelyn's two bags into the house, usually commenting, "I'll be your bellboy if you're a generous tipper."

Evelyn removed items from her rolling suitcase to toss into the laundry basket, and repacked it for her next flight. Michael always considered this to be an impressive display of discipline, and orderliness. She'd been up since seven AM in Germany, one AM in Virginia, and wasn't flying for four more days. Yet, Evelyn spent the fifteen or twenty minutes needed to get her suitcase ready, and placed in the closet by the front door.

After a quiet hour of conversation at their small dining room table, Michael used an Italian accent to ask Evelyn what she would like Chef Luigi to cook for her dinner.

"What are my choices?"

After Chef Luigi went over the short list, Evelyn chose

shrimp scampi on angel hair pasta. "With extra garlic, please."

As Michael arranged the small number of ingredients on the counter and started to peel the garlic, Evelyn asked, "What can I do to help?"

"Sit your cute butt down, and catch up on your magazines."

A short time later Evelyn looked up from what she was reading. "This article says the average male needs only thirty seconds to know if he wants to have sex with a woman. Do you think that's accurate?"

"It didn't take me nearly that long with you."

"Michael, it's a comfort knowing that in this constantly changing world you are an oasis of consistency."

Later, after enjoying the pleasing and garlicky meal, and one glass of red wine for Evelyn, two for Michael, he poured two small glasses of limoncello. They sat there, sipping, and silent. Evelyn's left hand held Michael's right. After a while, he said, "I have memories of my mother and father sitting at our dining room table and holding hands after clearing the table. Like we do. They used that quiet time to talk about what needed to be discussed, and listen to the other person, letting the conversation flow in any direction. Sound familiar?"

Evelyn smiled warmly.

Michael closed his eyes as he continued. "I can hear and see the love in their voices and their eyes."

He opened his eyes. "I always enjoyed sitting there, watching them, trying to solve the mystery of how they seemed so much in love. It wasn't a contest, but the parents of the friends whose homes I sometimes ate at never appeared to come anywhere near that level of genuine affection and caring.

"I asked my father about it one night when I was twelve. It was right before he and my mom were killed."

Evelyn squeezed his hands. "I'm sorry."

"I know you are. Thanks. My dad smiled, and said, 'Michael, having a great marriage is easy. I married my closest friend.' My mother kissed him. Then my dad added, 'When you start dating, you're going to have plenty of girlfriends. Be kind, and respect them. If you're lucky, you'll find a woman who's as right for you as your mother is for me.'

"I asked, 'How will I know which one that is?' My dad winked at me, and said, 'You'll know, son. Listen to your heart.' Well, I did. And he was right."

"That's sweet, thank you." Evelyn followed the example of Michael's mother, and kissed him.

Michael said, "I don't want to ruin this moment," he paused, "we've been married for eight years. Don't you think we need to do something?"

"What are you talking about?"

"I'm referring to your family, who doesn't know we're married. Like your parents. Who, in case you haven't noticed, aren't young anymore. Your dad is seventy-one."

Evelyn frowned. "I know. I think about that often. I'm embarrassed that we've been lying to them for so long."

Michael shook his head. "We haven't been lying. We didn't say we *weren't* married. We somehow forgot to mention that we were."

Evelyn fired a skeptical look. Michael ignored it and continued. "If we've deceived them, it was by remaining silent." He nodded to confirm the logic of that.

"Clever. I don't think my parents will see the difference."

Michael shrugged. "Then the solution is obvious. We won't tell them we're already married, it would hurt them that they didn't know about it, and weren't invited, even if it was just us and the mayor. We'll plan a new first wedding. In Germany."

"In Germany?"

"Yes, Germany. You know, the nation that sits

between France and Poland. It's famous for tasty beer, fine cars, and invading the rest of Europe every now and then. That Germany. Maybe you've heard of it?"

Evelyn slapped his arm. "For a world class wise-ass, you've come up with a good idea."

"I know I have. Since we can't get married in the U.S. again, we'll tell your family that it's easier, and cheaper, for the two of us to cross the Atlantic than it is for a bunch of them to come here. When you explain that, please don't forget to emphasize what considerate, gracious, and selfless souls we are. Especially me. I hate it when my magnificence isn't recognized. Or my modesty."

~ * * * ~

The wedding in Moerfelden was easy to plan. It would be a small civil ceremony, with Evelyn's parents, two widowed aunts, and several lifelong neighbors.

In keeping with the German tradition of *Polterabend*, they had a party in the large backyard of her parent's house the night before the wedding. Michael bartended, serving beer from a small keg, and pouring white German wine, while the handful of people ate from the platters that everyone provided.

At the end of the evening, to complete the custom, a happy Evelyn and Michael posed for pictures with the inexpensive plates they were about to smash. Michael asked about the meaning of this. The answer he got was that the pottery was sacrificed so that the marriage would remain unbroken. Whatever the origin, Evelyn and he enjoyed the custom, and everything about the evening.

In the morning, they all walked about ten minutes to the small government building in downtown Moerfelden. Evelyn's father wore his one suit, and Evelyn's mother wore her prized outfit. Michael wore his tuxedo from

The Mansion, Evelyn dressed in a plain black skirt and white blouse.

The civil ceremony in Moerfelden was like its American version, except that Michael didn't understand a lot of what was said. He had been coached when to say, "Ja," and to nod decisively when he said it, so that his intent was clear, even if his accented pronunciation of that one syllable wasn't.

Michael's limited German allowed him to understand numerous nouns and verbs that the civil servant said, and some adjectives. But big chunks of the ceremony were, well, like a foreign language. Michael watched the face of the older, distinguished gentleman performing the service for clues. His pauses indicated the need for a response, and it was helpful that he directed his look to Evelyn or Michael at those moments. Michael played with the idea of saying, "Ich weiss nicht," - I don't know – as a response a few times, then decided against it.

After the brief ceremony, the small wedding party drove to a local restaurant where a private room was reserved. The meal and the wine were impressive, and elevated by the celebration of the marriage of Evelyn and Michael. Michael decided that his normal limit of two drinks could be suspended, this was unique enough an occasion. During the dinner, Evelyn looked at Michael and said, "I'm sorry that your parents couldn't be here."

"Are you reading my mind? I was thinking the same thing." He smiled sadly. "They would have loved you. My mom would have fainted over you."

"Would you like to talk about it?"

"No. But, thanks for asking."

Evelyn's father drove them to the airport in the morning. They flew to Istanbul for their honeymoon. They'd gone there from Germany for a long weekend the year before, and that appetizer portion of Istanbul made them want the entire meal. Evelyn and Michael were fortunate to have visited a bunch of cities in the U.S. and Europe, none had been the capital of three empires. And, with name changes each time: Byzantium, Constantinople, and Istanbul. And no other city in the world sat on two continents, as Istanbul did with Europe and Asia.

Evelyn and Michael enjoyed those distinctions, and the exotic flavors that made up the spicy feast called Istanbul. Michael was proud of being American and the over two hundred years of history in his country. But, he was amazed every time he and Evelyn walked near the Hagia Sophia, a beautiful church, now a museum. Built by Emperor Constantine, finished in the year 537, it was the largest domed building in the world for nearly a thousand years.

Adjacent to that was the Hippodrome, a chariot racing area for the Romans, currently a park. An obelisk, tribute from Egypt, punctuated the large, grassy oval like an exclamation mark at the end of a sentence. At the other end of the Hippodrome was the Blue Mosque, an impressive, beautiful, and spectacular building. Evelyn and Michael enjoyed sitting on a bench in the Hippodrome, trying to absorb the history that flowed from all around them like heat waves rising from a hot paved road.

Travel, like eating, reading, and other things, is a matter of personal preference. Some people love London. Others yawn at the idea of going there again. Istanbul grabbed Evelyn and Michael in a way that nowhere in the world did. Each day that they explored it they found new things, large and small, to delight their eyes, mouths, and imaginations. They quickly realized this was a city they would need to visit again and again.

Chapter Thirty-Three

Evelyn and Michael had a few days left on their honeymoon in Istanbul. They were sitting at a small outdoor table of a café that overlooked the Bosporus Strait as it wandered between the Black Sea and the Aegean. Two coffee cups were on the red checkered tablecloth. Ferries left a v-shaped trail behind as they poked along between Europe and Asia, a twenty-minute scenic ride.

A refreshing breeze delivered the aroma of fresh fish frying over small wood burning grills on the decks of the tethered boats that caught them. The passing parade of locals and tourists handed over a few coins for the crispy fillets that were turned once, twice, then inserted into a fold of heavenly Turkish bread and eaten that way, or covered with the quick spread of a nameless and triumphant white sauce.

Evelyn put her cup down. "Michael, do you believe in reincarnation?"

"Interesting question. What brought that up?"

"I know that some years ago you told me about the shiny penny in the middle of your bed and the feeling of a spirit, or something, letting you know it was there. Being here in Istanbul, with all of its background, raised the subject back to the surface." She drank some of her coffee. "Life seems unfair. We spend all of our years growing wiser..."

Evelyn paused, then added, "Hopefully."

They both smiled.

She continued. “Then, when our accumulated wisdom and sophistication are at their peak… we die. Aside from the unbalance of that, we’re leaving everyone behind.” Evelyn sipped her coffee. Then she said, “Comments?”

Michael put his cup down. “I’d like to believe there’s some sort of life after this existence. Heaven, reincarnation, or something. Like you said, we spend decades becoming the magnificent people we are,” he used his left hand to caress his face in a fake show of self-love, “then we die. And, yes, you’re right, we don’t get to see the people we love ever again.”

“Wouldn’t heaven solve that problem?”

He paused. “Yes, it would. I’m hesitating because you’re asking my thoughts on things I haven’t made up my mind about. I’d like to know that either reincarnation or heaven exist. Since no one has come back with proof, we’ll probably never be sure.”

Michael sipped some coffee. “What about you? You sound like you’ve got an opinion about this. I’d love to hear it.”

Evelyn put the spoon back in her coffee cup and stirred it with circular motions. Michael knew this was something to keep her hands busy while stitching her thoughts together. “I would love for us to be together forever. There *is* something that I believe in.”

“What is it?”

“That some things are meant to happen. And they do when the time is right. Not one minute before.”

Michael smiled. “Are you talking about us?”

“I am.” She returned his smile. “I really believe this to be a universal truth. You and I are lucky to be recipients. Think about it. If everything hadn’t happened just so, we wouldn’t both have been at The Mansion when we were. Like the story of a butterfly flapping its wings that sets off a chain reaction changing the weather and people's lives. What if I'd liked being an interpreter after my language school? What if I didn't hear about The Mansion opportunity? What if you weren't working there? A lot of 'what if's' could have prevented us from being together."

Michael said, "Let me be the devil's advocate for a moment. Everything you're saying is true. But, if we hadn't met, you'd be with someone. A woman as beautiful and desirable as you are will always be pursued. And, I would have missed out on the best thing that ever happened to me. But, neither of us would know what did not happen."

Evelyn considered this. Michael enjoyed watching her. She shook her head. "I wouldn't have gotten serious with anyone else. You and I are perfect for each other. I can't imagine being with any other man."

He smiled. "Thank you. But if you hadn't met me, you wouldn't know that."

"Michael, I know what makes me happy. I wouldn't have been happy without you. Too many of the women I fly with tell me that they tolerate their marriages or relationships. They're content. Nothing more than that."

Evelyn paused. "I feel sorry for them. Would you want to go through life like that? That on its peak day, your relationship is acceptably adequate?"

"No."

She flashed her victory smile. "Then I guess you're lucky that you met me, aren't you?"

Michael reached for her hands. "Evelyn, if I haven't told you this often, please forgive me, because I should have. I'm the luckiest man in the world to be married to you."

"Yes, you are. And don't forget it."

Michael smiled. "I won't. You cast too strong spell on me when we met."

Evelyn blushed. "Michael, you were the one for me.

I made up my mind when I came to the U.S. that I wasn't going to get serious or even risk that by dating. I wanted to work hard, get a knock-your-socks-off letter of recommendation, and go home. You know all about this, we discussed it years ago. And we nearly broke up over it. There was something about you. Something that I sensed even when we first met."

"I don't mind if you flatter me. What was it?"

The blast of a ferry's horn made them look toward the water. Two ferries, one going to the European side of Istanbul, the other to the opposite shore, rumbled greetings to each other as they sailed about fifty yards apart. Some of the passengers on the deck of each ship waved to the other one. Evelyn and Michael watched them, lost in the peacefulness of the moment.

Then Evelyn said, "There was genuineness about you. And once I started to get to know you, I felt quite comfortable with you. It was like I'd known you for a long time. I have got a gift for reading people. To use a reference to your job, it's like my x-ray vision into people's souls. I see them for who they really are. Without all of the layers and layers of camouflage, and false clues, that some people use to fool others – and maybe themselves - into believing that they're different than what they really are."

She sipped her coffee and said, "Yes, I've been fooled. Not often, and not for a long time. A lot of the men I met before you seemed too smooth. Like they weren't real people, merely a package of artificial ingredients. Made of carefully rehearsed and practiced mannerisms. With counterfeit lines and insincere attention and compliments, whose single purpose was to get women out of their clothes as quickly as possible."

"Maybe I'm like them. But I'm better at hiding it."

Evelyn laughed. "OK, I'll concede that you might be. If you are, you're not doing it wisely."

"What do you mean?"

"Well, no one can keep up an act forever. They lose track of their lies, maybe forget their next phony line. Their true nature will somehow leak out, like light escaping from under a locked door. Revealing who they really are."

"Have I slipped up somewhere, letting you see the real Michael?"

Evelyn sighed. "Yes, I'm afraid you have. I've seen you put a cup over insects in the house, and carry it outside to release them in the grass. I've noticed the checks you never showed me that you wrote out to various charities and last chance animal shelters so that they don't euthanize for lack of funds. And shall I mention the expensive bird and squirrel feeders you maintain in our backyard?"

Michael raised his hands with his palms facing Evelyn. "Hey, I'm covering my butt. Piling up cosmic points in case I come back as one of those animals. Did you ever think of that?"

"Okay. What about the money that you hand to the sad looking homeless people, usually standing at long stoplights, holding the small handwritten brown cardboard signs that have 'Hungry' scrawled on them? And the clothes and food donations you make to charities for the less fortunate?"

"Those donations are tax write-offs."

"You're overlooking that I go with you to drop-off the items. You don't accept their receipts."

Michael smacked his forehead lightly. "I knew I was forgetting something."

"Oh, and you always pass on having your name associated with any of this, preferring it be anonymous. If I recall correctly, you recently told the woman at the food bank that if it comes from the heart, you don't need others to know about it."

"I said that to get her interested in me. You're gone three days a week."

"She was at least seventy-years-old!"

"Maybe she has a cute granddaughter."

Evelyn laughed. "Michael, let's face it, you're not going to make it as one of the users. You're a giver, not a taker. It genuinely comes from your heart. You're not seeking recognition or rewards."

"Is that good news, or bad news?"

"Neither. It's an honest description. You're a very special person."

"When we get back to our hotel tonight, I'll show you what special really means."

Chapter Thirty-Four

When Evelyn was growing up, her parents couldn't afford to take the family on vacations. Her father's commission-only sales job provided basic meals for the family, and a roof over their heads, but, no frills. Evelyn and Michael weren't sure whose idea it had been to take her parents along on vacations, they both enjoyed it. Evelyn's parents were enjoyable and appreciative companions. They never complained about anything, and were always willing to do what Evelyn and Michael suggested. They were grateful to travel to places they didn't believe they would visit.

Evelyn's father insisted on paying for their share of hotels and meals despite a small pension, and an even smaller bank account. That was handled easily. Michael said, "Since your parents don't read or speak English, unless we stay in Germany they won't be able to check the bill for the cost of their room. We'll tell them we got travel industry discounts at the hotels and restaurants, we can cut their portion in half. Problem solved."

"That's thoughtful of you. Be careful," Evelyn said. "If you tell them too low a figure, they'll get suspicious, and we'll hurt their feelings. They don't want to feel like we're paying for them."

"Don't worry, I excel at this. I've been overcharging you for years, and you never knew it."

"Overcharging me? You don't ask me for me money to pay for things."

"Who said anything about money?"

"I'm going to pretend that I didn't hear that. Now, where are we going to take them this year?"

That's how they all wound up in Marrakesh. Evelyn and Michael flew to Frankfurt, and stayed at her parents' house for a while. Then, a flight to Casablanca for two days of walking around that city, and a train to Marrakesh.

The four of them enjoyed a memorable vacation in Marrakesh. Their mid-range hotel was clean, comfortable, and well located. It was just far enough from the center of Marrakesh to be quiet, not so far that they needed a taxi to get around. Breakfast at their hotel was basic, and delightful. Crusty, warm, fresh baked baguettes - reminders of the French colonial influence - served with butter, jams, and cheeses. Enjoyed with strong, flavorful coffee, and freshly squeezed orange juice. The fruits were probably plucked that morning from the lines of orange trees growing along the sidewalks around their hotel.

Then, the four of them usually walked about ten minutes to the Djamaa El-Fna, the splendid main square in Marrakesh. Along the perimeter of that huge open area resided orange juice vendors with their small carts. Michael wasn't thirsty again after that short walk, but, he couldn't resist having another of the sweet, squeezed-to-order juices from the smiling and friendly locals.

None of the four visitors ever experienced anything like the Djamaa. Evelyn and her parents liked it, Michael believed it was as exotic as any place he ever visited, right up there with Istanbul, and Hong Kong.

During the day, the Djamaa was a circus of acrobats, jugglers, fortune tellers, snake charmers, musicians, vendors with local crafts, and other delights. Maybe the ultimate unusual sight was the occasional carpet on the ground displaying rows of various sizes of gleaming human teeth for sale. Evelyn said, "I don't want to know where they came from."

They enjoyed walking around, taking everything in, and trying not to stare at the teeth. Evelyn's parents needed to sit after this, so they all relaxed over late morning coffee at one of the cafes gazing at the Djamaa.

Almost hidden in a far corner of the Djamaa was the Mellah. This was a confusion of narrow streets that made up a part of Marrakesh that was as depressing as the main part of the Djamaa was appealing. Evelyn and Michael found out about it one day when they returned to the Djamaa while Evelyn's parents enjoyed their afternoon nap.

Evelyn and Michael slowly strolled around, filling their senses with things they knew they would not see back in the United States, or maybe anywhere. A young man, about twenty-five-years-old, approached them, and spoke a greeting in French. They ignored him. The local offered up a sentence or two in German. Evelyn and Michael continued walking. The man quickly tried English. He wanted to be their tour guide for an hour. "You don't need to pay me," he insisted. "Perhaps I will show you enough of hidden Marrakesh that you will thank me with a small donation so I may feed my large family."

Michael didn't stop walking. He smiled, shook his head and said, "No, thanks." The Moroccan smelled American money, and followed them like a hungry lion stalking a wounded gazelle. He maintained a rapid-fire sales pitch, not risking any pauses during which Michael might insert, "No."

Michael respected the guy's persistence. Michael wanted some quiet, alone time with Evelyn as they discovered Marrakesh, but finally accepted that he wasn't going to get that unless he turned unreasonably rough with the potential guide. And Michael wasn't that kind of person. *The story about the hungry family may or may not be true. But he's trying to make an honest buck instead of begging or pickpocketing.*

"OK, you've got thirty minutes. Then you need to find a new customer."

The young Moroccan's face produced a smile as large as the Djamaa. "What is your name, my American friend?"

"Michael."

"Mr. Michael, I am Nabil. I will not disappoint you. Please follow me."

Evelyn and Michael continued to hold hands as they walked alongside Nabil, who spoke rapid, understandable English as he pointed at things. He led them to the left, into a narrow, rundown street that was empty of tourists. Michael wondered if he'd made a mistake. If this was going to be an ambush by Nabil's friends as they turned a corner. With Evelyn there, Michael wasn't going to risk putting up a fight. If any thieves demanded his money, he'd hand it over. If they weren't satisfied with that, even if they flashed knives, Michael was confident that he would make them very sorry for their greed.

That readiness turned out not to be necessary. Nabil's tour continued down streets that lacked a single foreigner despite the shops. This was the Mellah. The heart of Marrakesh. Where many locals were born and lived. And died.

Evelyn and Michael silently soaked up the Mellah. The shops were contained the useful products essential for daily living, not touristy trinkets and souvenirs. Evelyn and Michael enjoyed fresh vegetables and fruits at the restaurants and cafes they ate at in Marrakesh, all of it as pleasing to their eyes as it would be to their mouths. There was no evidence of that quality here. The vegetables and fruits looked shrunken and tired. As if the choicest of them went to the foreigners, leaving the locals to pick through what was judged unfit to attract Western currency.

And there was the meat. Raw, bloody, and unrecognizable hunks of flesh that looked like they were ripped, rather than cut, from animals of some unknown species, were carelessly draped over the concrete and stone window openings of butcher shops. These totally unappealing scraps were landing zones for small clouds of flies that no one in the shop made any effort to disperse.

Evelyn and Michael didn't think the Mellah could not get more depressing. They were wrong. Nabil invited them to see the inside of a home in the Mellah. They smiled politely, and shook their heads, saying, "No, thanks."

Their guide led them onward. Just past the last store they turned a corner into a new narrow street. There were no shops. Nabil stopped in front of an open door on their left. An old woman, her age could have been anywhere between seventy and two hundred, she looked that wrinkled and used up, sat on a bare cot that occupied nearly all of a room that could have been a large closet in the U.S.

She was motionless, whether from the heat or some other cause, and stared down at the floor. She made no indication that she was aware of them standing outside her doorway. Nabil said something about her, including her name. She was a relative of some sort. Evelyn and Michael had already tuned him out to keep sane in all this sadness.

Michael looked at his watch and said, "Nabil, you've been a fine guide, thank you." Michael reached for his wallet and handed Nabil a twenty. He took out two more. "Please buy her something that she needs."

The Moroccan looked at Michael liked he'd handed him a gold bar, or a bag of diamonds. "Michael, my friend, you are very kind. I hope your god sees this and remembers."

Nabil thrust out his right hand. He changed his mind and moved in and hugged Michael, who returned the embrace. Evelyn and Michael thanked Nabil again, and left. After several wrong turns they emerged out of the Mellah and into the vastness of the Djamaa.

Michael and Evelyn were already thankful for the lives they had, even more so after the Mellah. They never forgot that old woman. Evelyn and Michael used the Mellah as a standard. If life presented them with something that wasn't pleasant, which didn't happen often, they would shrug it off with, "It could be worse. We could have been born in the Mellah."

Evelyn considered the Djamaa to be interesting, while Michael considered it fascinating and exotic. They both felt the optimum time to be there was late afternoon. That was when the hand-pulled food carts began to arrive, like the changing of the guard.

Evelyn, Michael, and her parents drank their afternoon coffee at the Café Argana overlooking the Djamaa, as the entertainers, sellers, and others stopped what they were doing as strictly as if a loud whistle had blown, ending their shift.

The daytime people exited as hand-pulled carts replaced them. The countless carts were arranged impressively and precisely in rows and columns. "If you didn't know any better," Evelyn said, "you'd think there were painted markers on the ground telling them where to be."

It didn't take long until the welcome scent of wood fires reached their noses. The sun continued descending, its receding light was replaced by the flickering of dozens of cooking fires. Black smoke was soon joined by the aromas of roasting meat, as both danced around the Djamaa.

Michael paid for their coffee, and they left the Argana to curiously wander and gawk. Many of the meats were recognizable, Evelyn and Michael looked at each other with questions marks about others. One that didn't need identifying was a grill that held about ten small brains arranged in two rows of five, roasting over the bright ashes. Michael pointed it out to Evelyn with his eyes. He moved closer to her, and quietly said, "I don't want to know what animal these are from. These people aren't stupid, and they're here every day. They know what number they're going to sell. They wouldn't have ten of these here if they didn't think they would go." Michael was pretty sure Evelyn was thinking the same thing.

They hurried away. Michael caught bits of German, French, and other languages from the tourists they passed, but no English. Maybe this was because they'd travelled there from Germany, a five-hour flight. It would take considerably more flying to get there from the U.S.

Evelyn and Michael lingered at one cart, tasting things with their eyes, trying to decide if their mouths should share the experience. A male voice said, "Isn't this one of the more provocative places you've ever been to?"

Michael said nothing, his silence deferring to Evelyn. She asked the other tourist, "Where are you from?"

"Israel." He added, "I've done a lot of traveling, and I think this city, this square, even more at night, is a dream." He paused, closed his eyes for a moment, and inhaled the spicy air. He looked back and forth between Evelyn and Michael. "What do you think?"

Michael turned to Evelyn, curious how she would

answer. She hesitated for a moment, and said, "I see how you would think that."

The stranger seemed pleased with her answer. "Enjoy your visit," he said, and slowly walked away, his attention focused on each cart as he passed it. Michael waited until the Israeli was swallowed by the masses of locals and tourists before saying, "I'm proud of you."

"Why?"

"Because your display of diplomacy was impressive."

"My diplomacy?"

"Yes. When he remarked that the Djamaa was a dream, I know that you saw on his face that he felt strongly about it. So, you validated his opinion. And you did it deftly, without agreeing. Which would have been a lie."

"Thank you. And yes, you know me well. Agreeing would have been a lie. I like it here. Is it a dream?" Evelyn shook her head. "I don't think so."

Michael reached for her hand, leading her through the crowd, passing cart after cart, seeing many of the same items as before. He looked over his shoulder at her. "I taught you well."

Evelyn stopped walking, still holding Michael's hand. She released his hand and crossed both arms across her chest. "You taught me well? Is that what you think?" she asked with mock surprise.

"You bet. When you first came to the U.S., how would you have answered that Israeli's question about the Djamaa being a dream?"

"I would have said that with these poor, hungry souls struggling to stay alive for another meal, another day, yes, it is a dream... a bad one."

"Exactly my point."

"But that would have been my truthful opinion."

"Yes," Michael said, "presented in a 'take-no-prisoners' manner. Instead of your current, smooth, tactful, and still truthful answer."

Evelyn considered this and smiled. Michael grabbed her hand and led her forward again. They both enjoyed the Djamaa for a while, then walked back to their hotel.

Chapter Thirty-Five

"I'M PREGNANT."

They had been home from Marrakech for about two weeks when Evelyn came out of the bathroom and said this. She added, "Isn't that fabulous?"

"It's *super* fabulous. Are you sure? I'm not trying to be negative, I don't want to get all excited for a false alarm."

"Michael, I'm sure. I wouldn't have told you if I weren't. I'm extremely regular with my periods. This one is so overdue that I sent out a search party. And my breasts are sore in a way that never happened before. I just did the pee-on-a-stick now, it was the third positive reading. I wasn't taking any chances!"

"I'm going out to buy a bottle of expensive champagne. Wait, you shouldn't be drinking. Okay, I'll drink it myself. No, bad move. I'll pass out, and miss the celebration."

"Michael, you already had your celebration. That's why I'm pregnant."

"Very funny. Hey, I realized something."

"What?"

"We flew to Moerfelden and stayed there before we went to Morocco."

"Yes."

"Between the jet lag, and staying at your parent's house, we didn't fool around."

"Correct, again."

"When we got to Casablanca, it was late. We strolled

around for a while, showered, ate dinner, and went to bed."

Evelyn closed her eyes. "I'm sure this is going somewhere. Please wake me when it arrives."

"Boy, you newly pregnant women are cranky. I'm nearly done."

She opened her eyes. "I really would like to hear the end of this before the baby is born."

"After exploring Casablanca from dawn to sundown the following day, we collapsed into a coma. The following afternoon we rode the train to Marrakech. Then, finally, in mid-week, we spiced up our sightseeing with some tropical naughtiness."

Evelyn looked up at the ceiling, thinking, as if an answer was written there. "That sounds about right."

"Let me summarize. We got naughty once."

"Yes."

"And you're pregnant."

"Delightfully so."

"From now on, please refer to me as One-Shot Michael. Well, maybe not in public. Other women will hear you and ask if I'm available for stud service."

~ * * * ~

Evelyn and Michael were thrilled with all sorts of pregnancy and parenting expectations. Her OB/GYN doctor wanted to see them. Since this was a first pregnancy, he wanted both future parents there while he went over what to expect during the nine months ahead.

They arrived early for their doctor visit. They arranged to have the last appointment of the day so Michael could go after work, despite knowing that this late in the afternoon the patient schedule had nearly all day to become backed up. Evelyn and Michael were neither surprised nor annoyed that they waited well past their appointment time. They held hands and talked about this glorious phase of their lives.

A nurse opened the door to the area behind the front desk and called their names. She introduced herself with a smile, and led them to a small examining room. She said the doctor would be in momentarily. Evelyn and Michael continued contemplating the upcoming year, and its impact on their lives. The conversation was filled with joking about the pleasures of middle of the night feedings and diaper changing.

Someone lightly knocked on the door and opened it. “Hi, I’m Dr. Perusse,” he said to Michael as they shook hands. Evelyn already knew him. Dr. Perusse was, as Evelyn had described, about Michael’s 6’1”, maybe early fifties, thin, with a full head of gray, nearly silver hair. Michael figured that his long, spotless white lab coat, and the stethoscope draped around his neck, combined with a grandfather’s kindly face probably made all his patients feel confident that they were in the hands of a caring and capable professional.

That impression was reinforced when Dr. Perusse spoke plain English, without a single medical term. And despite that he must have given this talk thousands of times, he delivered it with the freshness that each new parent deserves. Any pregnancy, especially the first, is an important event in the life of the parents-to-be. Dr. Perusse was at the end of what had surely been a busy, hectic, and maybe frustrating day. His voice conceded none of that. It remained calm, friendly, and reassuring.

When Dr. Perusse finished his brief summation of the highlights of the complete pregnancy, he asked if they had any questions before he continued. Michael looked at Evelyn sitting to his left. She shook her head slightly.

Michael said, “I have a question. You may know that Evelyn is a flight attendant, so we’re fortunate to travel a lot. I don't want to sound like a name dropper, we were in Africa when this baby was conceived. Will this child be considered African – American?"

Dr. Perusse stared at Michael for maybe three seconds, a long time under those circumstances. Then he laughed so loud that his nurse came back in the room, maybe to make sure everything was alright.

~ * * * ~

Michael told that story to one of his African co-workers. He laughed and said, "That's a funny story, Michael, but you're wrong. If that baby was conceived in Africa, he's African!"

One of the female technicians Michael worked with asked him if he was going to video the delivery of his child.

"No, I filmed the conception. That should be enough."

~ * * * ~

They were eating dinner at home. Evelyn asked, "What are you looking forward to about being a father?"

"Wow. You sure know how to ask big questions, don't you?"

She smiled. "Why not? You're a smart man. You'll give me an intelligent answer."

"Smart man? Intelligent answer?" Michael looked left and right. "Are you sure you've got the right person? When I was a kid, I wanted to grow up to have a strong back, and a strong mind." He shrugged. "One out of two isn't bad."

"Michael, this is serious."

"Okay, I would have to say that being the father that this child deserves, as we raise him or her, is my main priority. If I do this nearly as well as my father did, I'll consider myself successful."

"What do you think made him such a successful father?"

"Hmmm. For starters, he was genuine. There was no difference between Marvin the man, the husband, or the father. He treated everyone fairly and politely. He had a way of making people glad to see him. I'm not sure I ever saw him lose his temper. Yes, he needed to count to ten sometimes. I could swear I saw steam coming out of his ears occasionally, usually because of me. But, he controlled his emotions. They did not control him." A bittersweet look drifted onto Michael's face.

Evelyn gave Michael time to deal with his memories, and then said, "He sounds like quite a man. You must miss him."

Michael looked at Evelyn, his brief time travel over. "I miss both my parents. A lot."

"I'm sorry that I didn't get to know them."

"Me, too. They would have been crazy about you. Just like I am."

"I know you have a loving opinion of your father. I hope you realize that you could have been describing yourself."

Michael smiled. "You caught me off guard with that. I don't have a smart-ass answer to grab onto. I'll settle for 'Thank you.'"

Evelyn beamed one of her magic smiles. "You're welcome. I might add that you're the best person I've ever known."

"Most of the time."

"No. All of the time."

"Well, most of all of the time. And all of most of the time."

They both smiled.

Michael said, "Okay, your turn. What do you anticipate about motherhood?"

"Besides you doing the middle of the night feedings and diaper changes?"

"Yes, beyond that."

"This may sound repetitive... the same as yours. I want to be the mother that I wish I'd had. You know my mother. She's a terrific person, and did as well as she was able. She was a product of the time and culture that produced her. We all are. And I suppose that each generation feels more intelligent and enlightened than every generation before it."

Evelyn held Michael's hands. She said, "I feel like I'm capable of being exactly what I want to be, not what my circumstances, background, or upbringing have conditioned me for." She smiled. "I bet you didn't expect a speech when you asked that question, did you?"

"No, and I didn't get one. I got a deliberate, articulate, and honest answer. A typical Evelyn response."

"Thank you."

Michael said, "I think it's safe to say that if we don't win the Gold Medal of Parenting Award, it won't be from lack of desire or effort."

As the weeks zipped by, Evelyn's belly began to grow. She commented about her weight gain. "Michael, I know you're trying to pamper me, and I appreciate it. Bringing home chocolate chip muffins, glazed donuts, and other desserts, isn't helping me. You're not the one who must lose the weight later. *I* am. Thank you, but please don't do it."

"No problem. I'll eat yours. Think of any weight gain by me as my attempt to share your pregnancy experience."

"I'm always impressed by your capacity for sacrifice."

Chapter Thirty-Six

On Thanksgiving, Evelyn and Michael were enjoying their turkey dinner and the cooking aromas that lingered in the air. Evelyn put down her fork and said, "I don't feel well."

Evelyn's serious tone, coupled with the look of discomfort on her face, told Michael that this was serious. He instantly boiled with decisions and worry. But he needed to stay calm. Michael put down his knife and fork and said gently, "What exactly are you feeling?"

"My belly doesn't feel right. I know that isn't precise. It's the only description that I can come up with."

Michael nodded and stood. "I'm sure this is nothing except too much turkey." He somehow managed to smile, hoping that he was right, yet not quite believing it. Evelyn was too tough for that. "Let's go to the hospital to play it safe."

He deliberately avoided the phrase 'the emergency room' though that's exactly where they were headed.

Evelyn pushed away from the table and slowly stood. Her hands grabbed her lower abdomen. Her face told him all he needed to know.

Michael said, "I'll get your coat. Please lean against the wall if you don't want to sit down again." Evelyn closed her eyes and nodded. He knew she was in pain. And too stubborn, like him, to admit it, even to herself.

Michael had served with some truly tough dudes when he was in the Marine Corps, Evelyn was way up there on the grit and guts scale. For her to grimace was like a scream from anyone else. Michael made sure that he put his hospital ID lanyard around his neck before they left. He didn't expect preferential treatment, it certainly couldn't hurt to wear it.

The ride to the emergency room, while short with the roads nearly empty on Thanksgiving, took too long for Michael. He filled the time with what he hoped were soothing words, delivered calmly. Evelyn kept her eyes squeezed shut. He wondered what she was thinking. Michael didn't ask. He didn't want Evelyn to give life to her fears by speaking of them.

The emergency room was crowded, which surprised them. They figured there might be some 'I cut myself carving the turkey' patients there, but they believed that the main wave of 'my belly hurts from stuffing myself' would arrive in the early evening or night, not late afternoon. Despite the number of patients there, when Evelyn told the admitting clerk that she was four months pregnant and had abdominal discomfort, an orderly with a wheelchair appeared practically from nowhere.

Evelyn was promptly rolled through the automatic doors with Michael right behind. Unlike the usual visits to a physician's office, a doctor was already waiting for them in the examining room. His face and voice conveyed concern as he started scribbling Evelyn's responses to his questions on the clipboard in his left hand. He studied his notes. "We're going to do a pelvic ultrasound. Please take everything off below the waist and put on this hospital gown, with the opening in the front. Open the door when you're finished."

In a few minutes, Evelyn's wheelchair sped down a corridor, around a corner, and into an examination room in the ultrasound section of the radiology department.

Michael tossed a polite, unsmiling hello to the employees that he knew.

Dr. Landsnes, one of Michael's favorite radiologists, came out of her office. "Michael, I'm normally glad to see you," she shook her head, "not under these circumstances."

Michael asked Dr. Landsnes if she would be in the room for the ultrasound exam.

"Of course, I'm going to be there. I want to see the exam in real time."

Evelyn slowly climbed onto the ultrasound table and laid back. The female technologist covered Evelyn's abdomen and pelvis with a towel and reached under it. She opened Evelyn's hospital gown, keeping the towel covering her. "I'm going to gently rub some gel below your naval. I'm sorry, it will be cold." Evelyn closed her eyes and nodded. Michael held her left hand.

During the exam the technologist's ultrasound probe searched for, found, and lingered over the tiny person living inside Evelyn. Michael stared at the monitor, watching their baby's delicate little heart beating. It was breaking *his* heart not to know what was going on.

When the technologist was done, she withdrew the probe from under the towel. Dr. Landsnes held Evelyn's right hand with both of hers and squeezed it. "I'm sorry, this is not good news. The fetus is no longer attached to the wall of the uterus, as it should be."

Michael knew that Evelyn was emotionally drained, so he asked, "What does that mean?"

Dr. Landsnes hesitated. She didn't want to continue. "It means that a spontaneous abortion is taking place."

She looked directly at Evelyn. "Evelyn, I'm so sorry. Your uterus is rejecting the fetus. This is usually due to a birth defect. It's nature's way of protecting the species."

Dr. Landsnes gave them some silence to absorb this.

She continued, "This is probably difficult to accept right now, it's a merciful thing."

Michael knew that Evelyn needed to think about this. He maintained watching Evelyn, alert for any clues that she might need help.

Dr. Landsnes said, "The medical literature says that about thirty-five percent of all pregnancies end in miscarriages. I think the number is closer to fifty percent. In my opinion, many women don't even realize that they're in the earliest phase of pregnancy. And when they miscarry, they attribute it to a heavy period."

She managed a sympathetic smile. "Evelyn, you're young and healthy. You and Michael will have plenty of time to grow a family."

Dr. Landsnes continued. "When are you going on your next vacation? May I suggest Aruba? I honeymooned there. And whether it was the spicy food or the spicy evenings, our first daughter was born nine months later. Please drop by my office anytime if you want any hotel suggestions. I'm not trying to steal business away from your travel agent, I kept brochures as souvenirs and references for return visits. You can copy them."

Michael appreciated Dr. Landsnes's effort to lighten things up. "Thanks."

"You're welcome. Please do whatever they tell you in the emergency room. Here's my advice: Evelyn, take it as light as you can for a while. Are you able to do that?"

Evelyn nodded. "Yes. I'm not flying for four days."

"Excellent. You probably will experience some heavy spotting, maybe bleeding. That's normal. There may be some moderate cramping, that's also normal. If you feel anything other than that, call your gynecologist. And - I insist on this – if you have any concerns, please call me directly. Michael has my extension. Do either of you have any questions?"

Michael looked at Evelyn. His eyes invited her to ask

any if she had them. She looked at Dr. Landsnes and said, "No. I understand what's going on. I don't like it. But I have no choice, I must accept it."

Dr. Landsnes shook hands with Michael and put her hand on Evelyn's shoulder. "I know this is a tough time for you. Maybe the toughest of your life so far. Please believe me when I say that as difficult as this may be to hear, all wounds eventually heal." She gently squeezed Evelyn's shoulder. "Please let me be of any help that I can."

Michael nodded and Dr. Landsnes left. Evelyn reached out for Michael. "I can see why she's one of your top doctors to work with."

No words were necessary as Michael helped Evelyn to her feet. They embraced. Evelyn's head and body were pressed tight against him. It didn't take long for her entire body to shake. Michael whispered into her ear, "It's okay. Let it out. You'll feel better."

And she did. Evelyn cried for their dying child. Michael couldn't possibly comprehend how tortured she must feel, knowing that her tiny child is inside of her was dying, and there is nothing that she could do. Michael held Evelyn tightly until she was finished. He handed her a paper napkin from his pocket, he always carried several. She blew her nose and looked at him. "Thank you. You're right, I do feel better." She intensified her look. "When do you get your chance?"

"I appreciate your concern. I'm fine."

"Michael, don't try to fool me. Or yourself. I know this must be tearing you apart, losing our child. You're human. You need a release."

"I'm okay. How 'bout if we continue this talk later? Let's get you back into your clothes and go home." Evelyn nodded, and reached for the big white plastic bag that contained her folded clothes. When she was finished, Michael gripped the handles of the wheelchair. "Madam, your royal chariot is ready."

"If this is my royal chariot, then you are...?"

"At your disposal, of course."

"Why didn't I realize that?"

That night, and for many others, when they held each other in bed, it was tighter, more protective, more sheltering than before. As if their sanity, or their lives depended on that closeness.

~ * * * ~

Evelyn never forgot the images of that tiny heart quivering as it struggled to live. She tried to get Michael to talk about this, hoping to somehow reduce his pain. But he didn't understand how re-visiting a tragedy could lessen it. Evelyn gently insisted that although she was grieving, she accepted it. Neither of them ever got over the loss of their child. Both were forever silently wounded.

Chapter Thirty-Seven

Evelyn and Michael waited in line at the express check-out counter of a local grocery store. Michael glanced around casually. An old woman, maybe in her late seventies or early eighties, stood behind them. She was short and somewhat slouched over, as if back pain was a constant companion. She was wearing what used to be called 'Sunday Go To Church' clothes. The dress, while clearly not new, radiated dignity, just like the woman wearing it. Michael turned and smiled down at her. "Your earrings are very pretty."

The old woman's expressionless face came alive as if he had told her she'd won a trip to Hawaii. She touched her right ear. "Oh, these old things." She smiled. "My husband bought them for me after his first big promotion. God rest his soul. Our son loved them when he was child. He said they sparkled like the sun. We told him he could give them to his wife when he grew up."

She paused. "He died in the army before he got married."

The old woman went silent again, maybe thinking of her husband and son. "Thank you, young man," she said as she touched Michael's arm. "You made my day."

"You're welcome."

On the way to their car, Evelyn said, "I think that somehow you could tell she was widowed, lived alone, and needed a compliment. How did you do that?"

"As Sherlock Holmes would say, 'Elementary, my

dear Watson.' Old people usually don't go out without their spouse, either out of love for each other, or as a precaution in case there's a problem. And women tend to marry men somewhat older. Put those two together and...," he waved his hands like a maestro conducting a fine symphony, "voila, no husband alive."

Evelyn nodded. Michael said, "If she lived with any adult children, they would either do her shopping, or go with her so she wouldn't fall and break a hip carrying heavy grocery bags." He smiled and shrugged. "See, that was easy, wasn't it?"

Evelyn stopped walking and turned to him. "You are a special one. Not many people would have made the effort to brighten up her day. It wasn't a big deal, and that's exactly the wonderful part. You do the little things that are meaningful. I'm proud of you." She moved in and wrapped her arms around him.

Michael returned the hug and whispered, "When we get home you can show me how proud you are."

~ * * * ~

Evelyn was pregnant. She and Michael were again thrilled with all the possibilities. He bought a large button, one of those with a message or slogan on it that you pin on your shirt or jacket. His said, 'Proud Dad.' Michael put a small piece of tape under those words with 'To Be' carefully written on it. He proudly wore it constantly, on the pocket or front of whatever shirt he was wearing. Evelyn didn't want one. She was too shy. Michael told her she didn't need the button, her glow would declare her condition.

They planned the baby's bedroom once again, making pleasurable decisions about everything except the color. Evelyn's belly grew a small bulge that Michael insisted was sexy, despite her protests. Over dinner each night, they happily discussed different aspects of early parenthood, and enjoyed gradually eliminating names until two or three for each gender remained.

"Why are we wasting time with boy's names," Michael said, "The fertility gods know you want a girl."

"I never said that."

"You didn't need to."

Evelyn smiled.

Two nights later, over dinner, Michael asked, "How are you feeling?"

"My face is sore."

"Your face?" He got worried. "Why? Did something happen?"

"From grinning with relief, happiness, and anticipation all day."

They stopped eating and held hands for a while. Finally, Michael said, "This pregnancy is beyond words. I'll settle for 'spectacular'. What do you think?"

"I don't know that German or English has exactly the right expression, but I love the feeling that we have a fresh chance to be parents. And all that it means."

Evelyn and Michael sat like that, silently holding hands for a long time before they went back to their dinner.

~ * * * ~

The outward curve of Evelyn's belly was no longer small, or a bulge. It was an announcement, a proclamation, a decree. She modeled her new stretch-band maternity pants for Michael as proudly as if she had earned and not bought them.

The days sped into weeks, which accelerated into several months. Her pregnancy, and their lives, were moving along exactly as they wanted.

Until Evelyn's sudden and fierce abdominal cramping.

As Michael drove her to the E.R., he tried to reassure her that this could be anything, and that she shouldn't worry. Evelyn said nothing. She squeezed his hand. They signed in, and were taken to an examination room immediately.

Michael didn't bring it up, this was how the miscarriage started. He prayed this would end differently. He knew that soothing words would go only so far. Evelyn was listening to her body, and trying desperately to force away a pregnant woman's worst nightmare.

After being examined by the E.R. physician, a pelvic ultrasound was ordered. Michael walked alongside Evelyn's wheelchair, holding her hand as the nurse steered them to the radiology department. Michael knew the on-call radiologist. He had an excellent reputation among the staff as friendly and proficient. He greeted Michael, and said he would be in the room during the exam.

Michael stared intently at the monitor, and the technologist's face as she moved the probe around Evelyn's lower abdomen, stopping over select areas. *Why is she lingering there? What does she see?* Michael's eyes leaped back to the monitor. But this was totally different from an x-ray. Michael strained to understand the constantly changing shapes.

The radiologist looked at them and said, "I'm sorry to tell you this, I detect no fetal heartbeat."

Evelyn and Michael stared at each other, sending messages that made words unnecessary. The radiologist put his hand on Michael's shoulder and said, "I'm going to leave you two alone. I'll be right out here if you need me." He quietly left the examining room and shut the door.

Evelyn sat up. She and Michael clung to each other. He said, "I don't have a miracle to offer you. All I can say is that I'm sorry."

"I know you are. It wasn't meant to be." She paused. "Next time."

~ * * * ~

Evelyn was returning from a flight to Munich on a Saturday. It was Michael's birthday. When he had spoken to her on Friday, she'd mentioned that her carefully monitored hormone level was rising and this should be a rewarding weekend to conceive. On Saturday, Michael worked out in the morning and did some chores. He made a tuna salad sandwich on toast with tomato rice soup for lunch, then enjoyed a long, hot shower.

Michael decided to spoil himself with a mystery novel for about an hour. Evelyn would be home around five that afternoon. He sat on the sofa with his book and somehow dozed off. He was deep in a pleasant dream when a gentle rubbing on his left arm slowly brought him back to the surface.

"Wake up, birthday boy. You have work to do."

Evelyn didn't get pregnant that month. Or the month after that. Or even that year. Michael sensed that her confidence in getting pregnant, and successfully carrying the baby to term, was gradually being eroded the way a steady drop-by-drop assault by water could eventually destroy a powerful boulder.

Evelyn never complained. The closest she came was to say, "I got my period today," with the words floating on the smallest wave of frustration. Someone who didn't know Evelyn probably would not have detected the disappointment. Michael heard it.

Chapter Thirty-Eight

MICHAEL WAITED FOR THE RIGHT time, and the right moment. And over dinner one night, he decided it had arrived. "I think we had this conversation before. I believe that things happen for a reason. We may not realize the reason at the time, we may never know it. Call it fate, predestination, God's will, whatever label you prefer to give it. I believe in that. I think there is a powerful force at work in our lives."

He paused to let Evelyn absorb that. Michael continued. "I don't mean that we should sit around waiting for things to happen. Or that we're powerless, controlled by something larger and dominant, the way a puppeteer manipulates a puppet. The older I get, and the greater perspective on life that I acquire, the more I'm convinced of that. What do you think?"

Evelyn put her fork down. "Two things. First, I agree with that one hundred percent. Second, I've felt that way since I was teenager." She smiled. "Apparently, I'm either smarter than you are, or I learn things quicker. Which one do you think it is?"

~ * * * ~

United Airlines changed its health insurance carrier the following year. Evelyn and Michael felt this was done to save money. And they agreed that if they controlled the benefits for any company, certainly one with tens of thousands of employees like United, they would have done the same thing. Their benefits remained the same, they needed to pick a new family doctor. Evelyn soon met Dr. Sim when she needed a referral for a routine mammogram. Over dinner that night, Michael asked about her appointment.

"It went well. She's friendly and professional. I'd say mid-thirties, asks sensible questions, and she listens to the answers - solid bedside manner. When I answered her question about pregnancies, she asked if any blood work had been done. She was surprised when I said no. She wrote out a lab slip, I'm going there tomorrow."

Two days later Evelyn received an email that her blood-work numbers were available online. When she went on her health insurance company's website to look at them, there was a message from Dr. Sim requesting that Evelyn schedule a follow-up visit to discuss the lab findings, and their consequences. Evelyn secured an appointment for the following day. When she got home from it, she went over everything with Michael. "I'm so mad! I could...what is the expression...swallow nails?"

Michael made a pained face and drew in a breath. "Ouch, that would hurt. Especially when they came out."

Evelyn silently lectured him with a faux angry 'must-you-be-so-disgusting? look.

"OK, I'll stop. Anyway, it's 'spit nails.' Please don't ask me where that came from."

"Well, whatever you do with nails, that's how angry I am."

"Why?"

"Because when Dr. Sim went over my blood work, she pointed out that my progesterone level was nearly non-existent."

"Evelyn, I spent high school biology and chemistry classes looking out the window and daydreaming. What does that mean?"

"She said that was probably why I couldn't carry a fetus to term. And that it was a miracle that I got pregnant in the first place with that progesterone level."

Evelyn paused. "I'll bet that's why I needed so long to get pregnant the first time. And no one ordered the right test to discover that." Evelyn smiled. "That was the bad news."

Michael rubbed his palms together rapidly and repeatedly in front of his face and said, "I know I'm going to like this next part."

"She recommended progesterone supplements. She felt that once my level was back to where it should be –"

Michael interrupted, "You'll be a hot mama. With the emphasis on *mama*."

Evelyn raised her eyebrows, "Are you saying I'm not hot now?"

"You're not a hot mama. You're the *hottest* mama. Did I add that fast enough?"

"Yes. Barely."

A big smile invaded Michael's face. "That is good news. No, it's *great* news." He stood up, and Evelyn did, too. They hugged each other. Michael breathed in deeply, and let it out in relief. Their long maternity nightmare would finally end.

Michael asked, "When do you start the progesterone, and how long will it take for your body to reach a normal level?"

"I was saving that bit of news. Dr. Sim gave me a prescription for what she called bio-identical hormones. This means that the supplements are an exact match for what my body would produce on its own. And, they're made from natural sources, plants, not a synthetic chemical produced in a giant lab somewhere."

"Natural sources sound better than drugs. And I like the idea of the supplements being matched to your specific needs, not pulling a one-size-fits-all bottle of pills down from a shelf. Now, how 'bout the time-frame?"

"Dr. Sim said that it should take a month or two. She warned me, there is one fairly common side effect."

As soon as Evelyn said that, Michael started gathering soothing words. "Don't worry. We'll deal with them as they occur, if they ever do. I think that most side effects are listed as a legal necessity, and don't actually happen."

Evelyn said, "The reaction she warned me about is pretty universal in women. She said she'd be surprised if I didn't experience it."

"She *has* to say that. It's CYA."

"CYA?"

"Cover your ass. I don't mean this negatively about Dr. Sim, if she didn't warn you about this, she runs the risk of some lawyer suing her."

"I don't think she was worried about being sued. She was concerned about you thanking her."

"Huh?"

Evelyn smiled. "It increases my sex drive."

Michael was silent. Then he said, "Please hand me the phone book. I need to find a florist to send her a dozen roses. No, make that two dozen. And a 'thank you' note. And a bottle of champagne."

"I suspected you might enjoy that. How many vacation days do you have saved up? I may keep you home as my sex prisoner every now and then."

"Do I get time off for bad behavior?"

"Only if you're *very* bad."

"Hold that thought. We'll get to it later. This is amazing news. My wife becomes a sex demon *and* we become parents."

"And while you're enjoying yourself, what do I get?"

"Don't be ridiculous. You get the privilege of gaining about thirty pounds and having hormonal storms yank your emotions around like a toy boat on an angry lake. Did I mention that you'll bounce back and forth between wanting to hug me and then planning to kill me in my sleep? And you'll be exhausted all the time. Then there's morning sickness. Which I don't want to get into, it will ruin my appetite. Sounds charming, doesn't it?"

"Yes, I can't wait. And it's gratifying to know that all the hard work I've put into the gym and on my treadmill will be wasted." Then Evelyn got serious. "I'm not twenty-six, like when we met. I'm not even thirty-six. That was last year. I want our baby as much as you do, maybe more. But Mother Nature and Father Time don't wait for anyone."

"What are you saying?"

"That the odds of me getting pregnant are no longer in our favor. The calendar has seen to that. I'm on the wrong side of the timeline. I don't want you to set yourself up for disappointment."

Michael smiled genuinely, not out of false hope. "Have I ever let you down?" He quickly added, "That you know of?"

Evelyn shook her head.

He said, "I'm too old to start now. Relax. Let's see if One-Shot-Michael will come out of retirement and hit one more game winning home run."

Chapter Thirty-Nine

EACH MONTH THEY HELD THEIR breath as Evelyn's periods approached. And each month she came out of the bathroom and shook her head. Evelyn did not get pregnant again.

Michael became wary as Thanksgiving approached. He always did. It was Evelyn's favorite American holiday until her first miscarriage on that day. He was so tuned in to her after their years together that he could sense her feelings with laser precision. *I'm not going to bring up what happened. Why re-open an old wound?*

Their meal that Thanksgiving featured the usual conversation that started in one place, and delightfully wandered all over. Then Evelyn stopped eating and looked at Michael. "If I hadn't lost that first baby, she'd be five now."

Michael put his knife and fork down and reached for her hands. They held hands like that, not saying a word. Finally, Michael said, "Yes, and if she was lucky she would have been a clone of her mother."

Evelyn tried to smile. The tears had already formed. He used his napkin to gently dab at them as Evelyn sniffed. Michael stood up. Evelyn did the same. They embraced.

Michael spoke softly, "You would have been the world's best mother. I can see the two of you, rushing from store to store, buying pink outfits in various sizes. Those that fit her now, and those she could grow into to. You would need two shopping carts. I'd have to get a second job to pay for all of that. And I'd be too busy working to be at home, which is the way you both planned it. The two of you would spend the day together, our daughter saying, 'Mommy, it's so awesome to be alone with you.'"

Evelyn smiled, as he hoped she would.

They held each other for a long time. Michael pulled back a bit, he kept his arms around her waist. "I'm sorry."

Michael maintained his probing eye contact. Evelyn said, "It wasn't meant to be."

"I'm still sorry."

She pulled herself into Michael again and pressed her head against his chest. Her crying began silently and delicately, he knew she was resisting. He whispered into her ear, "It's alright. Let it out."

Michael's words and tone generated the desired response. Evelyn needed to purge the poison that had accumulated. She held onto him as tightly as clinging to a tree for safety in a tornado. Michael matched her embrace; he wanted to be certain that she felt secure. He said nothing as Evelyn cried herself out. Her body shook lightly as evil spirits were expelled. They continued to hold each other, standing in the middle of their dining room. Michael tried to think of some new magic words, words that would heal Evelyn. He couldn't.

~ * * * ~

Evelyn's fortieth birthday was one week away. Michael looked at the calendar in their kitchen and acted surprised. "Forty? I'm going to have to trade you in for two twenty- year-olds."

"That's a great idea. I'm sure you'll have no trouble. Twenty-year-old women are lining up for forty-three-year-old men whose idea of a late night is not turning out the reading lamp until eleven o'clock. And should I mention that only rich men need apply? Trophy girlfriends want to see what's in your bank account before they care about what's in your pants."

"You're getting quite clever and funny as you get older. You may even kill my theory."

"What theory might that be?"

"That the toughest job in Germany is being a stand-up comic."

"You're on a roll tonight."

"OK, then I'll continue. What's the toughest job in China?"

After about five seconds Evelyn said, "I give up."

"Police sketch artist."

"You really need sensitivity training. You know that don't you?"

"Thanks for the compliment." Michael pulled Evelyn in. "Do you know what I see when I look at you?"

"No, what?"

"The beautiful twenty-six-year-old woman who walked into the kitchen of The Mansion on the luckiest day of my life."

"Thank you."

"Of course, my vision isn't as sharp as it used to be."

Evelyn slapped his arm.

Michael squinted. "And the lighting is dim in here."

Evelyn laughed.

He said, "Other than that, you look the same."

"And you haven't lost any of your diplomacy or tact as *you've* gotten older."

They stood there, holding each other, not moving, barely breathing, savoring the closeness.

Michael said, "You were the most beautiful woman I'd ever seen when we met. And you're even more beautiful now."

Evelyn pulled her head back. “Thank you. But how is that possible? I’m not twenty-six any longer.”

“Because then you were not as fascinating and endlessly interesting on the inside as you are now. Aging is a natural, unavoidable part of life. Doing it gracefully is a choice. You’ve developed inner beauty while remaining ravishing. And I have been the luckiest man in the world to be with you during those years.”

“Thank you.” Evelyn returned her head to his chest. They resumed their silent embrace for a long time.

Finally, Michael said, “We’re at the ideal age. Old enough to appreciate how terrific we have it. And young enough to enjoy it.”

~ * * * ~

Evelyn called Michael. “I’m in my car. I just left the imaging center.”

“How did it go?” He knew the answer about her routine mammogram would be, “Fine.”

That’s what Evelyn always said.

She didn’t say that.

“They found a lump.”

Chapter Forty

EVELYN HUNG HER KEYS ON the set of hooks at eye level on the wall to the right of their front door. They sat at their dining room table, holding hands. Michael said, "Please start at the beginning and tell me everything."

"There isn't much to tell. The mammogram was over and the technician asked me to wait in the dressing room area. She said the doctor wanted to speak to me. That was my first clue that something wasn't right. They never did that before. A doctor came in and introduced himself. I forget his name, I was so focused on what he might tell me."

Michael squeezed her hands. "That's understandable."

"He said they found a lump. He used the word *mass*. He added that statistically the majority of these are benign. He said that a biopsy is needed to make sure."

Michael stared at Evelyn, unable to focus. He tried to sort everything that flew around in his head. He didn't want this lump, this mass, this invader, to feed and grow from his emotions - to become stronger, more powerful, and more dangerous.

"Evelyn, I have a suggestion." He forced himself to move his mouth into what he hoped looked like a smile, a real smile was not attainable. "Let's not come to any conclusions until we have all of the facts."

She nodded. Michael knew she wasn't convinced. He had work to do. "I know you're worried. You wouldn't be normal if you weren't. Worrying about something that may not happen doesn't make any sense, does it?"

Evelyn's eyes were watery as she nodded again. Her tiny smile was eager to be reinforced. Michael said, "Most of these lumps turn out to be nothing, as the doctor told you." Michael was reasonably sure he believed this. He knew that he wanted to believe it. *It doesn't matter what I believe. Evelyn needs the peace of mind of believing it.* He said, "When are you going to call and schedule the biopsy?"

"I did that before I left the doctor's office. I'm their first patient after lunch tomorrow afternoon. I want this nightmare of uncertainty cleared up right away."

Michael summoned every bit of optimism he was capable of. "I'll bet you a donut that we'll laugh about this when the results are negative."

~ * * * ~

As soon as he got to work, Michael tapped on Dr. Landsnes's open office door and told her about Evelyn's mammogram. Dr. Landsnes pulled up Evelyn's exam on her monitor and slowly scrolled through the entire study, going back again and again to the images where the abnormal density appeared. Michael stood alongside her, silent.

Then Dr. Landsnes swiveled her chair and looked up. "Ninety percent of these are benign. I'm sure that you've already been informed of that. I'm equally sure that you confirmed it by looking it up on your own."

Michael nodded.

Dr. Landsnes said, "Nine to one odds are the numbers you want to have on your side." She smiled. "You could clean up in Vegas with that."

Michael called Evelyn and told her about his conversation with Dr. Landsnes. He could tell that Evelyn was somewhat relieved, yet still nervous. Michael tried to lessen her fears. "After we get the thumbs up about the biopsy, I'll cook you a dinner so delicious that your taste buds will have involuntary orgasms."

~ * * * ~

Each day they hoped that Evelyn would get the call that contained the one word she wanted to hear: negative. This dominated every hour of every day. Because Evelyn and Michael were such private people, they seldom got phone calls. Each time the phone did ring, it startled them due to their apprehension and anticipation. They looked at each other, simultaneously wanting to answer it, and not wanting to answer. They let their answering machine screen away the many telemarketing calls.

Evelyn and Michael faced this head-on. They didn't pretend that things were normal, that a life-threatening monster wasn't prowling, and salivating about Evelyn. They spoke of this openly, hopeful with optimism, knowing that the medical statistics were on their side.

The days dragged by without the news they wanted from her doctor's office. Over dinner on the fourth day, Michael said, "You're one of the bravest people I've ever known. I'll bet you that anyone else would have crawled into a corner, and hid there, sucking their thumb and crying."

"What makes you think I don't do that during the day when you're at work?"

"Evelyn, you're a lot braver, and funnier, than I would be in your place."

"Thanks. I know you're exaggerating for my benefit, and I appreciate it. I refuse to let the fear of an uncertain future ruin the present. I have no control over what the lab says. I do have control over whether I let it turn me into a bowl of quivering Jell-O while I'm waiting."

In bed that night, like the nights before that, they held each other extra close. Michael encouraged Evelyn not to keep anything inside. She insisted she was fine. Michael was awakened twice by Evelyn twitching wildly. Then she jerked like she was having a spasm. Michael hugged her tighter without waking her. He lay there awake, wondering what was going on in her subconscious mind.

~ * * * ~

Michael called Evelyn from his car to tell her he was on his way home. She said only four words. “The biopsy was malignant.”

The nightmare had jumped feet first into the middle of their lives.

Michael couldn’t process the word malignant. It sent shocks to his brain. He felt dizzy and wasn’t sure where he was, or what he was doing. Michael regained enough composure to say to Evelyn, “We have a bad connection. I’ll call you back.” He barely had enough presence to steer his car to the side of the road and put his hazard lights on. Michael knew he would probably hit a car or drive into a ditch if he didn’t pull over.

He sat there, staring ahead, breathing deeply, forcing his body to pump richly oxygenated blood to his brain. After a lengthy pause, he called Evelyn. He said, “Please repeat that.”

Nothing changed with the second telling. The feeling inside Michael was so toxic, so evil, and corrupt, that it felt like it would burn right through him and spill onto the floor. *What must Evelyn be going through? I’ve got to get to her.*

Michael drove home aggressively, and just about ran to the front door where Evelyn waited, holding it open. They embraced. After a long silence, he said, “We caught this early and we'll beat it. I promise." He hoped Evelyn believed him.

~ * * * ~

"Breast cancer involves various levels of concern, and assorted treatment options." That's how Dr. Murcia, their oncologist, began her first meeting with Evelyn and Michael.

Evelyn and Michael briefly looked around Dr. Murcia's office after she led them in and seated them. Dr. Murcia came highly recommended, but Evelyn and Michael were looking for clues. Even small ones, to help them start to build their own opinions of Dr. Murcia. Her office was what they expected, with the usual diplomas, textbooks, and photos of her with her husband and two young blond children, a boy and a girl.

Dr. Murcia wasn't behind her desk. She sat in a chair facing them. Evelyn liked that. It reduced the sense of separation, and let her know that the oncologist wanted to talk *with* her, not *at* her. "The treatment we recommend," Dr. Murcia said, "will be determined by the precise nature of your cancer and the success, if any, of its ability to invade other areas of your body."

Dr. Murcia leaned forward and stared at her newest patient as intently as if she were trying to hypnotize her. "Evelyn, we're going to work together as a team to defeat this. I promise you that we'll apply every up-to-the-minute medical insight, the combined years of experience of me, my partners, my staff, and any other resources to cure you."

She paused to let Evelyn and Michael fully comprehend that.

"We feel that we have the ideal medical setting here in Fredericksburg. We're close enough to Washington, D.C. to have big city technology, know-how, and equipment. And we're small enough to give you the personalized treatment and care that you deserve. Before I get into specifics, do you want to ask anything?"

Evelyn and Michael looked at each other, their eyes asking each other the same thing. They turned back to Dr. Murcia, and shook their heads.

"Okay, let's move on," Dr. Murcia said. "Evelyn, I read your test findings. You have a particularly nasty little demon inside of you. That's the bad news." Her next words were as reassuring as her face. "The good news is that it doesn't seem to have found its way around your body. If we can keep it isolated, we have a superior cure rate."

"I like the sound of that," Michael said.

Evelyn's look of dread melted into a tentative and brief smile for the first time.

Dr. Murcia said, "So do I. We don't believe in wasting time. This cancer is aggressive." She paused, and smiled a smile that contained no warmth, or humor. Those words didn't describe the look on her face. Merciless and relentless did. "And so are we. Evelyn, can you give us a few hours today? This cancer has a head start. We need to catch up as quickly as we can."

"No problem. When we made this appointment, your staff told us to allow for this. We're glad you have that attitude. I'm ready to do whatever you need for this disease to be gone."

Michael noticed Evelyn's eyes begin to moisten. He squeezed her hand to reinforce that he was there for her. Large tears slid down Evelyn's cheeks. Michael quickly used the tissue that he'd hidden in his shirt pocket to dry them.

Dr. Murcia gave Evelyn a sympathetic smile, and reached out and patted her shoulder. "You're doing better than I would in your place. I'd be running around the room, screaming, and pulling my hair out."

"Then you won't mind if I do that right now, will you?"

Dr. Murcia smiled, and then she discussed the different forms of treatment available - chemotherapy, radiation, and surgery. She highlighted the advantages, disadvantages, and likely effects of each. Dr. Murcia then went over how they were used separately, or in collaboration.

Evelyn noticed how full the waiting room had been when they arrived. Despite that, Dr. Murcia never glanced at her watch, or gave any indication that she was in a hurry. Instead, she paused often, allowing Evelyn and Michael to fully absorb and process this critical information. And she periodically asked, "Do you have any questions about that before I go on?"

Evelyn noticed that Dr. Murcia's eyes flitted back and forth from Michael to her, probably checking for traces of confusion. All of this added up to Evelyn being satisfied that she'd been referred to Dr. Murcia. After Dr. Murcia finished, she asked Michael to leave the room. She said she wanted to speak briefly to Evelyn alone. Michael nodded and left.

After he shut the door, Dr. Murcia said, "In addition to my incredible skill as an oncologist," she and Evelyn both smiled, "I'm a world class judge of people. You and Michael seem to have a pretty solid relationship. I wanted to make sure that you have the chance to tell me in private how much to have him involved in our discussions and your treatments. It's entirely up to you. If you don't want him as part of the team, for any reason, I'll tell Michael that it was my decision."

Evelyn shook her head. "He means the world to me. And I value his opinions. Thanks for asking. Please have Michael come back in."

"Like I said, I can size people up accurately. I thought you would say that. You're a lucky woman. Some husbands sit in our lobby reading sports magazines while their wives face this alone. Some men don't even do that. They drop their wives off in the front and go somewhere. Then there are the ones who sit with their wife, and you can tell they'd rather be somewhere different. Anywhere. But not here. This isn't a comment on the people involved, but their relationship." Dr. Murcia stood. "I'll ask Michael to join us."

When they were all seated, Dr. Murcia outlined what she called Operation Annihilate. "Think of this as a military mission. We knew who the enemy is, and where their headquarters is located. First, we isolate the enemy by making reinforcements, or advancement hopeless. Then we remove any chance of escape. Finally, we use overwhelming force to kill the evil bastards. There will be no survivors."

Dr. Murcia gave specifics of each phase of the war on Evelyn's tumor. She didn't become bogged down in medical-ese or unnecessary details. "I've touched on what I would want to know if I were you. Now it's your turn to talk. Concerns? Questions?"

Michael looked at Evelyn. This was about her, not him. It was important what she thought or felt. He knew Evelyn well enough to know that she was probably overwhelmed by all the possibilities of this potentially life-threatening situation. *Who wouldn't be?* Michael said, "Dr. Murcia, you've explained this well." He was buying time for Evelyn to sort out the avalanche of information.

Evelyn remained unreadable and silent for long seconds. Dr. Murcia and Michael both looked down, not wanting Evelyn to feel their gaze and think they were rushing her.

Then Evelyn said, "I think I understand everything. I'm sure I'll have some questions later."

Dr. Murcia nodded.

Evelyn continued. "There's a lot to think about. All I can say right now is that I hope Operation Annihilate doesn't get confused and annihilate me."

Chapter Forty-One

Evelyn and Michael sat on their sofa. Her left thigh was up against Michael's right thigh. They were holding hands, comfortably silent, absorbed in private musings. Michael squeezed her hand. Evelyn turned her face to him. He said, "Everything will go well." He paused for a moment. "Try to relax. I'll do enough worrying for both of us."

Evelyn managed a small smile.

She needs to be distracted. "Let's go upstairs. I can be the dignified doctor, and you can be the naughty patient. Or, I can be the naughty doctor, and you'll be the gullible patient."

Evelyn smiled again. It wasn't one of her five-star smiles, but it was real. "You are such a pig."

He pulled her close. "Only for you, Evelyn. Only for you."

~ * * * ~

Two days later, Evelyn and Michael had their second appointment with Dr. Murcia. This time she got specific about Evelyn's treatment plan and her recommended approach. Dr. Murcia finished by saying, "Evelyn, we're all eager to start this, to have it succeed, and give you a big hug when you're done. Please sleep on this. Go home, talk about what I've said, and ask any questions you may have."

Operation Annihilate involved a three-part assault. First, surgery to remove the tumor in Evelyn's breast. The breast could probably be saved. It might need some reconstruction, conditional on the amount of tumor involvement. Then, radiation to carpet bomb the site where the tumor had been, to destroy any hidden survivors. Finally, some chemo to make sure that the rest of her body was cancer-free.

Evelyn checked into the hospital the night before her surgery. Michael stayed in her room until a nurse gently reminded him for a second time that visiting hours were over. He sat on the edge of Evelyn's bed. "I'm sorry that I have to go."

A tear spilled out of each of her eyes. "I know you are."

Michael presented a smile that he hoped would fool Evelyn. He knew better. "Everything will be fine." Michael used his fingers to emphasize each positive point as he said, "You caught the lump early. The tests showed no other cancer. You're young. Uh, let's move past that one."

She smacked his arm. "You did your job, you made me smile. Now give me a kiss, and get out of here." He hesitated. Evelyn continued, "I'm fine. You know I need to deal with this in my own way. Just be here when I get back from the surgery tomorrow."

"I promise." Michael got to the door and turned. He surprised Evelyn with their lucky words, "Vaya con Dios."

~ * * * ~

Michael greeted Evelyn with a big smile when the stretcher was wheeled into her room. The two nurses moved it to her bed, and they gently slid Evelyn over. She had an IV in her left arm with two plastic bags dripping into the tubing from an IV pole. Michael waited until the nurses were gone before he kissed her. "How the heck are you? Be honest."

"Groggy. Glad to be alive. Thank you." Evelyn pulled the loose hospital gown down below her left shoulder. A large bandage, held in place with white tape, covered the upper part of her left breast. A red stain occupied the middle of the gauzy material. Evelyn saw Michael's face. "I'll be fine."

Michael breathed in deeply and let it out. He said, "One phase of killing bad cells down, two to go."

"That's how I look at it."

"You're drugged, and you've been through a lot lately, emotionally and physically. I'm going to sit here while you take a cat nap. Don't worry about me. I'll use the time to try and solve the three biggest mysteries of the ages."

"And they are?"

"Do UFO's really exist? Is there life after death? And the biggest mystery of all-time, what do women really want?"

Evelyn started to laugh and then groaned quietly. "Please, nothing funny, my chest hurts. Just be here when I open my eyes."

"You know I will be."

~ * * * ~

Evelyn was released from the hospital two days later. Early that morning, before her breakfast tray was delivered, the surgeon who had sliced Evelyn open and cut out the cancerous chunk of flesh, lightly tapped on her door before entering. The friendly looking man of average height stood at Evelyn's bed. "I wanted to see you before my first surgery today. If everything looks good, I'm going to kick you out of here." He smiled. "If that's okay with you."

Evelyn smiled.

The surgeon pointed at Evelyn's left upper chest. "May I?"

Evelyn nodded.

He opened the snaps on the left shoulder of her gown and inspected the surgical site. "I want to be sure that there are no early warning signs of an infection and that healing is taking place." He gently lifted the paper tape on two of the edges of the large gauze pad covering Evelyn's incision. He bent over for a closer look. He tilted his head toward each side as he attempted to see it from different angles.

Then he smiled at Evelyn as he snapped the shoulder area of her gown shut. "The answers are 'no' to the infection, and 'yes' to the healing."

He held both of Evelyn's hands in his. "We removed all of the cancer and only enough of the surrounding tissue to be prudent. You were lucky. We caught this early. And the tumor was small. I operate on female patients as if they were my wife. I keep in mind that you will want to wear a bathing suit without being self-conscious about scars."

The surgeon smiled again and squeezed her hands. "Evelyn, you're young and healthy. The tumor is gone, and your body is in healing mode. The statistics are on your side for a complete recovery and a long life. The next time I see you I hope that it is while you are walking around downtown. Good luck."

Michael arrived five minutes before the official start of visiting hours. The nurses gave Evelyn a small white plastic bag with the hospital logo on it and a thick collection of large gauge pads and paper tape inside. And prescriptions for antibiotics and pain killers. Michael knew that Evelyn would faithfully take the antibiotics, and equally faithfully ignore the pain killers. *She is one tough hombre.*

Michael walked alongside Evelyn's wheelchair as

a nurse pushed it to the entrance. Evelyn's dark blue Honda Accord waited there. It was bigger than his black Civic, Michael hoped it might be easier for her wounded body to slide into and out of.

Evelyn somehow didn't notice them until Michael turned into their driveway. First, she saw the flotilla of brightly colored balloons, pulling their strings tight as they tried to escape, floating about two feet above their front porch.

Then, the big, sparkly 'Welcome Home' letters taped above their garage door came into view. Evelyn turned to Michael. Her mouth opened, no words came out.

Michael said, "Whoa! Look what someone did while I was gone."

Chapter Forty-Two

THEY CONTINUED WITH THEIR LIVES. Evelyn stayed home for two weeks on medical leave while her surgical site continued to heal. Dr. Murcia didn't allow her to work. Any lifting, like heavy items into the airplane overhead bins, was out of the question. Although Evelyn was paid out of her accumulated sick time, her pay dipped a little. While on sick leave she didn't receive her hourly German language speaker supplement, or the additional per diem rate for international flying. She was concerned about this. Michael told her not to worry. "We aren't going to miss any meals, and all of the bills will get paid."

The two weeks of her recuperation went quickly. Too quickly. They cherished having Evelyn home seven days a week. Then Evelyn mentally readied herself to go back to flying. "Michael, I know you're concerned about my going to work. Please don't worry. I promise that I won't overdo it, especially with my left arm." She smiled. "For the next several weeks, even if a passenger has only one arm, they will be lifting their own heavy items into the overhead bin."

Their lives were quickly filled again with normal activities. The main difference was that Evelyn didn't work out with her usual poundage when she lifted weights at the local Y. She didn't want to put stress on any ligaments, tendons, and muscles that were sliced apart to get at the tumor. Evelyn compensated by doing a marathon worthy amount of cardio on a treadmill.

About three months later, over dinner, Evelyn said, “Dr. Murcia called today. She wants me to have a scan as a routine precaution.”

“That’s a smart move.” They were casual about this. Evelyn and Michael felt guardedly comfortable with the way things turned out. The surgery went well. The radiation and chemo were brutal, but effective. The main source of their optimism was that Evelyn’s one-month follow-up scan had been negative.

“Do you want me to take the day off and come with you?”

“Thanks, no. I’ll be fine. This is routine. And since I’ve been through it before, I know what to expect. The soonest slot I could get was for tomorrow afternoon at three. You may be home before me. I’ll share my wonderful news with you then.”

Evelyn was right, Michael was waiting for her. He bought the fanciest ‘Get Well’ card he could find. He drew a thick black line through ‘Get’ and wrote above it, ‘Stay.’ A bottle of Dom Perignon proudly stood in the front of their fridge, anxious to be popped opened. Michael wanted to remind Evelyn of their early dating days at Arthur’s Steakhouse in Hoboken.

When he heard her car pull into their driveway, Michael went to their front door with his hands behind his back. One of them held the card, and the other gripped two chilled champagne glasses. Evelyn’s key scratched at the lock before she got it right. Then she came in. Tears rolled down her face.

Michael quickly placed the card and glasses on the small table by the door where their mail belonged. He embraced Evelyn and made sure he kept any alarm out of his voice. “What happened?”

“It’s back.”

Michael felt like the world heavyweight boxing champ had somehow punched him in the head and the gut at the same time. He had to stay in control of himself. For Evelyn. Michael instinctively summoned the discipline needed to calmly say, "Let's go sit down so you can tell me all about it."

At their kitchen table Evelyn said, "Everything went smoothly, no surprises. When the technician came into the scanning room to get me off the table, he wouldn't make eye contact with me. That's when I knew."

"Hold on a minute..."

She stopped him. "I'm late is because Dr. Murcia asked me to come into her office after the IV was out, and I changed back into my clothes. She shut the door, and we sat there, neither of us speaking. Then, she said, 'I wish I had better news.'"

Evelyn reached for the tissue box. She wiped her eyes. Michael tried hard to keep a neutral expression on his face. Evelyn did not need a reminder or emphasis of the danger that waited for her in the darkness ahead.

Evelyn's voice was heavy with emotion, "It gets worse. The cancer came back. And it spread to other parts of my body."

Michael felt dizziness trying to take over. He couldn't absorb this. He struggled to summon every piece, every particle, every molecule, of his self-control to not scream out loud in frustration for his wife. *I can't even begin to imagine what Evelyn must be feeling.*

The only sound in the house was the ticking of a wall clock.

Then Michael said, "Did they tell you what happens now?"

Evelyn sighed. "Another biopsy. Maybe more than one."

He stood and held out his hands. Evelyn rose, and

they hugged. Her self-control melted, and she nearly collapsed into Michael.

"We'll do everything imaginable to conquer this. I promise." He said it with the absolute certainty as if he were announcing, "Water is wet."

Evelyn's eyes and face reflected her trust and faith in Michael. If any doors needed to be opened, she knew that he would do it. If they didn't open easily, he would kick them down if necessary.

But Michael didn't have a magic wand. Or the ability to snap his fingers and make the cancer disappear. And, no matter how dedicated or caring her doctors were, there were understandable limits to what they also could do. Regardless of how skilled, talented, and experienced they were, doctors woke up each day with the same number of hours that everyone has. They had other patients, other obligations, and other commitments that demanded, and deserved, servings of those limited hours.

Evelyn always believed in facing the truth: she was a chart in a rack, a time slot in a doctor's busy schedule, a medical record number on a form. She didn't think this in an unkind or critical way of doctors, or the medical profession. And Evelyn didn't expect anything other than that. *If I were a doctor, I would have no choice. I'd be the same way.*

Evelyn knew that not just doctors, but carpenters, lawyers, auto mechanics, any member of any profession, might be fully involved in your situation. Yet, the reality was that they had other customers, other responsibilities, other obligations, pulling on their sleeves for attention.

That's how the world works. But there is a single exception. Evelyn knew that there was one person in the world who would put eating, sleeping - even breathing - at a lower priority than curing her of the disease that was killing her. And she was looking at the face of that person. "Michael, I know you mean it, and will do everything you can. But you aren't an oncologist. Or God."

"That's true. I am a few credits short of my medical degree." Michael made a face of surrender. "Okay, make that all of them. Here's how I see things - sports are a microcosm of life. Or, maybe it's the other way around. Anyway, I know you don't like anything about baseball, but let's use a major league team as an example. Each player is a highly skilled professional, or they wouldn't be there."

Evelyn nodded.

He continued. "These are world-class athletes. To be able to throw a baseball ninety-five miles an hour, and make it dance up or down, in or out, of the small strike zone is a gift not many people possess. And, to hit that round ball, coming at you at nearly one hundred miles an hour, from sixty feet away, with your round bat, requires the incredible reflexes, coordination, and strength that only the elite of the elite are capable of.

"So, the question is, why do these athletes, who make millions of dollars a year, and have been playing baseball since they were pooping in their diapers, need a manager?"

Michael paused to let Evelyn appreciate that.

Evelyn knew no response was expected.

He continued. "Well, one reason is that the players are so involved in their portion of the game that they may not see the big picture."

"And you're going to make sure that the doctors see the big picture."

"No. The *biggest* picture."

Chapter Forty-Three

IN THE DAYS AND WEEKS that followed, Michael scrutinized Evelyn's disease from every direction, and every angle. He analyzed each available piece of information, and reviewed all the tests, all the lab work, and all the notes of all of the people treating Evelyn that were in her chart.

Michael believed that if he investigated them as part of the big picture that he'd described to Evelyn, and not as stand-alone data, he would discover what everyone missed – the key to her survival.

Michael limited his life outside of work to two activities: taking care of Evelyn, and searching through thick files of copies of her medical records and test results. He understood many of the medical terms thanks to his training and job. Some words required a medical dictionary, so Michael bought the same one that the radiology department used.

While hunting for this elusive clue, Michael always heard the loud ticking of the bomb that was Evelyn's spreading disease. It challenged him to think faster, harder, and extra clearly. There had to be something, some crucial factor that somehow, even with all the tests, biopsies and scans, had stubbornly persisted in remaining invisible.

Michael read, and re-read, every sheet of paper. He checked, re-checked, and triple-checked each test. Michael made notes in the margins, desperate to find that one critical, secret insight that would bind everything together. And open the magic door to saving Evelyn's life.

It didn't work. There was no obscure, secluded solution that was hiding; waiting for a different, fresher, wider perspective to reveal itself.

~ * * * ~

Evelyn and Michael held hands as they sat in Dr. Murcia's waiting area. An older, pleasant looking couple, they looked to be in their seventies, was also holding hands. The woman smiled. Her front upper teeth revealed a small smudge of red lipstick on them. She and her husband were dressed as if they were getting ready to meet somebody important. Michael always admired that about old people. Even on a hot summer day, the men preferred jackets and ties, and ladies wore the equivalent.

Michael found a reason to chat with them, and discovered that they had been high school sweethearts. They married right after graduation, before he went into the army, as men of his generation were expected to do. The old woman was terminal. Her voice was strong with defiant acceptance as she said, "At least we had all these years together." Then she asked, "What about you two lovebirds?"

Michael said, "We're hopeful."

Dr. Murcia's nurse came for Evelyn. They were taken to Dr. Murcia's office and seated. She was waiting in a chair in front of her desk, as usual, and not behind it. She held up a thick stack of papers in her right hand.

"These are preliminary developments of a new cancer drug. It isn't available to the public. It's on the edge of approval. One of the doctors I did my fellowship with faxed these to me. He's in Georgetown. I called in some IOU's from taking call for him, and got you into his test group if you want. That's the good news. The bad news comes as a one-two punch." She paused for a moment.

"The bad news, part one, is that this is still experimental. It doesn't seem to work on everyone. They're not sure why. When it works, it's a killer-diller, as my grandmother used to say. When it doesn't..."

"Now for the other bad news. It's a bitch on your body. No, it's a super bitch. You'll have nausea and cramping so bad, you'll question what's worse, the cancer or the cure."

Dr. Murcia paused again, maybe to let them fully absorb this. "Evelyn, if you weren't as tough as you showed during the chemo and radiation, I'm not sure I would tell you about this." Dr. Murcia looked back and forth at Evelyn and Michael. "Do either of you have any questions so far?"

Evelyn said, "I'm not asking you to make a guarantee, or a prediction. How are my chances with this?"

Dr. Murcia tilted her head back and looked up toward the ceiling. Michael thought he saw her eyes close. In about five seconds she lowered her head and looked at them. "I think the relevant way I can answer is that if I were you, I would do this."

"I've never believed in sugar-coating things," Evelyn said, "I know I'm dying. This seems like an easy decision to me. Michael, do you have any questions?"

"One. When can we get started?"

~ * * * ~

"Dr. Murcia was wrong. This drug isn't a super bitch. It's the queen of the super bitches."

That's what Evelyn told Michael when she came out of the bathroom at Dr. Murcia's office. "I think I vomited up food I ate when I was five years old."

That was the first time Michael heard her say anything about any of her treatments other than, "This isn't so bad. If this is the worst thing that ever happens to me, I've had a charmed life."

The new, experimental treatment was a six week, severe, nuke 'em into oblivion, attack on the cancer. The new IV drugs were strong, but they weren't smart enough to know the difference between the cancer and healthy organs. They crushed and killed everything they came into contact with.

Evelyn didn't complain when the nausea grew so bad that she was gagging and vomiting even when there was nothing left to bring up. When that happened, she simply slowly walked out of the bathroom wiping her mouth with a damp cloth. She didn't say a word when abdominal cramping kept her up virtually all night. Or when the headaches started. Headaches that felt like a jackhammer crew was determined to open her skull. Headaches that no amount of over-the-counter or prescription medication or pain-killers could reduce.

There were other nasty side-effects, and Evelyn didn't feel sorry for herself during those, either. Michael could see the pain in her eyes, and did everything he could. He knew it didn't help.

The six weeks of treatment finally ended. Evelyn was pushed through additional tests to check the success, if any, of the torture she had endured. Dr. Murcia called two days later. All the lab and imaging results were back, and she wanted to go over everything in person. Evelyn asked Michael nervously, "Would she ask us in to give positive results? Or, do you think she doesn't want to deliver bad news over the phone?"

"Excellent question. I can see both sides of this. I'm sorry, I know that isn't any help."

They waited in Dr. Murcia's office. Her nurse said that she would be right in. The door opened, and Dr. Murcia walked in. Evelyn and Michael knew the outcome by the absence of the usual smile on Dr. Murcia's face.

This was confirmed when she looked at Evelyn and said, "I'm sorry."

~ * * * ~

That evening, Michael asked Evelyn where she wanted to go to for a getaway. Anywhere in the world was okay. "I know you're out on disability leave. You can still use your travel benefits, I checked. I'm sure that you could use a break from everything." Michael nodded. "Especially after the last six weeks." He paused. "Maybe somewhere with a plush spa? You're not a 'pamper me' kind of person, and I've always admired that. But, maybe this once." Then he added, "Don't get used to it."

Evelyn smiled. "Are you offering a dying woman her last request?" She tried to be casual, yet they both know that's what this really was. Michael started to say something. Before he could, Evelyn said, "It's okay. I don't want to go anywhere. I don't want to share you with cafes, restaurants, and other sights. I want to spend the time that I have left alone with you."

~ * * * ~

Evelyn was back in the hospital. Whatever battles were taking place in her body, the bad guys were winning. It was toward the end of afternoon visiting hours. Michael looked at her with worry and concern as she untwisted her thin IV tubing. She turned to face him, and nearly caught him before he summoned a look of nonchalance. It was important to Michael that Evelyn not realize how scared for her he was.

She said, "I know you won't do this," and stopped to let him know that something important was coming, "I'm going to ask anyway. When I'm gone, I want you to see other women."

"Evelyn, half of the people in the world are women. I

see them all the time. They're everywhere. I'm surprised you haven't noticed."

"You're impossible. I'm wasting my words, aren't I?"

"Yes, you are. In case you've forgotten, which I doubt, Semper Fi is short for Semper Fidelis, which means Always Faithful. The last time I checked, always means forever."

Michael moved to the edge of the bed. "Anyway, the only place you're going is home with me after we kick some cancer butt."

Tears were already descending as Evelyn reached out. He embraced her as tightly as he thought she could handle. They stayed like that.

Several minutes later Evelyn said, "I feel like I've become an old woman while I've been in the hospital. Worse, I look like an old woman."

He tried to disagree, she used her right hand to shoo away his attempts as if they were annoying mosquitoes. They held hands in silence until Evelyn's face revealed her need for rest. Then Michael left so that she could nap. He went home and leaped online. "I guess that high school sophomore literature class finally paid off," he said as he entered the title he wanted.

Michael was at Evelyn's room the moment evening visiting hours began. He had a folded piece of paper in his pocket. After a greeting, a kiss, and a hug, he pulled his chair to her bed and sat down. He reached into his shirt pocket. "Today's sonnet is from William Shakespeare." With love, Michael slowly read it to Evelyn:

Shall I compare thee to a summer's day?
Thou art more lovely and more temperate.
Rough winds do shake the darling buds of May,
And summer's lease hath all too short a date.
Sometime too hot the eye of heaven shines,
And often is his gold complexion dimmed;

And every fair from fair sometime declines,
By chance, or nature's changing course, untrimmed;
But thy eternal summer shall not fade,
Nor lose possession of that fair thou ow'st,
Nor shall death brag thou wand'rest in his shade,
When in eternal lines to Time thou grow'st.
So long as men can breathe, or eyes can see,
So long lives this, and this gives life to thee.

When Michael finished, he handed a tissue to Evelyn to catch her tears. She asked him to read it again. His voice thickened, and he nearly couldn't finish it. Evelyn held out her arms to Michael. He rose from the chair, and leaned across her bed to hold her damaged body as she cried softly.

After a while, Evelyn said, "I need another tissue, please." She wiped her eyes. "That's the most beautiful thing I've ever heard."

Chapter Forty-Four

THE NEXT DAY, AS EVERY day, Michael pulled one of the visitor chairs to Evelyn's bed and held hands with her. Her breathing, even helped by oxygen flowing through plastic tubing in her nose, was difficult. Evelyn started to say something, and then stopped. She needed to gather some strength. "Do you remember our conversation about reincarnation some years ago?"

Michael considered that for a moment. She helped him. "We both said it would be miraculous to be together again. Maybe even over and over."

He nodded with recognition.

Evelyn continued. "Being in this hospital bed has given me plenty of time to think about that. And a lot of other things." She squeezed his hands. "I know I'm not going to live much longer..."

Michael felt his eyes beginning to moisten. He needed to stay strong. He didn't want Evelyn worrying about him. Instead, he sat on the bed and held her. His voice came out thick. Michael could barely say, "You will live forever in my heart."

"And you will always live in mine." Her weak body pressed against him. Evelyn gave in and cried. They swayed delicately. Michael gently rubbed Evelyn's back the way she always liked. The cancer, the treatments, and her diminished appetite had stolen Evelyn's body. The carnivorous disease was literally eating her alive.

Michael's heart suffered even more at what Evelyn was enduring. *And she has never complained.*

After a while, Evelyn pulled away, she wanted to look at him. "I'm not afraid of dying, I don't want to be apart from you." She managed a small smile. "I always believed we would grow old together. Protesting about wrinkles, gray hair, and achy joints."

Michael opened his mouth to reply. Evelyn shook her head, a signal not to interrupt. "I hope that heaven, or reincarnation is real, so that we can be together forever. If we're in heaven, I'm sure that we'll recognize each other, even with wings and a harp." They both smiled. "If we're reincarnated, I hope that we're lucky enough to find each other again, out of all of the billions of people in the world."

Evelyn went silent. Whether she was finished, or unable to continue, he wasn't sure. Michael used the quietness to speak. "If there is any type of existence after this life, no matter what it's called, I'll find you. I'll do whatever it takes. Wherever you are."

"I know you will." Her voice choking with emotion, Evelyn tried to finish her thoughts while she could. "That's one of the things I've always treasured about you...you didn't hold back in any way on your love. I always knew there were no boundaries to what you would do for me."

Michael hugged Evelyn silently. Sometimes words got in the way.

~ * * * ~

Evelyn looked more pale, thinner, and in greater pain than the day before. Michael made sure that his eyes and face did not communicate this. He said, "I would take all of your pain for you, if I could." He paused. 'No, I would take your entire disease."

"I know you would."

They sat in silence. Then Michael said, "If I had your cancer, it wouldn't live."

"Why?"

"My body's cells are barely smart enough to support me. There wouldn't be anything left over to nourish the cancer. It would die of hunger."

Evelyn smiled. "Your humor is always the highlight of my day. Thank you."

Michael shook his head. "This wasn't supposed to happen. You were meant to become the white-haired and sophisticated elderly lady with the hint of a mysterious accent, who made every room she entered a better place by her being there."

~ * * * ~

"How are you feeling today?" Michael asked. Visiting hours had just begun.

Evelyn's weak voice said, "Not so hot."

Michael knew that Evelyn's 'not so hot' was the average person's unbearable pain.

He sat on the edge of Evelyn's hospital bed and held her hands. Michael always secretly loved those strong hands, a legacy from generations of hard workers. Now, they were barely able to return his grip.

"Michael, it's time. We both knew that."

Evelyn struggled to get her words out. Her breathing was rapid, shallow, and labored. "I want you to hug me as I close my eyes. Then I'm going to go to sleep."

She used what little strength she had to squeeze his hands. Then, amazingly, Evelyn smiled. "When I wake up, I'll be waiting for you. Please don't show up for a long time. I'm quite patient."

Evelyn breathed in as deeply as she could and continued. "Do you remember our first date? At Wallace's Jazz Club?"

"Of course, I do." A warm feeling spread through

Michael's body. "That was not a typical first date. And it wasn't with a typical young woman."

"Do you recall what you said when you started to kiss me in the parking lot?"

That memory generated a sad smile for both.

She turned her head and coughed. "You'd been interrupted from trying to kiss me in the bar, and said that we had unfinished business. I corrected you, and said that it was an unfinished kiss."

"I remember it perfectly." And he did.

Evelyn tried to smile, she coughed again. She wiped her mouth with a tissue and said, "I think I remember every moment of our lives together." Evelyn somehow accomplished a smile. It lingered on her mouth and in her eyes. She closed her eyes. Michael did not stop staring at his wife's thin face.

Evelyn opened her eyes. "Michael, my love, we've already said everything that can be said. Neither of us likes long good-byes. You've been my closest friend and the greatest thing that ever happened to me."

She paused, struggling to continue. "I'll love you forever. Please give me one more unfinished kiss and hold me."

Michael couldn't speak. His eyes had already teared up. Big drops rolled down his cheeks. He gently kissed Evelyn. Then he placed his arms around his wife.

Michael continued to embrace Evelyn long after the nurses turned off the beeping alarms of the monitors that brought them running to her room.

Chapter Forty-Five

"EVELYN, HOW DO YOU FEEL about being forty?"

"I can't honestly say I'm thrilled about it. It seems like I was twenty-six just yesterday. Since the alternative is not turning forty, I'll take it."

Those words about Evelyn's final birthday haunted Michael for the rest of his life. Michael always considered his superb memory to be a valuable and useful tool. Now he wasn't so sure. November 26, Evelyn's birthday, was the worst. Birthdays are supposed to be a day of celebration. Not this one. It personified everything about Evelyn that Michael missed.

And, The Disease. *That damned disease that kidnapped and killed the finest person I've ever known.*

Looking back on Evelyn's fortieth birthday, Michael sometimes wondered if they would have done things differently if they had known what was lurking. He asked himself over and over how he and Evelyn would have, maybe should have, lived each day if they knew there weren't many of them left for her.

Evelyn and Michael had loved each other beautifully and completely. And their friendship flowed naturally. They were always amazed at how lucky they were in finding each other. Michael didn't regret a single day with Evelyn. Only that there hadn't been more of them.

Evelyn's closet in their home still smelled like her. Her seldom used, and barely applied perfume, along with her personal scent on some clothes she'd briefly worn, lingered, although faintly. Michael realized that eventually these would fade away, to be replaced by, well, nothing.

Someday I'll surrender to common sense and donate everything to the needy. Not yet. The clothes stay for now.

Michael received flying benefits from United as the spouse of a deceased employee. He knew he would never travel again. And he didn't mind. Michael couldn't go somewhere they'd been, it would have been painful without Evelyn. And if he went somewhere new, he'd spend the entire time thinking, *If only Evelyn were here to see this, to taste this, to smile once again.*

~ * * * ~

When Evelyn was sick, Michael was distracted and too busy to do anything other than keep their home clean and tidy. Ready for her return. After Evelyn died, he didn't change anything in the master bathroom of the house they built at the end of the cul-de-sac for their anticipated children.

Michael couldn't bring himself to remove her hairbrush, with its strands of Evelyn. It lived alongside her sink in their large master bathroom. He didn't move the small towel that she dried her hair with after she showered for the last time before going to the hospital. Michael left it on the metal ring attached to the wall right outside the shower. He smelled it sometimes, and the aroma of Evelyn stayed with it for a long time. Or maybe he thought it did.

Michael wondered if these reminders of Evelyn around the house were helping him cope with her death, or making it worse. He examined that for a while, and then decided that he wasn't going to be an amateur shrink and second guess himself. He wanted the items to remain, that was good enough. Michael didn't remove the tangible, visual items that helped fill the huge hollowness ripped open in his heart and his life.

He had rituals that he maintained as small memorials to Evelyn. He didn't decide to do these, they just happened. He always let the last of his coffee grow cold before drinking it. This reminded him of young Evelyn in Germany, before he knew her, nursing her coffee as she sat in coffee shops with her laughing and happy girlfriends, without enough money to afford a full charge refill.

Michael was somehow reminded of celebrities whose long-time spouse died, and then they re-married within a short period. He decided that they hadn't really loved their partner if they could so quickly leap into marriage. Then, he realized that he didn't know the truth about their relationship. Maybe that couple hadn't been in love for a long time, and could barely tolerate each other. *Who knows what's really going on with other people? And more importantly, who cares?*

He never considered dating. *I can't.* There were opportunities. Women who in ways both subtle and not, announced their availability. Michael pretended not to notice, allowing them an easy out. His thoughts, feelings, and memories of Evelyn provided all the happiness he needed. That didn't change.

Evelyn and Michael had seldom socialized; they were each other's closest friend and favorite company. Michael gradually withdrew from the handful of people he stayed in contact with. He wasn't feeling sorry for himself. If he couldn't be with Evelyn, he preferred being alone.

Michael responded to the inevitable coaxing of "Join us for dinner and meet a lady we think you would like," with a smile and a polite decline. The phone calls and visits gradually vanished like early morning haze being burned away by the morning sun. Michael was alone, not lonely. When Evelyn was alive, she and Michael enjoyed a pure, uncomplicated life. He continued to do that.

Evelyn lived in the very front of Michael's heart, but not in a sad or weak way. She had been the one woman for him. No one ever gets over, or replaces a loss like that. Healing was something seen in TV shows or movies that needed a happy ending before the credits rolled. There wasn't any calamity, or disaster that they couldn't resolve with some empty bumper sticker slogans or phony happy talk. Michael knew that life wasn't like that. Some wounds never heal. Some scars never go away. Some pain never lessens. We just limp along, diminished.

~ * * * ~

A black, four-drawer metal file cabinet lived in a corner of the room in their home that Evelyn and Michael had intended to be their children's playroom. The cabinet waited patiently, knowing that Michael grieved. He realized that he shouldn't put this off, that nothing in the files would mean anything to anyone once he died. Maybe it was pointless, but Michael wanted to empty the cabinet drawers and recycle the paper, not leave them for some stranger to do. Those papers and documents represented his life with Evelyn. A life blessed to have overflowed with love, tenderness, and friendship. He didn't want the hands of a stranger to toss out the memories of their lives like meaningless trash.

The travel folders were heartbreaking. They bulged with hotel check-out forms from around the world, airline boarding passes, city maps, and receipts from foreign shops for items Michael donated to charities. Each sheet and scrap breathed with moments and memories.

As Michael held each piece of paper, he closed his eyes, and was back in that city, that coffeehouse, or on that beach with Evelyn. Michael savored the warm love of her smile, and the irresistible pull of her presence. He could feel her squeeze his hand. They had been truly fortunate to have found each other, and to have travelled together like they did. Michael was sorry, so sorry, that Evelyn was gone.

He continued to empty the file cabinet. *I was wrong.* The travel folders weren't the saddest. The medical records were. He pulled the first file, the one with the initial cruel diagnosis, and sat at his desk with it.

Michael looked at the thick folder in front of him. It pretended to be an innocent collection of harmless sheets of paper. Michael knew better. Pain and Death hid in there, disguised as words - hurtful words, evil words. Words as dangerous and destructive as any weapon ever invented. He couldn't force himself to open the folder. His heart didn't need to be stabbed again and again. Michael knew he would be better off taking the medical files to a recycling bin. He put it back into the cabinet. He never opened that drawer again.

Michael stayed in the one house he and Evelyn ever lived in. Years before, when Evelyn's mom broke her hip going down some stairs in Germany, they planned that when they got old they would move to a one-story home to avoid those potential problems. Evelyn didn't live long enough for that to happen. When Michael walked downstairs in the morning, he didn't bounce like the young man he was when they first had their home built. Instead, he held onto the railing and took his time. His left knee, injured in an ancient motorcycle accident, was getting worse as Michael aged, notably when he tried to pivot on it or bend down. *That's okay. This is a cheap price to pay for being alive.*

He didn't use the dishwasher, preferring to stand at

the sink each evening while cleaning that day's rinsed utensils, plates, and cups, or glasses. Michael enjoyed looking at the picture of Evelyn that he'd enlarged, framed, and placed on the counter near the sink. The close-up photo showed her shoulders and head. It had been on that counter since long before she got sick. Michael couldn't remember exactly when the photo was taken, or where. And because it was a close-up, there were no unique background landmarks to identify. It didn't matter. Evelyn appeared to be in her late twenties, smiling with the unburdened and unlimited joy of someone who knows that the gods are truly gracing them. Michael would often sigh. *I'm glad she had no way to know about the future miscarriages and the cancer.*

~ * * * ~

The years staggered by slowly. Michael retired from his job and settled into a routine. He read a lot and became knowledgeable on all kinds of things, although no one ever knew.

Michael often visited the nearest big, chain bookstore on quiet weekday mornings and carefully walked through each aisle, scanning the shelves for books he might be interested in. He made sure to look at the lower shelves for some treasures that might be hiding there. Then he wrote down the titles of books he wanted in the small notepad that fit perfectly in his shirt pocket.

Michael would drink a cappuccino at the bookstore coffee bar while using his phone to search the local library's website for the titles he chose. He put checkmarks in his notebook to indicate the books that the library carried, and he bought the ones that they didn't.

At some point while holding his cup, Michael always thought of Evelyn and their afternoon coffee custom. He ached for her to be there, even for a single sip. *I would settle for one look at her. One touch of her hand. The heat of one smile.*

~ * * * ~

While thinking of Evelyn one morning, Michael shuddered as if splashed with a bucket of ice water. *I have trouble remembering Evelyn's voice. Everything visual is there. That magic smile. Her gestures. Her habits. Not the sound. I don't remember her voice well, but I remember it deeply.*

~ * * * ~

Michael volunteered at a local animal shelter several days a week. He did whatever they asked, which was usually cleaning the cages and making sure that the animals had enough food and fresh water. Michael liked the people there, though he spoke mainly to the animals. And he stuffed bills into the donation jar when no one was looking.

The other volunteers and employees, predominantly young people, enjoyed Michael's company, and treated him like their beloved grandfather. They tried to get him to talk about himself. Michael smiled sadly, and told them that he had once been lucky enough to be married to the best person in the world.

He started talking to himself at home. A morning of silence was cracked open with an unexpected, "Look at that!" when Michael saw three hummingbirds taking turns at the feeder on their back deck. His voice startled him, and he laughed about it. *If only Evelyn were here to see this.* And for a moment... just the briefest moment... he started to call out for her.

It didn't take long for Michael to sip his morning coffee and say, "Well, that's a little too hot." Soon, the house enjoyed his comments on sports, politics, and the books he was reading. And, of Evelyn. She was never further than one thought, one memory, one glance at a photo away from front and center in his mind.

Whenever Michael got his blood pressure checked, he wanted to put a tranquil image in his mind. He closed his eyes as the blood pressure cuff was inflated, and there she stood, timeless and unchanged. Twenty-eight-year-old Evelyn on the beach in Negril, Jamaica, ankle deep in the clear, calm, warm water.

Her left hand held a beach bag with their sandals and shirts in it. Evelyn's eyes and posture urged him to hurry and snap the photo so they could continue walking in the luscious Caribbean. Evelyn wore the black one-piece bathing suit that was cut high enough on the sides that she'd been reluctant to buy it. He remembered that day so well that it could have been yesterday. Michael had no idea why some things possessed this quality. Maybe the subconscious mind was trying to tell you something.

On the days he didn't do volunteer work, Michael read in the morning, ate a plain lunch, enjoyed a nap, and laughed about it, often saying out loud, "I used to make fun of the old people who napped every day. Now I look forward to it. I've truly become an old man." And he was right.

Dinner was often two pieces of bread with a thin layer of butter and a slice of meat or cheese, perhaps with mild pepper rings or sweet pickles placed on it, German style, the way he and Evelyn had done hundreds of times. And a glass of red wine. "Maybe I'll splash a little more into my glass."

He sat in the same chair as always, at the same place of the table as if Evelyn were still to his right. Michael didn't move his utensils, plate, or glass into the empty space on the table that for years been occupied by Evelyn. He wasn't stupid or in denial; he long realized that there was a very narrow gap between honoring your loved one's absence in a healthy way, and pretending they were there. Michael was firmly in the former, aware of what he was doing, but missing Evelyn too much to behave differently. That never changed.

Each night Michael read in bed until his eyes started to close, which required less and less time as the years tip-toed by. Then he put the book down and turned off the light. Michael always slept on his side of their king-sized bed. Sometimes he sleepily reached for Evelyn before he realized why she wasn't there.

Chapter Forty-Six

IT HAPPENED EARLY IN THE morning. Michael was carrying the laundry into the basement. Maybe he wasn't fully awake when he wrapped his right forearm around the plastic basket as he opened the basement door with his left hand. Michael didn't put the basket down, and immediately realized he had made a mistake. He lost his balance for merely a small piece of a second. That was all it took.

Michael began to lean the wrong way. He tried to compensate by forcing his weight the other way. It worked. He smiled gratefully. *That was close.* Then his left knee, arthritic from his long-ago motorcycle spill, buckled from the sudden twisting. He stumbled toward a bad place – the hard basement floor far below. Michael released the laundry basket. He grabbed for the wooden railing with both hands. It was too late. A message flashed through his brain, *If I'd been younger, I could have caught myself.*

Michael crashed down eleven uncarpeted wooden steps, accelerating and tumbling. Then he collided with the unyielding, and unfriendly cement at the bottom.

The fall happened so abruptly that Michael didn't feel anything during it except disorientation. Lying broken and bleeding at the bottom was different. The pain was worse than anything he'd ever experienced. Michael tried to move. He couldn't. He knew he was in serious, serious trouble.

Michael hoped to recover enough to somehow crawl up the stairs and get help. His body would not cooperate. Michael was old, but still a tough Marine. He lay there, pulling together his strength. Then, he tried to squirm forward. After three days, he hadn't been able to drag himself further than a few inches.

Evelyn was on Michael's mind the entire time. On the evening of the third day, Michael struggled to open his lips. They felt like they'd been glued shut. All moisture in his mouth had dried up during the first twenty-four hours. Michael nearly didn't recognize or hear his own weak words, "Evelyn, I'm finally coming to join you."

When Michael didn't show up at the animal shelter for his scheduled volunteer shift on the fourth day, the staff got worried. This wasn't like him, he would have called. They phoned the police.

After Michael's body was discovered and examined, the coroner said to his assistant, "Bob, come over here, please. This is strange. It looks like Mr. La Rue has a smile on his face. Like he'd been thinking about something pleasant. That couldn't be. Not after a fall like that, and a painful, slow death."

Chapter Forty-Seven

THE YOUNG MAN LOOKED IN the mirror and saw a slightly nervous, confident, and eager twenty-five-year-old. He didn't want to leave his apartment and show up for his first day at work with his shirt buttoned wrong, or specks of toothpaste around his mouth. He wasn't worried about making a positive first impression, he'd interned with EESW International for the past two summers while finishing his graduate degree from a top university last week. He'd been near the top of his class.

Other companies pursued him, yet there was something beguiling about EESW. It was the leading company in its field and a great place to work. This was like playing ball in the major leagues. He would be working with, and competing against, some of the most talented people in the world.

That wasn't why he felt this was where he needed to be. Other companies were nearly as appealing, while offering the same money and benefits. And a couple of them dangled more. Something he couldn't quite identify pulled him toward EESW, as certainly as a beach beckoned to the morning tide. The young man didn't like unanswered questions, and several nights he postponed sleep while trying to figure out what aspect of EESW seduced him. He never solved that riddle.

He flashed the ID from his internship to enter the parking garage under the modern and huge corporate headquarters building, and found an empty slot. One of the elevators delivered him to the lobby where he said, “Good morning, Ralph,” and showed the smiling face on his ID to the security guard.

He knew the building well, and went directly to the conference room where the orientation for new, full-time associates was scheduled. Just inside that large room, placed against the wall on the right, were two wooden tables covered with fancy white table cloths. One table held three large, metal coffee urns labeled regular, decaf, and hot water. They were highly polished, and not blemished by even a fingerprint smudge. The other table offered equally shiny silver oval trays of tempting pastries, and small glass bottles of chilled orange and apple juice, and imported mineral water. Stacks of white paper napkins that he knew would be the softest ones available stood there like sentries on guard duty.

The young man had already eaten breakfast, but a gooey pastry whispered his name until he grabbed it, knowing how satisfying it would taste with a steaming cup of coffee. With both hands occupied, he searched for the right seat. The room contained fifty chairs arranged in rows of ten, with a wide space in the middle of each row. He wanted to be close to the coffee pot without climbing around other new hires, so he sat in the last row, nearest the wall.

He arrived early, as always, and did some people watching as he enjoyed his refreshments. The room soon filled with the buzz of several dozen conversations. He sat alone, as preferred, glad that no one else wanted to sit in the back row if there were seats closer to the well-polished and expensive looking dark wood podium.

He checked his watch, betting that the first speaker would start five minutes early. EESW was a company that valued promptness. At five minutes of eight, the doors in the rear of the room shut, and a tall, older, well-dressed, and handsome man strode to the podium. The welcoming was about to officially begin. The young man listened carefully, though his eyes were steadily tugged to another newbie. She sat in the middle of the section of seats to his right, two rows ahead. One time, he glanced at her, and she was looking at him.

Three speakers, and forty-five minutes later, the new hires earned a break to get coffee, use the bathroom, or maybe stretch their legs. He went back for one more coffee, his second and final one of the meeting. The young woman he'd noticed stood by herself, twisting open a water bottle.

She was exceptionally attractive, but not with the vacant beauty of a model or actress. He was close enough to feel the pull of her allure, and he closed the short space between them. She looked up.

He said, "I know this sounds like a lame pick-up line from an even lamer movie, I'm certain that I know you from somewhere."

She stared at him. Her blue eyes seemed to be searching his face. He wondered if he had offended her.

Then she said, "I'm not sure what to say. When I entered the room, and looked around for a seat, my attention was drawn to you. I felt the same way." She had a look on her face that he couldn't identify.

"Um..." she paused, and looked down like she was embarrassed to go on. Then she did. "This isn't easy for me." She stopped again, and turned her head to the left and right as if checking to see if anyone was close enough to listen.

She lowered her voice, "This has never happened to me before. I don't feel like you're a stranger. It's like I know you. And very well. How could that be? I'd remember if that were the case...wouldn't I?" She looked at him for an answer. He didn't have one. He was as confused as she was.

She said, "I'm sure I'm not making any sense. This feeling that I know you is so strong that I struggled to pay attention to the speakers." She blushed, and then smiled. "I'll bet now I sound exponentially more inept than any lines from even the worst grade z movies you mentioned."

"No, not at all. Inept maybe, not exponentially inept." They both smiled at the needed relief. He looked at his watch. The break was nearly over. "How does this sound? Let's get together after work today for coffee, and see if we can figure this out? Never underestimate the value of a caffeine jolt."

He added, "I'm sorry, this mystery has made me forget my manners." He put his hand out. "I'm Michael."

She smiled back, and shook hands. "Coffee and a solution sound like a brilliant idea. My name is a little old-fashioned. I'm Evelyn."

Acknowledgements

No one completes the journey of presenting a book to its readers by themselves. I was not an exception. Glendon and the talented team at Streetlight Graphics are that rare combination of talent and professionalism blended with friendly helpfulness.

And then there is Evelyn. Sweet Evelyn. After twenty-eight years together, there still aren't enough hours in the day when I'm with you. Simply put, I am the luckiest man in the world to be married to you. And we are the luckiest parents in the world to have Sacha for our son. Evelyn told me that Sacha is not to hear any of my Marine stories until he's thirty. He was born in 1999. If you meet him before that birthday, please don't mention this book.

M & J: I never stopped loving you.

About the Author

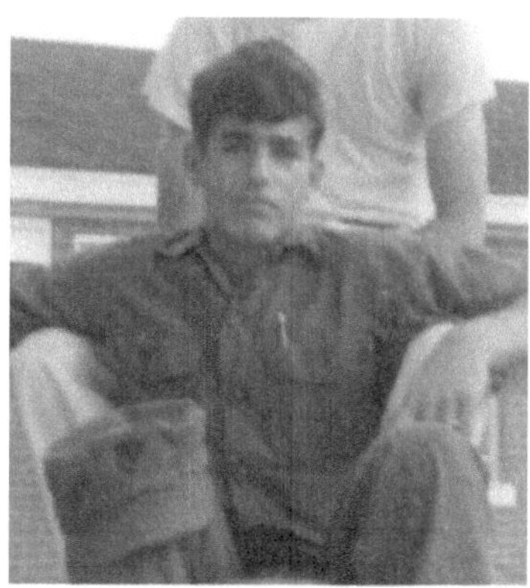

Tim Weller lives in Fredericksburg, Virginia with his wife and son and can often be found in line at Carl's. Thanks for buying his book. He hopes you enjoyed reading it as much as he did writing it. A chunk of proceeds from book sales will be donated to charitics such as helping wounded/disabled veterans, hungry children and Last Chance Animal Rescue.

www.ingramcontent.com/pod-product-compliance
Lightning Source LLC
Chambersburg PA
CBHW031707170626
46808CB00005B/1648
* 9 7 8 1 7 3 3 6 8 3 1 0 4 *